FATES ENTWINED

FATES ENTWINED

USA TODAY BESTSELLING AUTHOR

J. BARNARD

JBARNARDAUTHOR.COM

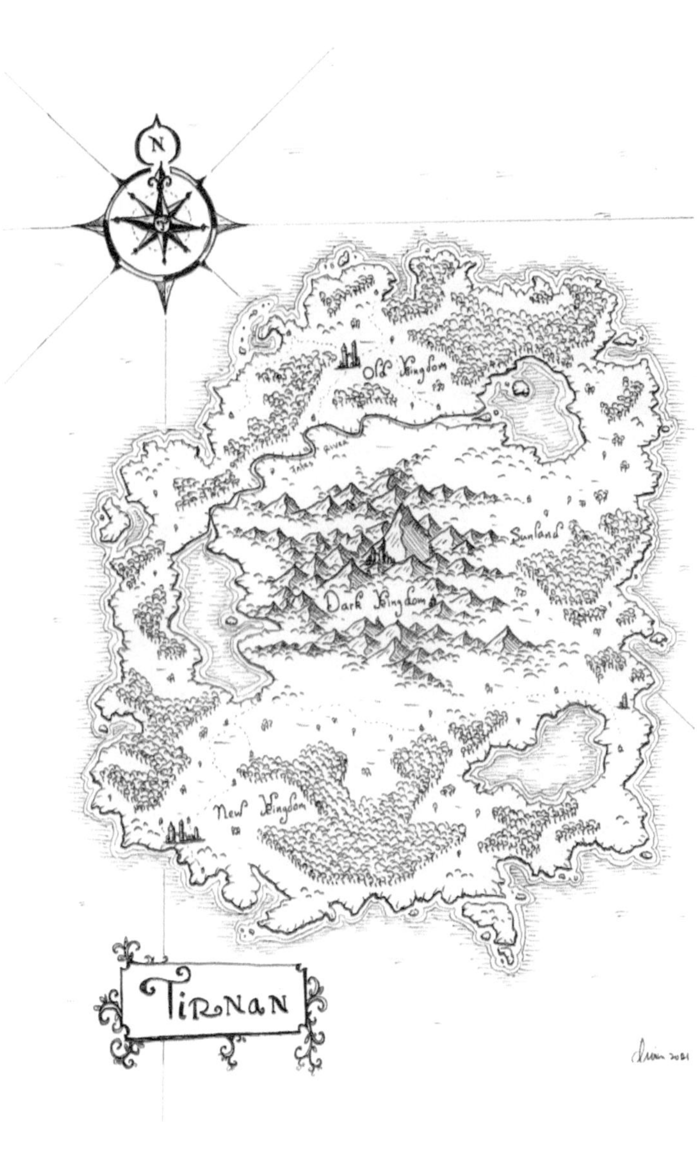

N
Old Kingdom
Isles River
Sunland
Dark Kingdom
New Kingdom
Tirnan

CHAPTER
ONE

Reese woke with the mother of all hangovers.

The inside of her mouth felt like cotton, and her head pounded so hard that white lights winked behind her eyelids with every heartbeat.

She lifted her face off a wool rug that reeked of arthritic dog, and peered around the unfamiliar room. White wicker furniture with floral cushions surrounded her—definitely not a student dorm.

Where the hell was she?

Reese waited for the spinning to ease before attempting to push up to a sitting position. She was sprawled in the center of the room like someone had dumped her there. Given the soreness in her hipbone and the right side of her face, anything was possible.

She rubbed her eyes, thinking back. The last thing she remembered was going to the fraternity party by herself. And, granted, it had been a stupid move to go alone. But there was no way she was staying home the night of her eighteenth birthday. That was just pitiful. Her roommate

Elena had said she would meet her there, but Elena never showed.

Even more distressing, Reese couldn't remember much after she'd arrived at the party. The last thing she recalled was taking a shot of alcohol.

Footsteps sounded down a dimly lit hallway on her right and Reese's heartbeat picked up. She tried to rise to a sitting position, but her body wasn't cooperating.

Two men entered the room...and last night—how wrong this situation was—came crashing down over her.

Her breath sawed in and out of her chest. Her hands grew cold and her stomach rolled with nausea.

The first man—handsome, middle-aged—studied her like she was some kind of insect. But that wasn't what had her freaking out. It was the younger man beside him: the hot fraternity guy she'd met at the party, before everything went blank.

"Whoa." A handsome guy with dark hair and wearing a rugby shirt rubbed his eyes dramatically after Reese entered the fraternity house. "Can I get your picture? I want to prove to my friends that angels really exist. Here—" He handed her a shot glass of something purple while his gaze traveled down her body in the tight red dress her mother had picked out on their last shopping excursion.

The fraternity guy's pickup line was pure cheese, but she hadn't cared at the time. She'd needed the attention of some innocuous, nameless boy. It had been a hell of week.

Reese had learned that Elena, her roommate and closest friend at Dawson, was half Fae. *Fae!*

What was a Fae, anyway? All Reese knew was that Elena suddenly had the ability to change water and other compounds and elements into different forms—because that wasn't weird. If Reese hadn't seen Elena make water boil with a wave of her hand, she wouldn't have believed it. Then there was Elena's Viking-looking Fae bodyguard who'd been sleeping on their couch the last few nights. As if learning her friend was part Fae wasn't bad enough, Reese had to discover that Fae men were just as self-centered as human guys.

Not an uplifting realization.

Considering her fragile mental state after all these bombshells, Reese shouldn't have gone to the party by herself.

And now she wished she'd been more careful before she snatched the shot glass from the hot fraternity guy. Because inside this unfamiliar room, with the two men staring down at her, fraternity guy wasn't looking at her with admiration anymore.

He wore a white button-down—no more rugby shirt— and his hair was combed back instead of haphazardly ruffled the way it had been at the party. More important, his smooth-shaven cheeks and angular jaw were set in hard lines, a touch of repulsion in his expression.

This wasn't right. Not right at all.

Reese moved to stand, but couldn't bear weight on her arms or legs, and she wound up slumping to the ground.

It didn't take a genius to figure out that the fraternity guy had put something in the shot glass at the party. She hadn't been there long enough to drink anything else. That was the only explanation for why she couldn't remember anything afterward. And why she still struggled to move.

"Did I pass out or something?" She leaned on her elbows, her hands shaking like crazy, from the drug he must have slipped her, from fear—she didn't know. In any case, her hands gave the lie to her ditzy words. But she'd be damned if she'd admit how frightened she was.

The older man crouched before her, his dark eyes intent, as though cataloging her features. His mouth, cut in a straight line, and lightly creased face gave nothing away, but she got the distinct feeling he was angry.

He reached out and Reese attempted to scoot away, but her body shook violently and she barely moved an inch. He caught her arm and slid his hand down to the coiled-snake bracelet her mother had given her when she was a girl.

His gaze met hers, some fathomless, eerie emotion in its dark brown depths.

Reese swallowed past the cotton mouth and tried to pry herself from his grip.

He released her abruptly and she fell back. "Keep her alive. For now," he said to the younger man, "we'll bring her with us." He turned and started walking away.

Keep her alive?

Elena needed a bodyguard for reasons she wouldn't explain to Reese. Did this have anything to do with that? Did these men think they could get to Elena by capturing Reese?

She ignored the pain in her head and glanced around frantically. The drapes were drawn and the place seemed empty. No one to call out to, no place to hide… "There's been some mistake," she said.

Halfway to the hallway, the older man didn't slow or acknowledge her.

Before she could make a move—even if she could get her limbs to work—the fraternity guy crouched in front of her and pulled out a syringe.

"Wait. Don't do this!" Reese's voice rose with each word, her tone no longer smooth and calm.

Without pausing, the fraternity jerk jabbed the needle in her arm.

She stared at it sticking up, felt the cold of its contents releasing into her system, before everything blurred and the world disappeared.

~

No matter how tight a ball Reese curled into, she couldn't get warm. The surface she was lying on was somewhat soft, but the air was freezing cold.

She pried her eyes open. And stared at a stone wall.

No wonder she was freezing.

Reese's heart raced, her last memories of the men in the empty house rushing back.

She looked over her shoulder—and saw vertical metal bars half a dozen feet away.

She was in prison now?

An armed man in black peered at her from behind the bars. He was in a uniform, but it wasn't like any police uniform she'd seen. There were no emblems or badges on it. And in addition to the all-black pants, fitted long-sleeved shirt, and combat boots, he wore a sword strapped to his back. *A sword!*

Reese sat up abruptly, her arms stronger than they had been the last time she'd woken, but her head hurt like she'd knocked it against these stone walls, her vision swimming.

She clutched the sides of her head. First the men, then the needle, and now this? "What is going on!"

The guard was tall and beautiful, like that jackass bodyguard of Elena's. But unlike Elena's bodyguard, Keen, this guy had short light brown hair instead of the longish white-blond hair Keen sported. And suddenly Reese realized something.

Those men in the abandoned house might have been

human, but this soldier was not. He wasn't a policeman with a strange military uniform. He was Fae.

And that explained *everything*.

Mister Tall and Beautiful was too perfect to be anything less. Plus, he wore the same clothes Keen had worn, before Keen started dressing down his Faeness on their college campus.

This was all *his* fault.

If Keen hadn't given her such a hard time while he was guarding her roommate, Reese might not have left for the party without Elena.

The expression on the man in front of her was severe, his stance powerful. Elena hadn't wanted Reese to get involved in her business with the Fae. She'd said it was too dangerous. Considering the way this man was looking at her, it appeared Reese was officially involved.

"Hey, hot guy." She snapped her fingers to draw his attention to her eyes. He hadn't said anything. Just stood there, his gaze flickering down every couple of seconds, scorching her bare legs. Granted, her legs were revealed almost to her crotch, thanks to the Herve Leger bandage dress her mom had bought her. Reese's mom had a taste for trashy couture. "Why am I here?" she asked, now that she had his attention. "And can you bring me a blanket already? It's freezing." The air in the stone prison smelled of mold, and it was as cold as a meat locker.

The Fae smirked and his gaze slid to her mouth. "I could heat you up if you wish."

Oh, good God. Now she had to deal with perverted Fae too? This night just kept getting worse. Or day? She wasn't sure what time it was anymore. Given the hollow feeling in her stomach, she had a sneaking suspicion many hours had passed.

The guard thought he was clever, did he? Well, she'd heard it before! Men were all the same. Untrustworthy. Arrogant. Users. Which was why she was a card-carrying commitmentphobe, and proud of it.

"No thanks." She smiled sweetly. "But you could let me out of here. I'd be most grateful."

He huffed out a breath through his nose, then turned his back on her.

The bastard!

Human men stumbled over themselves to get up her skirt. Fae men were crushing her pride. Not that she would have put out just because this guy let her go free, but he didn't know that.

Reese looked down at her legs, now bluish-tinged, thanks to the cold. They were slim, her toenails prettily painted red and strapped inside spike heels. Unless the drugs these people had dosed her with had given her a sudden case of the uglies, she resembled her golden-haired mother, a retired Hollywood beauty.

"Hey! Quit screwing around and let me out of this box of rubble!"

He looked back and lifted a brow. "You do not know?"

Reese had never met a man she couldn't run circles around. Well, maybe one, but *he* was the reason she was in this mess. Keen had insulted her. Repeatedly. *Her!*—a scholar, tae kwon do badass. Keen was the reason she'd needed a slutty fraternity guy to boost her self-confidence.

She wasn't sure what was more pathetic—how shameless guys could be in order to get laid, or her emotional weakness when it came to that stupid Fae bodyguard. She wasn't proud that she'd gone to the fraternity party to get attention. It was dumb. Desperate.

Never again would she allow a guy to make her feel that way.

Reese relaxed her face and curled her shoulders innocently inward. "Do I know *what*? No one's told me anything."

Okay, so it was a shameless move to appear the needy female, but desperate times and all that. Plus, it worked.

The guard's wide mouth softened. He crossed his arms over his massive pecs. The Fae had insanely hot bodies—if she were into manly Fae physiques. Which she was *not*.

"You are in the New Kingdom dungeon for observation."

Reese's heart stumbled over itself. *The fuck?* "Um, and that would be where?"

"Tirnan. Fae realm." He turned around as if the conversation were over.

What the hell, what the hell!

Reese patted down her body, searching for anything— her purse, her wallet, better yet, a phone. The chamber she sat in was empty except for the cot she lay on, which didn't contain a sheet, never mind a blanket. Electronics of any kind were out of the question.

How did she get from the fraternity party, to the house, with those two human assholes and their needle, and now to the Fae realm? As far as she knew, Fae and humans didn't work together.

During the brief, mostly frustrating moments she'd spent around Keen, she'd learned that Fae thought humans beneath them, which explained Keen's shitty attitude toward her. The only reason they'd worked with Reese's roommate Elena was because of Elena's powers, which were supposedly unusual in Halven, the Fae term for people who were half human and half Fae. In fact, working with

Halven of any kind was a huge exception—as in, *never been done before.*

According to Elena, she'd been the Fae's last resort, and that was why they'd approached her. Fae never got sick, but some psycho had created a virus that was killing them.

And now they wanted Reese for observation? She was human; what could she possibly do to help?

Though her head no longer pounded the way it had when she'd first awakened, her limbs were weighed down by a thousand pounds of exhaustion. She wasn't getting anywhere with the guard, so she sank back onto her shitty cot and curled into a ball to keep warm. She would close her eyes for a second only, just enough time to rest up while she considered her next move. Whatever that would be. They couldn't keep her here forever. This was ridiculous.

After a few minutes, her stomach cramped with hunger. Her mouth sticky and dry, she said, "How about some water?"

"Ah," came a woman's voice. "She is awake." Reese rolled over, blinking dazedly. A tall woman with thick, wavy gray hair stood beside Reese's jailer. "You may wait by the door, Ulric."

The guard retreated and the woman approached the metal bars of Reese's cell, along with the older man from the house. The human.

But the woman was Fae.

Though her gray hair reflected middle age, like the man standing next to her, the woman's skin was supple and smooth. Only light lines around her eyes came close to indicating the years her hair represented. And she was tall—crazy basketball player tall. This woman had perfect, pretty features and a narrow, flawless figure. Nothing like the physique of the muscular Fae guard, but the height, the coloring... She had to be Fae.

"You are certain, Marlon?" The woman stared at Reese.

"Yes. The bracelet. It is my father's emblem. And her face..."

The bracelet?

Reese glanced at her wrist. The bracelet she wore had been an odd gift from her mother when Reese turned nine. The snake curled in a figure eight and...well...ate its tail, for lack of a better description. But Reese hadn't cared at the time. The gift was different and it had come from her mother, who never bought anything that wasn't expensive clothing. Though beautiful, the jewelry wasn't trendy, and that made it special. Along with the message her mother had given with the gift.

"This represents who you are," she had said.

Reese always wore the bracelet. But now she wondered what it really meant.

"I also noted that she is changing," the man said.

The older Fae woman and the man she called Marlon spoke freely in front of Reese, as if her presence didn't matter. Underestimating and misjudging her like everyone else. If Reese hadn't been so damned tired, she'd give them a piece of her mind.

"This one has abilities, I can sense it," he said. "Further proof she is my father's child. If we keep her, we can use her to get to him. To control him."

His father's child? Abilities? They must think Reese was Halven like Elena.

This was one huge mistake. Reese wasn't Halven, and her parents weren't Fae.

Reese's father was a screenwriter from Orange County, busy writing the next blockbuster in between banging his assistant behind her mother's back. Her mother knew about her father's infidelity, of course—and retaliated with the twenty-four-year-old personal trainer she kept on salary.

The Fae woman chuckled and cut Marlon a look. "You surprise me. Your ruthlessness shows no limits." She tapped a blunt fingernail on the metal bars and stared at Reese. "We will keep her. For now. I am curious to see what ability she possesses. You are correct in using her to gain access to your father."

The woman's head shifted slightly and she studied Marlon out of the corner of her eye. "He never viewed you the way the rest of my kind do. He accepted you, to a certain degree, and he will accept her as well. Particularly if she possesses powers. He will not wish to kill his Halven daughter the way most Fae do. But are you certain of this path? Your father stood beside you when no other would. I will be most displeased if I find your fealty remains with him." Ice cut into the woman's tone, and suddenly Reese was happy to be on her side of the bars.

Marlon's gaze remained inside the cell. "Would I have created the only virus capable of killing my father—had that Halven not intervened—if I'd sworn him loyalty?"

The virus. This guy had created it? And he'd said a Halven intervened. He must mean Elena. Had she managed to cure it?

Did they really believe Reese was like Elena? A Halven? Reese's parents were known for their infidelity...

It was possible.

The woman paused for several seconds. "We will press forward with the plan."

That didn't sound good.

The woman glanced at someone out of view. "Do not indulge her, Ulric."

"Yes, Your Majesty." It was the voice of the Fae guard.

The woman's gaze returned to Reese—hard, cold, like the cell Reese lay in. "I want her weak."

CHAPTER

TWO

The flashing lights and rainbow of colors were always disorienting while traveling through a portal, but Keen's nerves manifested more from his return home for the first time in years than from his mode of transportation. And because of the task before him.

Failure wasn't an option.

Landing on the rich Tirnan soil inside the Fae realm, Keen looked up, expecting to see a horde of soldiers running toward him.

He wasn't disappointed.

The moment he'd entered New Kingdom, a Presence Charm would have notified the castle of an intruder. At least fifty soldiers gunned for him.

Keen took a deep breath of Tirnan air that smelled of allon trees and a sweet herb that resembled Earth's lavender, glanced up at the native patchwork of red stars in the darkened sky, and braced himself. He raised his palms in a display of submission. Any signs of aggression wouldn't get him what he wanted.

Fortunately for Keen, after a tense but brief conversation—in which he'd been knocked from his feet and pinned to the dirt—the soldiers detained him instead of killing him, while they confirmed his claim that he'd worked with the queen in the Fae realm embedded on Earth.

Keen's boots, along with several of his captors', were nearly soundless on the stone floors of the palace as they made their way up two flights of stairs with ornamental balustrades. They entered a room that could have been a guest suite.

So not a prisoner. Not yet.

"We will see what the queen has to say about your uninvited arrival," the first commander said as he exited the room, leaving several soldiers behind to stand guard.

Keen turned and took in the space. He'd never entered New Kingdom Palace—few Oldlanders had and lived to see the next day. He couldn't help but notice the differences compared to his native Old Kingdom, a land and castle that was more of a hardened fortress. The soldiers and people there were taught that luxuries such as these—upholstered chairs, gilded ceilings, and masterpieces of unimaginable fortune—were extravagances meant to distract from magic and power. To weaken Fae.

It wasn't until Keen had traveled to Emain, the Fae realm embedded on Earth, that he was exposed to such finery. And to televisions and vehicles—human technologies Keen found particularly enjoyable.

New Kingdom didn't hold the same beliefs as Old Kingdom. The palace possessed great wealth, thanks in part to trade with humans. Tirnan was ripe with precious minerals, and New Kingdom rulers mined and sold valuables to humans in exchange for goods. It didn't make up for the magical weaponry Old Kingdom possessed, but it kept its inhabitants fed, clothed, and never wanting. Which made them strong in other ways.

A familiar older woman with silver hair and flawless skin breezed past the guards at the door and entered the room. "Keen," she said, her eyes shrewd as she took him in from head to toe. She'd exchanged the simple black attire his people wore for a courtly smock with bejeweled sleeves and a collar of emeralds around her throat.

Portia was an Oldlander, like Keen, but she'd spent centuries as a companion to the New Kingdom royal family. Keen had detected ambition in her thoughts before she'd joined forces with the Halven Army, but she'd hidden her true intentions. Keen possessed telepathic abilities. Few could hide their thoughts from him. Unfortunately, Portia was one of them. He'd never suspected the perfidy to which she would succumb. Betrayal of her own people? Mass murder? All to wrest control of New Kingdom from her supposed friend and its rightful ruler, Theda Rainer Rosales, the mother of Keen's Halven charge, Elena.

"To what do we owe the pleasure of your company in our humble palace?" Portia waved her hand at the opulent furnishings of velvet drapes, silk-covered furniture, and crystal vases. "And why should I keep you alive after you fought my men in Emain and dared to enter my land?"

Keen had battled alongside the Emain guards to fend off Portia's attack. She'd wanted to wrest control of Emain the way she had New Kingdom.

She'd lost.

"We are aware you hold the human, Reese Fisher. Emain wishes to ensure her health and negotiate her release."

Portia tilted her head. "Human." She said the word as though it tasted wrong. "And negotiate, you say?" She chuckled, and then her expression grew serious. "I am curious. What do you feel you have to offer me?"

He remained still. The truth was, he had very little to offer in exchange for the girl's release, though secure it he must.

Portia didn't say anything for a long moment. "I'll allow you a visit with the girl," she finally said, "and then I'll tell you what I want."

She snapped her fingers, and two Newlander guards just outside the room entered. "Take him to her, but cut off his head if he tries anything." A smile spread on her face as she stared at Keen. "Reese Fisher resides two levels belowground. In the dungeon."

Keen's heart pounded beneath the walls of his broad chest as he descended stairs made of dark stone. He'd searched for Reese for nearly a week—a fact that infuriated him. It should not have taken him this long to find one small human.

At the bottom landing, an eight-foot timber door, blackened with age, blocked passage to the dungeon. One of the guards assigned to him used both hands to lift the wooden bar that secured the door. He grunted as he heaved the bar upward, which said more about its weight than the guard's might. Fae possessed unparalleled strength.

The guard swung the door open, and they strode down a narrow hallway, the air growing stale and chilled.

Another soldier at the end of the hall faced a cell, his arms crossed, his expression pensive. Keen recognized him as Ulric, one of the Fae who had led the full-fledged attack on Emain. But Keen and the Emain soldiers were not weakened by disease the way the New Kingdom soldiers in Tirnan had been. Ulric and his men had lost that battle and barely escaped with their lives.

Ulric turned at the sound of Keen and the two guards entering. He stepped away from the cell and pulled out his sword from the sheath at his back.

"A pleasure to see you again too, Ulric," Keen said.

One of the guards beside Keen held up a hand. "He is here at the command of her majesty. Put away your weapon."

Ulric hesitated, then re-sheathed the sword. His expression shifted from aggressive to furtive as his gaze flickered back to the cell.

Keen had spotted the bars in his periphery before Ulric's weapon had drawn his attention. Now he took a closer look.

And nearly stopped breathing.

Inside the cell, a small female figure lay barely clothed atop a filthy mattress, her skin as pale as death.

The air inside the chamber was too cold for Keen's comfort. For a human with little clothing, it was deadly.

Ulric stepped back in a courtly bow, his arm wide as he gestured to the prisoner. "By all means. Visit. She is a pretty thing, though not as lively as she was when she first arrived."

Pressure built behind Keen's temples. Having a sword pulled on him hadn't bothered him, but now Keen wished to crush Ulric's skull into the stone wall.

He paced to the door between the bars. "Open it. Now!"

Ulric glanced at the other guards, who merely shrugged, then used a large skeleton key to unlock the metal door.

Keen swallowed the knot at the back of his throat,

steadying his breathing as he searched for movement from the girl. Her eyelids flickering, her chest rising—anything to indicate she lived. "What happened to her?"

Ulric pushed the door open and tucked away the key. "She was already shaking when she arrived. She hasn't stopped shaking, and now her coloring..."

"And you did not think to give her a blanket?"

The idiot looked momentarily surprised. "Wasn't told to."

Keen let out a steadying breath. It would be okay. She was simply cold. "What have you fed her?" he asked as he entered the cell.

"Fed her?" Ulric said as he entered behind Keen and peered curiously over at Reese on the cot. "Her majesty wanted her weak."

The pounding beneath Keen's temples spread down his neck, knotting the muscles along his shoulders. "She is a human, you idiot. They cannot go without..." He let out a harsh breath. "Never mind. How long has she been here?" Afraid to harm her in such a fragile state, Keen paused before reaching out. It was dark in the cell, but he detected a blue tinge to her flesh, her lips a purplish hue.

There was a pause, and then the sound of Ulric's feet shifting came from behind. "Three days."

Fury blazed through Keen. "Three—" He closed his eyes and compressed his lips. Nothing would come of killing Ulric right now, other than a battle. And Keen needed to care for Reese. "The girl comes with me," he finally said.

"Her majesty—" Ulric began.

Keen shot him a deadly look he dragged to the other guards as well. "Her body shivers and I sense her shallow breathing, but she barely lives. Should anything happen to her, you will not like the consequences. Neither will her majesty." It was a threat—one that could get him killed—but he didn't care.

He stared down at Reese. The girl was innocent, and they'd—

The red fabric covering her body caught his attention. It was stained with dirt. And one of the smudges appeared to be a large handprint. Keen swiveled his head to the others. "Has she been touched?" he said in a deadly tone.

Ulric stepped back and gripped the hilt of the blade at his waist. "She has not been—*touched*—other than to secure her inside the cell."

Keen drew stiff fingers across his lips. Had Ulric given him any other answer, he would have made sure the Fae suffered a slow death.

He bent over and slid one arm beneath Reese's knees, the other beneath her back. Her small body vibrated with spasms. Her skin was too cold. He rocked her toward his chest and lifted her.

She immediately curled into him—toward the heat.

Shifting her so that he held most of her weight with one arm, he swept the hair from her face. Her lips were cracked and bleeding, her breaths barely visible. "Reese, can you hear me?"

No response.

His throat went dry, his thoughts suddenly disorderly. *She must live. For... She simply must.*

"Didn't know," Ulric said. "Most prisoners don't require food during their time down here."

"Her majesty will hear of your threat and she will have your head," one of the other guards said from outside the cell. The man spun on his heel, presumably to inform the queen of what had transpired.

Let them try to take my head, Keen thought.

"See that the queen does hear of it. And inform her that if the girl dies, Emain will attack."

He didn't know how he'd follow through on that warning while trapped in New Kingdom with no means of reaching Emain. He was in no position to go up against this queen—a queen without honor. But he would worry about that later. Once he'd gotten the girl to safety.

Reese had been kidnapped by the Halven Army on Earth at the command of Fae. No matter the military skirmish, all agreed on a code of conduct toward the innocent. What harm had the human female caused? She had frustrated Keen while he'd gone about his duty protecting her roommate Elena—severely so—but he'd never wished Reese ill.

This crime—this torture of *her*—defied the code.

Keen rarely allowed anger to distort his thoughts, but at this moment, his duty to his people was the last thing on his mind. "Someone will pay for this."

CHAPTER

THREE

I'm dying.

Reese's thoughts came in fragments. The fraternity party. Angry men. Fae. She had never so much as broken a bone, but somehow she knew she was close to death.

Where were the flashbacks of good times? Where was the sense of peace she was supposed to feel?

Her body shook, but that was all it would do. She couldn't get it to move, not even to open her eyelids. And a tight band of heat wrapped around her.

Uncomfortable. She whimpered.

"You will be all right," a deep, melodic voice said, though the man's tone appeared laced with fear.

That voice. She knew it, didn't she? Was he one of the men who'd captured her? No. They were cruel. This man wasn't.

"Open your eyes," he said.

She wanted to, but they wouldn't cooperate.

"*Please,* Reese."

This time there was anguish in his tone. He worried for her.

She was going to die and she'd done nothing with her life, not really. She wasn't ready.

She must have drifted off, because her next thought was that the tight band of heat around her was still suffocating, but she was beginning to feel sensation in her limbs. And someone was running a very large hand up and down her back.

Okay, maybe she wasn't dying. She snuggled closer to the heat in front of her face and brushed her nose against —skin?

Reese blinked her eyes open. She squinted and waited for them to focus...on a man's chest.

He was the warmth she'd sensed surrounding her. And he wasn't wearing clothes.

What the...? Reese tried to move away. But even though she got her eyelids to cooperate, her body was more sluggish.

"It's okay. You are safe, but you need to stay close to me. You were too cold," he said. "The blankets weren't working."

Reese angled her head back and peered up, up...at the face of an angel. White-blond hair that brushed his shoulders, and the most beautiful masculine features she'd ever seen.

Oh, hell no. "You?" she croaked, her throat dry.

She wiggled until some much-needed inches separated her from the hot Fae guard who'd protected her roommate this past week—and frustrated Reese to no end with his pompous attitude. "Where's Elena, Keen? And what am I doing here?"

He reached over and tucked blankets around her like a

mother hen. She could see that he wasn't as unclothed as she'd first thought; he'd only removed his shirt. And, of course, he had an amazing body underneath all the black he typically wore.

She frowned and slapped his hands away. "Knock it off!"

"You must stay warm. I didn't think you'd…"

"I was dying."

He lifted his emerald gaze to hers. "Yes."

The jewel tone of Keen's eyes had been alarming when she first met him. They still unnerved her. They were beautiful, there was no getting around that, but the way he looked at her now, with intensity and a confusing air of fear, set her mind whirling.

Reese drew in a steady breath and accepted the glass of water he handed her. She gulped down the liquid and choked.

"You have gone too long without food or water," he said. "You must drink slowly."

She took another sip and handed the glass back to him. "Why are you giving me water and keeping me warm? Aren't you here to finish me off?"

Keen's head notched back as if he were surprised.

Well, what did he expect after his people kidnapped her?

The arrogant look he normally wore replaced his worried expression.

This was more like it. This was the Keen she knew.

"I am here to help you," he said. "Elena insisted on it. The Newlander queen who imprisoned you was…forgetful. She left you in the care of someone unfamiliar with the needs of humans. I pointed out your dire physical state, and she allowed me time to help you heal. You must relax. You are not well, and this excitement cannot be good for your body." His gaze dipped.

Even though she was completely hidden beneath the ten inches of covers he'd packed over her, Reese's legs shifted under his stare, her flesh slipping across cold sheets. *All* of her flesh, with the exception of the thin pair of panties she wore. She hadn't bothered with a bra under her fitted dress. "You took my clothes off while I was unconscious? Goddammit, Keen!"

He let out a long-suffering sigh. "I assure you, it required little effort with the amount of apparel you wear, or lack thereof. That red bandage you call a dress barely covered your—"

"You arrogant—"

"Reese, I did not save your life only to argue with you." He propped up on one elbow, his broad shoulders encroaching on the space between them, and cocked his head. "It is impressive that after all you've been through, you have the energy to yell at me."

He made a good point. She felt like hell.

She took a deep breath and closed her eyes. When she was calm again, she opened them. "What is going on? Why did they leave me down there to die?"

Keen lay back and stared at the ceiling. "They didn't intend to kill you. Most Fae have never spent time on Earth and don't understand the needs of humans. Ulric didn't realize you require food and warmth to survive. Fae are nearly immortal. We only die under extreme circumstances, and until recently, we've never known disease. We do not get sick, and injuries and malnourishment are not enough to kill us, unless the deprivation goes on for months."

So they hadn't meant to kill her. "What about the things they said? That woman—the one with the gray hair

—she suggested I was Halven. I thought she was confused, but then she and that man, Marlon, mentioned my father. And they weren't talking about my dad. They were talking about a Fae."

Keen's gaze snapped to Reese. *"No."* His eyes were wide, intense again.

She snorted. "That's what I said."

He took in her body, as though he could see through the blankets. Then he reached out and tried to pull back the covers. "It cannot be."

"Hey!" She slapped his hand away a second time.

She might wear the sexy dresses her mother bought her, but Reese's body was *hers* and she didn't give free looks. In fact, only one guy had seen what lay underneath her clothes, though everyone believed differently. Didn't matter if they thought she slept around. And it didn't matter what Keen thought either, because she knew the truth.

Keen grabbed her trembling hand, twisting it this way and that. "The signs: shaking, which happens when Halven come into their powers; surviving for days under extreme circumstances no human could have survived." His bright gaze lifted to hers. "I sense it now." He stared past her. "I try not to sense anything around you, but if I pay attention—I sense it. The energy level you give off...different from before. You are Halven." A hint of fear touched his voice.

Reese swallowed and looked away. Her roommate Elena was Halven, and she had strange abilities. Reese didn't want that. She wanted to be normal. Badass, but normal. "If it's true, that would mean my mom slept with one of you. I don't think my father could have slipped a newborn in under my mother's nose." She rolled to her back and covered her face with her hands.

What was happening? She was supposed to go to

college and build a new life—far away from the deranged one her parents had subjected her to. And now she found herself in a world more complex and disturbing than the one she'd left behind?

Keen's large palm covered her hands, and she realized her cheeks were damp with tears. He lifted her still trembling hand and twined their fingers. Sliding closer, he bridged the gap she'd created between them. And then his arm was surrounding her and pulling her close. "It will be all right."

She breathed in his scent. He smelled of cedar and something masculine and good. Comforting. *Dammit.* "Why are you being so nice?"

She felt his heart skip a beat beneath her cheek. "Rest," he said. "You need sleep in order to recover fully."

That wasn't an answer, but she was too tired to argue.

IT SEEMED like seconds later when Reese woke again. She was wrapped in Keen's arms. And her bare chest was flattened against his without the blankets separating them.

Reese sucked in a breath. Keen had a firm hold on her, but his breathing was even, a light vibration coming from his throat—not a snore, more like a deep purr. Kind of cute, but shit! At some point the blankets had fallen, and she was still nearly naked. She must have snuggled up to keep warm. How the heck was she supposed to get out of this without waking him?

She gingerly reached down for covers and slowly pulled a blanket higher.

Keen shifted, his breathing less modulated. He tightened his hold on her, and the precarious grasp she had on the blanket broke.

His head dipped into her hair and he seemed to breathe in, his nose nuzzling her ear.

She froze, her heart pounding in her chest.

A second later, the press of Keen's fingers on her back stilled. "Reese?" His voice was groggy and deep.

"Yep, still me."

He let out a harsh sigh, and one by one lifted his fingers from her back, until his hand was no longer on her at all. He rolled away and swung his legs over the side of the bed. He sat there for a moment, forearms on his black-clad thighs, staring straight ahead. "My apologies."

Reese gathered the blanket and brought it up and around her. "Do you always snuggle with your prisoners?"

Another harsh breath escaped his chest and he stood. "You're not my prisoner. But no, I do not."

For a moment, her heart was jumping all over the place. At his words, and at the appearance of him without his shirt on, which had her belly somersaulting. The man had an amazingly broad, muscular back.

But this was *Keen*—the arrogant, aloof Fae who protected her roommate. Reese had never liked him, and it was best to remember that. Especially when he wasn't wearing his shirt.

Her stomach rumbled loudly. Embarrassingly. "Would it be too much to ask for some food? I will take unseasoned broth at this point. Matter of fact, that sounds heavenly."

He ran his hand through his hair, the breadth of his back and shoulders and the movement of muscles beneath his skin distracting her again. He shook his head and pulled a black long-sleeved shirt from a gold-upholstered chair, tugging it over his head. "Of course. I should have had something brought up."

He strode to the door of the large bedroom and opened it no more than an inch, then mumbled something to someone outside. Without looking at her, Keen crossed the room to a wooden wardrobe. "You should dress."

Actually, come to think of it, Keen hadn't looked at her since he'd awakened. He'd been avoiding it entirely.

"Well, I would be dressed if someone hadn't decided to take off my clothes," she said saucily.

This time he glanced over, his expression stony. "You were dying. Removing that piece of fabric you used in place of a gown was the only way to save your life. You needed heat."

Reese swallowed and plastered a sarcastic smile on her face. She didn't want to remember the dungeon and the fear that had smothered her while she lay there unable to move, barely able to breathe—wanted to forget it entirely. "Heat? You mean your body?"

He growled. Actually growled. "You will dress." He grabbed something from the wardrobe, seemingly without thought, and tossed it at her. "Then we will see about getting you out of here."

Reese raised her hand and caught the gown in midair, the billowing skirt flouncing down around her arms.

She pulled it forward and stared at the pale blue monstrosity, scrunching her nose. "You can't be serious. Don't you have anything from this century?" Keen frowned, and she rolled her eyes. "Fine. Turn around so I can put this thing on." She'd glimpsed other doors in the room—likely a bathroom among them—but she had no energy to stand.

He did as she asked—*shocking*—and faced the wall. The one with a green mural depicting winged warriors in a bloody battle. Not exactly the motif she'd go for in a bedroom, but it was luxury compared to the dank cell where they'd originally held her.

The stone dungeon, the four-poster bed she'd just slept in, and the rest of this ornate room—it was as though she'd entered another century. "We are in the same time dimension, right?" she asked. "I didn't get sent back in history or anything, did I?"

He sighed in exasperation. "Time travel is a human fiction. The Tirnan timeline coincides with the Earth realm...for the most part."

For the most part?

She shook her head. Did it matter? She was stuck here and had bigger things to worry about. Like why they wanted her. Where Elena was. And how she was going to get home.

Reese attempted to slip the puffy dress, which had enough fabric to cover three women, over her head. It took forever, but she managed to pull her arms through the proper holes and get it fastened with a bit of wiggling and stretching. At least Fae utilized modern conveniences like zippers.

She tried to lift her arms over her head, but only managed to get them halfway up. The cut of the gown prevented full mobility.

Whenever she'd seen Keen he was in a slim black uniform and military boots. This couldn't be what his people wore on a regular basis.

"You can turn around now." She tugged on the collar that covered her neck. "What's with the double standards? I don't see men walking around in frilly shirts."

Keen's mouth quirked as he took in the gown. "Finally, you wear clothing."

"Why in the world would you prefer a woman in this?"

"It is proper. It is also what those at the palace don. Not everyone in this realm has such luxury. You should feel fortunate." Keen tilted his head toward the door. "Your food has arrived."

A knock sounded a second later, and Reese started. "How did you know someone was at the door? I didn't hear anything until they knocked."

He walked away, ignoring her.

Typical. Did he ever answer a straight question?

She craned her neck to see if her food had in fact arrived as Keen predicted.

He greeted the person at the door and accepted a large tray, deftly toeing the thick wooden door closed behind him. He strode to the bed and placed the tray on top of the mattress beside her.

Reese leaned over and lifted lids off plates. Pastries, there were pastries...and tea, butter...some kind of fruit thing shaped like a purple heart. She'd pass on the weird fruit, but yay for pastries.

Breaking off a hunk of croissant, she shoved it in her mouth and closed her eyes, moaning with pleasure. "How do you plan to get me out of here?" she said around a mouthful of food. Not exactly elegant, but given she was hungry enough to ingest her arm, manners went out the window. "They didn't seem anxious to let me go." She eyed a dish of jam and slathered it on her next bite. "Said they wanted to monitor me for powers."

Keen shook his head. "Not all Halven acquire powers. It is extremely rare. Your roommate was one of the exceptions. A Halven must be of royal blood—the closest lineage to the angels—to have a chance of possessing abilities. Even then, it is not guaranteed."

Reese stopped chewing and raised her eyebrow. "Angels? No wonder you're all so high and mighty. In any case, that Marlon guy said he sensed powers in me, and the woman agreed."

Keen strode to the window, staring out. "It is highly unlikely you will gain powers."

"But they told me—"

"I will go to them and discuss your release," he said. "They kidnapped you in order to get to Elena before she could create a cure for the disease. She managed to cure it anyway. They have no more use for you." He leaned his wide palms against the frame of the window. "If they do not wish another war with Emain, they will negotiate your release."

Reese shrugged and kept eating. Keen didn't believe she had powers, and why should she care? It was a far-fetched notion.

She considered the bracelet Marlon had been interested in. She pulled up the sleeve of her dress, because the darn thing covered every inch of her skin. As though her body were shameful—which made her hate the dress even more. "While you're down there, find out about this emblem. They said it's my father's. If nothing else, I'd like to know who he is."

Keen turned, eyes narrowing on her arm. He walked over and went to one knee in front of her, lightly touching the bracelet.

Up close, Reese saw the smoothness of his pale skin and the light beard that had grown overnight along his square jaw that was a few shades darker than his hair. His lips were full, a light raspberry. She could believe Keen descended from angels. His beauty was otherworldly and annoyingly distracting. Fortunately, his irritating personality offset all the hotness.

Keen made a sound deep in his throat. One of frustration. He said something in a language she didn't understand, but that she'd bet was a curse, given the vehemence behind it. He stood.

"What's wrong?" she asked, preferring this side of Keen. Cuddly Keen had her going all gooey inside. Grumpy Keen was much easier to handle.

He strode toward the door. "Remain here until I return."

Reese was about to argue with his order, but then she reconsidered. The food was in this room and she was starved; no need to get sassy now. But Keen could damn well expect a full interrogation once he returned.

Her bracelet had meant something to him; she could see it on his face. And she wanted to know what that was.

FOUR

Keen left the palace guest bedroom while Reese ate her first solid meal in days, and descended two flights of stairs to the queen's quarters.

It couldn't be. Reese Fisher could not be the daughter of Hakon Radnor. That would make her... No. There was a mistake.

After he'd attempted to leave the dungeon with Reese, a regiment of the queen's guards had come to take him away. Or kill him. Then they'd seen the state of their small female prisoner, who was near death.

Portia was no fool. She'd kept Reese captive for a reason. Once her men had confirmed Reese's physical state, she'd given them the order to provide Keen a room in which to nurse the small human back to health. Now that Reese lived, Keen had to negotiate a new deal.

Seven New Kingdom guards waited outside the queen's chambers. They sized Keen up before grudgingly allowing him entrance. There was no need for another weapons search. They'd removed his weapons days ago and he'd not been left alone since he arrived, except inside the bedroom with Reese. Even then, he'd been too busy keeping Reese warm to find a way to arm himself.

Inside the suite, Portia reclined on a ruby chaise with her eyes closed while a serving girl rubbed her shoulders. Marlon St. Just, the mastermind behind the virus that had nearly wiped out Keen's entire race, sat at a nearby table typing on a laptop. Marlon was a brilliant scientist, and it seemed he'd brought his work with him to Tirnan. Which was not a good sign, considering the man's interest in creating diseases that killed Fae.

Beatrice, Portia's daughter, sat across from St. Just, polishing her sword and looking bored. Her strawberry-blond hair was pulled back in braids that ran along the sides of her head in a traditional female warrior pattern.

The last time Keen had seen Beatrice, no one had known her mother was behind the disease sweeping their land. Beatrice had taken Keen by surprise and glamoured him into forgetting his duty to protect Elena. The results could have been catastrophic. Fortunately, Portia and Beatrice were still lying low and hadn't dared make an attempt on Elena's life. They'd merely wished to distract the girl and delay her work on the antivirus.

Keen would never forget that Beatrice was just as sadistic as her mother.

One of the guards closed the door behind Keen, but not before Keen caught the angry glint in the man's eye as he glanced across the room at Marlon.

So not all of Portia's soldiers approved of the Halven's presence? *Good.*

For a moment, Keen considered taking all three of them out. What they'd done to his people... So many deaths on their hands. And what they'd done to Reese. Keen was one of the Fae's best warriors; he could disarm them and kill them in seconds, along with the guards outside the room. But he could not escape the palace along with the girl. Reese would be at the mercy of his people, and Fae barely tolerated Halven, even after the Halven Elena saved them.

"I wish to return the girl to the Earth realm," Keen said to Portia. "Her health is stable for now."

Portia glanced over, then closed her eyes again. "No."

Keen might be a deadly warrior, but like all Fae, he was capable of keeping his emotions in check. "You have no more use for her. The Halven Elena cured our people of the disease. Holding on to her friend as bait no longer serves a purpose." Though Keen knew that wasn't true. They held Reese for another reason. If he restated the obvious, perhaps they'd reveal it. "You nearly killed Reese in your attempt to keep her here. Every moment she remains puts her at risk."

This time Portia didn't bother to open her eyes before speaking. "The Halven stays. She will be useful."

Keen clenched his jaw. "If you wish her to survive, then allow me to guard her. Our brethren do not understand humans or Halven, and there is little tolerance for her kind."

Portia swatted the serving girl's hands away and sat up. "And why should I allow you to remain in my kingdom? You are not an ally, Keen Albrecht. You are fortunate I do not have you beheaded. Even now my curiosity as to why you risk your life for the girl is the only thing that keeps you alive."

Portia would not believe him if he told her the truth. That Keen had made a promise to Elena to find her friend and bring her back safely.

Halven were considered unnecessary. To make such a promise would seem foolish, but the Halven Elena was special. Powerful in her own right, she'd saved his people. Keen knew firsthand the sacrifices she'd made for them.

He'd taken a great risk in traveling here. But in all of the battles he'd fought, no one had managed to extinguish his immortal life—and he had no intention of giving it up now. He'd keep his promise to Elena and return Reese safely. "If you wish control of Emain, you will need my assistance. The girl's health is integral to gaining what you want."

"Utter rubbish!" Portia stood forcefully. "She is only Halven. One I may dispose of at my will."

"If she were merely Halven, you would not have allowed me to save her. As Elena Rosales has proven, Halven are not so useless as we once believed. They can wield great power. The power to kill"—he glanced at Marlon, who was paying attention now—"and the power to heal."

Beatrice sat forward, her gaze hardening.

Portia held up her hand to stay her daughter. She tipped her head to the side. "Continue."

"Emain will see proper care of Reese Fisher as an act of diplomacy. I will remain here to ensure she is kept safe and alive, and report as much to Emain when the time comes. That will give you the power to negotiate a truce with them."

Portia chuckled humorlessly. "And why would I wish a truce? I could have Emain under my control at the snap of my fingers."

"Possibly. Or not. You attempted to take control of Emain days ago, and were not successful."

Portia's mouth twisted in a cynical smile. "The disease spread more widely than I'd planned. I assure you, if we'd had all of our warriors, we would have taken over the Earth stronghold too."

"Or you could gain it now without bloodshed and notifying the humans of our existence. The last battle on Earth took all of Emain's diplomatic resources to cover up. You will not be able to keep a second battle quiet. Humans are not that gullible."

"Do not tell me what I can or cannot do, Keen Albrecht." Her eyes were as cold as the Land of Ice, where no Fae dared venture. "You have no idea of the power I wield. The palace knows what they have in store should they test me, as does my military. You'll soon find that everyone is at my mercy. I don't need your help with Emain. I will take it and there is nothing and no one who will stop me." Her hands balled into fists at her sides and she stood. "I am descended from Oldlander kings, and they made me a servant to the New Kingdom royal family. I deserved a place on Old Kingdom's throne!" She was breathing heavily, smoothing down her skirts. "But that is in the past. I rule New Kingdom now, and I will take both lands as payment for what I've suffered."

She tapped the side of her mouth. "You too have lost what was rightfully yours... If you wish to remain in New Kingdom, I will consider it. As long as you agree to my conditions."

She was hiding something—holding it over the heads of the Newlanders. Nothing else explained why the strong hadn't lashed out for what she'd done, unleashing the disease on their land.

Fae could not lie. Whatever he agreed to, he must uphold. It was that or be sent back to Emain without Reese.

Or killed—either was a possibility.

Keen had ventured to New Kingdom knowing the danger it posed, but he'd sworn an oath to Elena, and he would keep it. "What are your conditions?"

Portia stepped around the chaise and rested her hands on the back. "You will remain Reese's guardian—to keep her healthy, as you say—and to ensure she does not escape my land."

He waited for her next condition, for there was surely more.

"We hail from the same place, you and I," she continued. "Are you still an Oldlander, or has the human realm poisoned you?"

"I have no fealty to the human realm." *Some of the humans that reside there, yes, but not the realm itself.*

"Good. My second condition is that you promise to keep me and mine safe...and third, when the time comes, you will do my bidding in Old Kingdom. If you promise me this, I will reward you with a return to our beloved homeland. You wish that, do you not?"

"I wish to protect my brethren in Old Kingdom," Keen said cautiously.

"Yes, of course you do." She grinned, but Portia smiled with teeth instead of eyes. "Follow my orders and I will ensure you return to our native land unharmed."

"What of the girl?"

Portia strode to the window overlooking the palace yard. "Do not worry about the girl. She will remain safe as long as you abide by my wishes. Leave me now." She flicked her hand over her head. "Return to the girl...or practice your swordplay with my guards. Whatever you wish. Just keep the girl out of my way."

Keen could make certain Reese was safe, as he'd promised Elena, and walk out with his life by agreeing to Portia's demands. Returning to Old Kingdom after so long held appeal, though not to do Portia's bidding. But he would worry about that later. What bothered him now was why Portia wanted Reese. "She claims you told her she possesses powers."

Portia looked over her shoulder, then slowly turned and faced him. "She remembered that, did she? The girl was more aware than I assumed."

Marlon, who'd been silent throughout the conversation, stood and moved closer to Portia. Beatrice merely sat with her arms crossed.

"Reese Fisher is Marlon's half-sister, Hakon Radnor's daughter," Portia said. "You are aware of Hakon's claim to the Old Kingdom throne?"

Keen nodded woodenly.

"Only you, Keen, come before Hakon as heir to the throne, but you gave up the right to reign, did you not?"

There was no need to agree. She knew his history, as did all Fae.

"It was that or lose your life to Osulf Niall with the rest of your family. He spared you because you were an infant at the time. Most generous coming from Niall, who showed little mercy during his reign. Before you came of age, he had you swear an oath to never take the throne. Perhaps he allowed you to live because he knew you'd be a powerful ally and weapon one day? It's that I am counting on."

And here was the next part to Portia's demand.

"Osulf is dead," she said. "The rights to the throne you signed away when you came of age are nullified, and Old Kingdom needs a new leader."

"Niall's son, the Halven Derek, leads Old Kingdom now," Keen needlessly informed her.

She visibly bristled. "And many do not agree that he is the rightful heir."

That was not what Keen had heard. Portia did not want Derek in charge, but the Oldlanders were not so opposed to the Halven's rule. Derek had made minor strides in winning them over and gaining the respect of his soldiers. It could have something to do with the magical strength he'd wielded in taking down his father.

"Reese will come into an ability," Portia continued. "And Radnor will want his Halven daughter. I wish to leverage his desire."

The ouroboros emblem Reese wore told Keen of her Fae parentage, but he'd hoped he was mistaken. "St. Just is also said to be Radnor's Halven child, and he does not possess an ability. It is possible Reese will not either."

Portia looked toward Marlon. The Halven nodded at her silent communication. "She will possess powers. Marlon has none to speak of, but he can tell human from Halven, and Halven from Fae. He has enough angel blood to detect magic, and he senses it with Reese. As do I. As do you."

Keen did. He'd always sensed something unusual about Reese. He simply hadn't wanted it to be so. "What ability do you anticipate in her?"

Portia raised one hand, palm up, and shrugged lightly. "That remains to be seen, does it not? She comes from a strong, noble line. There are many powers that could manifest—all, of course, mental abilities. You will watch Reese Fisher, and when she comes into her powers, you will inform me. Then, and only then, will I tell her father she is here. The girl turned eighteen six days ago. Her ability will manifest soon, if it has not already."

Keen had managed to negotiate a way to remain in New Kingdom, where he could watch over Reese, but in doing so, he was giving up his freedom and binding himself to Portia. She also wanted him to betray the Halven Derek by helping her take over his land. Keen wasn't opposed to returning to his homeland of Old Kingdom, but not at Portia's bidding, and not as her puppet prince.

But he would not leave the girl. Not here, where she was sure to be used or killed.

He turned to leave.

"Ah, ah, ahh," Portia said. "Aren't you forgetting something?"

Keen stopped and faced her, catching the smirk on Beatrice's face. He dropped to one knee. "I swear on my life to protect you."

Portia smiled. "That will do for now." Her smile dropped. "You may go. But don't forget whom you answer to from now on. You are no longer an Emain soldier, or that silly Halven Elena's bodyguard. Whatever oath you gave her is void—my Fae blood overrides it. You fight for me now."

REESE GLANCED up as Keen entered the room, his handsome face tense with anger, his gaze focused inward.

Her stomach tightened. He'd gone to negotiate a way for her to return home, but by the expression on his face, things couldn't have gone well. "What happened?"

He took her in for the first time since he'd entered, and frowned even more, if that were possible. "What have you done to your dress?"

Reese glanced down. She'd tied the hem of her skirt into a knot. "I'm not Fae, Keen."

He raised an eyebrow. "What does that have to do with the manipulation of your clothing?"

"I'm not six feet tall! This thing you gave me to wear was tripping me."

He sank into one of the plush Louis XVI?—XVIII?—whatever—some ancient fancy chair. "Tying your dress up will not do," he said. "You may not show your legs."

"My *shins*—and why not? How prudish are you people?"

He pressed his thumb and forefinger to his forehead. "Do not argue with me right now. Do as I say and you might survive."

She took in his slightly bowed shoulders. What exactly had happened in that meeting?

She walked over and touched his arm.

He flinched and glared at her. "Do not touch me."

Heat suffused her face. She wrapped her arms around her waist and turned away. Keen had never been the soft sort, but his rejection hit home.

She'd been taken for granted, ignored, betrayed by men—why did she think Keen would behave any differently?

The way he'd held her with such tenderness this morning didn't matter. Or that it had felt like the most natural thing she'd ever experienced. She was a burden to him and he didn't want her around.

"Your father is Hakon Radnor," Keen said, drawing her attention. "Radnor is part of a noble Fae line. He would have ruled Old Kingdom had Osulf Niall not defeated him in a battle that nearly killed his entire family—a practice Niall was known for in his campaign to gain power."

Reese looked over her shoulder. His expression was serious. "A nobleman? Elena is a Fae princess, or her mother is. How is it possible I am one too? How many noble Fae can there be?"

"You are not a princess; Radnor does not rule Old Kingdom at the moment. And Elena's mother, Theodora Rainer, is the rightful queen of New Kingdom, not merely a princess. However, to answer your question, there are little more than a handful of families between the two kingdoms with noble blood."

Reese sank onto the edge of the large bed. "Are you sure that man is my father? Maybe there's been some mistake."

"Portia, the woman you described? She is currently leading New Kingdom. Though the crown rightfully belongs to Elena's mother, Portia took control of New Kingdom while the disease weakened our realm. She is ruthless and ambitious. She would not make a mistake regarding your parentage. She feels it will benefit her to keep you near. And the bracelet you wear... The gold charm is your father's."

Reese shook her head. "It could be a coincidence that my mother gave me a charm that happens to be some Fae dude's emblem."

Keen gave her a mocking look. "It is identical to the unique ouroboros design of Hakon Radnor's house. You are also Halven and coming into your powers. There is no mistake."

She was Halven and her father—a Fae who would have been king—was from Old Kingdom?

This was insane.

Reese swallowed the fear threatening to choke her, and gave him a false grin. "You think I'll develop some amazing ability like Elena? I'd love to be able to manipulate fire and singe a few jackasses who've crossed me over the years."

Keen frowned, and even Reese couldn't hold on to the smile.

She stood and paced in front of him. "I don't understand how this even came to be. You hate me, and I'm getting the feeling that Halven aren't highly esteemed, in general. Why do your people come near humans if we're detested? Why mate with us to begin with?"

"I do not hate you." His eyes were intent, something she couldn't read hidden in their depths. Then his gaze flickered away. "As to your question of mating, some Fae are led astray and find humans attractive. Your father sired you and Marlon after his battle with Niall, when he was particularly vulnerable after losing so many of his family. The only reason Radnor returned to this realm was for his daughter—his *Fae* daughter. I've heard Radnor is more stable in this last decade. It is possible he would challenge Elena's friend Derek for the throne."

Reese froze in her pacing. "What throne? And *what the what*? Derek—our hot neighbor—is Halven too?"

Keen's gaze flashed to her and he stood. He strode closer. Too close, the jerk. He didn't want her to touch him, but he could crowd her space?

She stepped back.

"Derek and Elena were in Tirnan to create a cure for the disease. Elena succeeded, but they nearly lost Derek. He is the Halven son of the previous king of Old Kingdom, Osulf Niall. He was Niall's only child, and the king did not wish to release him. Niall would have killed Elena if Derek hadn't taken his father's life. As Niall's only living child, Halven or not, Derek now rules Old Kingdom."

Reese rubbed her forehead. "Derek is *Halven*?"

"We established that, yes," he said, exasperated.

Reese stepped away and stared out the window at the men milling in the massive courtyard below. They looked like toy soldiers from this vantage point. Hundreds of them. But they weren't small. They were seven-foot Fae warriors prepared to maim—to kill. "Why didn't Elena tell me about Derek?" She cut her hand through the air. "Never mind. She was protecting me—I get it." Reese spun around. "How many Halven are there? And how can we all be descended from noble Fae?"

Keen returned to his chair and sank into it. "There aren't as many Halven as you might think. We persuade young Halven to attend Dawson through scholarships and other means. Once there, Halven with potential powers are assigned to the dorm you live in."

Her eyes widened. "Are you kidding me? You're saying they herded us there?"

He shrugged lazily. "It was an efficient way to keep track of you. Though not all in your dorm are Halven. The Emain scientists mixed in regular students to maintain an appearance of normalcy. Halven tend to be taller than the average human. Only the scientists knew who was Halven and who was not. I didn't know you were one when I was assigned to protect your roommate."

Reese began pacing again, her arms swinging in agitation. "You all suck, you know that? Why didn't your people just come to us? Tell us what we are?"

"As I said, there was no guarantee you would manifest abilities. A Halven without abilities is useless and no threat."

She stopped abruptly. "Right, like Marlon was no threat? He doesn't have abilities and he created the only virus capable of *killing* Fae."

Keen ran a hand down his face. "We were not prepared for that. However, St. Just had Portia, a powerful Fae, at his side. Many others helped him as well."

"Well, I'm not here to help Portia. I *won't* help her, no matter how long she keeps me in this place. She might as well let me go."

He sat forward, forearms on his thighs. "That will not happen. You must be patient until we negotiate a release."

Keen had saved her—ass that he was. He might push her away, but in some twisted fashion, he'd also been there for her.

Reese had to listen to him. It wasn't like she could get out of here on her own. Not with hundreds of toy soldiers surrounding the grounds. "How long do I have to wait?"

He threaded his fingers dangling between his knees. "I don't know."

She peered around in blind exasperation. "Well, what do we do while you're figuring it out?"

He lifted his head. "We wait for your powers to manifest, and pray they are not powerful."

"And if they are powerful?"

"If they are...Portia will use you, whether you want her to or not."

FIVE

Keen must have gotten the hint about Reese's clothes being too long, because soon after he left for guard duty, or whatever he did around this place, a team of seamstresses flooded her room. The women poked and measured, showing her dozens of fabric swatches. Reese prayed it was for something practical like jeans and a comfortable shirt, but the fabrics they presented didn't look cozy, or even stretchy. They looked shimmery and elegant. Which would have been fun back home, but not here amid the Fae and their dungeons.

What was with dressing her up like a Victorian doll? It was one thing for her to wear the dresses her mom bought for her back home. They were on the sexy side, but they were fun, and Reese loved her mom. The Fae taste in women's clothing sucked.

Reese stood still while the women did their thing. She was in nothing but a flowing white undergarment that was thin but covered her from collarbone to knee. So basically, she was clothed beneath the clothing she'd eventually wear. She'd hate to see what they wore for bathing suits.

A light rap sounded, and the large wooden door to her room opened.

Ulric entered, his eyes darting away at the sight of her. "You are well?" He stared at the wall, seemingly embarrassed.

Reese shook her head. She wasn't fully dressed, but she was wearing her potato sack underwear. Ulric hadn't had a problem with her tight, short dress when she'd been in the dungeon, yet now he blushed?

"Are you talking about after you starved and nearly froze me to death?" she asked.

He turned to her and his handsome mouth pulled back in discomfort. "I did not know you were so...fragile. Please forgive me."

So far, Marlon and Portia, and even Keen, at times, acted as if she were inferior. Why would Ulric care how he'd treated her? "Are you trying to gain information by being nice to me? Because I'll tell you right now, I know nothing."

His eyebrows drew together, and suddenly Reese experienced something that made her think she hadn't fully recovered from her dungeon stay.

She couldn't tell by his expression—yet somehow she sensed sincere guilt for the way he'd treated her in the cell.

"I will leave you to your—" He waved his hand vaguely at the fabrics. "I merely wished to apologize for how I enacted my orders. I should have confirmed your—uh —needs."

A Fae with a conscience?

"Hold on. Before you go, let me ask you something. You treated me like a piece of meat when they dumped me in that cell. Is this change of heart all because you feel bad?"

He shifted his feet. "I thought you were a human when you first arrived."

"So?"

"It would have made you...less."

"Less, as in no biggie if you'd used my body for your pleasure?"

He winced lightly—only it was *mental*. He'd made no physical movement.

She was losing it. Discovering Fae existed—that she was a part of it—her mind was beginning to snap.

"I would have never touched you, or anyone, without approval," he said. "But I've heard humans are...easy." He lifted one shoulder. "I was curious."

She sighed. There might even be some truth to that. Fae were beautiful; they probably never got turned down. "You realize there wouldn't be Halven if you guys weren't so eager to sleep with the riffraff?"

Ulric exuded light remorse. Again, not from something he did; she'd *sensed* it. "Halven are considered a distasteful side effect. No offense, miss. The Halven Elena saved our people. Some are worthy."

"All Halven and humans have value."

"As you say."

Reese took a deep breath. Ulric was trying, even if he was extremely misled. Fae had been raised with these beliefs for who knew how long? That they'd changed their thinking at all was probably miraculous.

One battle at a time. "Before you go, can you talk these ladies into making me something comfortable to wear? Pants and a top? Something I can move in."

He nodded and approached the head seamstress. She wore a matronly high-necked gown with her measuring tape tied like a belt around her waist. Reese wasn't optimistic, but she was desperate for something other than Victorian dresses, and Ulric seemed in a charitable mood.

He spoke in a low tone to the woman. The woman's mouth pinched, but she gave him a curt nod.

Ulric dipped his head toward Reese, then headed for the door, exiting the room. It was a simple gesture, that head dip, but Reese picked up on so much more.

Emotions he hadn't shown or in any way expressed.

Ulric still felt shame, but he was cheerier than when he'd entered...and Reese knew this because she could tell his emotions like her own. The same way she knew the head seamstress was irritated, and that the younger one was excited.

What. The. Hell.

The excitement from the younger seamstress she might have read from physical cues, because the girl was bubbly, but detecting the other Fae's emotions? No way.

This couldn't be the powers Keen had talked about. It wasn't the ability to create fire or move objects. This was just...weird.

She was hungry, that was all. She'd not eaten nearly enough.

Reese reached for a sandwich from the food tray. It contained some mysterious meat substance she tried not to think about while she ate.

And if she could tell her seamstresses' emotions as they flittered around the room, she kept it to herself...until two days later.

~

"Where are we going?" Reese nearly jogged to keep up with Keen's long stride, all the while taking in her surroundings.

The New Kingdom palace was bigger than she'd imagined—long corridors with beautiful light stone flooring and intricate wainscoting along the walls and niches. The niches and built-in shelving were filled with statues of warriors and angels. Paintings on the walls looked like masterpieces, only no masterpieces she'd ever seen in the museums she'd visited with her wealthy parents.

"You said you wanted exercise," Keen replied without slowing his pace. "We will train."

Reese peered in an open doorway they passed. It led to the biggest room she'd ever seen, and that was saying a lot, considering the ballrooms and homes she'd been in, growing up in Hollywood. The stunning passageway where they walked looked miniscule compared to the room, which seemed to extend the length of a city block.

And then Reese's brain caught up to Keen's words. "Train? For what?"

His jaw firmed. "You need fighting skills. The longer they contain you, the more concerned I grow about their intentions."

Reese swiveled her head distractedly at the statue of what looked to be a woman making love to a tall, muscular man with wings. *What the...* She shook her head and raced to keep up. "Right, well, you said they wanted to use me. We just don't know how."

Keen stopped suddenly and Reese almost ran into him. "What do they expect to gain from you? And what do they hope to gain from your father?" he asked rhetorically and with a great deal of agitation.

"Father? You mean that guy my mother had the affair with? Who cares? It was a one-night stand. I doubt he cares I'm alive."

Keen sighed harshly. "Your kind might be blasé about coupling—"

"Whoa, *coupling*? You mean sex. Are Fae really that uptight that you can't say the word?"

He stepped forward, but Reese held her ground. He might be big and striking, but she was no pushover. "Coupling is not considered an act one does for the simple pleasure of it."

Reese snorted. "I highly doubt that. Ulric..." The look Keen leveled at her made her pause before continuing that train of thought. Keen could be a scary-ass warrior when he wanted to be, and the look he was giving her right now said he was on the brink of rage.

Interesting.

He quirked an eyebrow, but the tension in his jaw didn't subside. "You were saying? Ulric what? He told me he did not touch you."

"He didn't, but he made it clear he'd be happy to warm me up." She grinned, enjoying the figurative steam coming out of Keen's ears. "In other words, he flirted with me when he thought I was nothing but a lowly human only good for...*coupling*. You do know what flirting is, don't you?"

He let out a long, slow breath. Was he even listening? "I will make sure he pays for his words."

Okay, that wasn't the reaction she'd wanted. Well, maybe a little, but not that extreme. "It was nothing. The point is, I highly doubt Fae don't find pleasure in the act."

"I never said that." Something flickered in Keen's eyes.

Oh God, he needed to stop looking at her that way. Every once in a while, he'd shoot her a heated gaze, like the one he was giving her now, and it messed with her head. When he crowded her with all of that arrogant warrior rolling off him, his words giving a different message than his body—it was confusing as hell.

Keen glanced to the side. "It takes most Fae centuries to

sire a full-Fae child, and some never do. There are social rules to ensure paternity. If a man chooses a woman, she must be faithful to him. They may part after a time and partner with another."

She raised her finger. "Hold up. Do you mean the woman has to be faithful...but not the guy?"

"It is our way. The man must know he is the father."

"Kind of a double standard, don't you think?"

"It is the only way to ensure the child belongs to her mate."

"*Or* you could see a doctor and ask him or her to run a paternity test."

"We've never needed doctors; there are no such tests in Tirnan. Running a human test, with the physiological differences between our two species, would be impossible. A human doctor would have to make allowances in Fae and human genetics, and our existence has remained a secret from humans for millennia. It must continue to remain so. Our forefathers insisted on it."

"Your what? You mean the angels?"

"Humans have varying beliefs about religion. Different gods and deities—each religion claiming to own us. Knowledge of our kind would be controversial at the very least, and would cause war in the extreme."

Reese didn't know how many wars had been fought over differences in religious beliefs. *A lot.* "Fine, human doctors are out, but you could still use human science in Tirnan to determine the father of a child. Not like you guys aren't already utilizing other modern conveniences. Or— now here's an idea—Fae could use birth control and then you wouldn't have to worry about who the father was. You could be intimate for pleasure." She made sure to give him a sultry smile on that last word.

Keen scowled. "Birth control? Our greatest wealth is furthering our race, particularly the noble lines closest to the angels. We do not prevent conception."

"Okaaay." She held up her hands. "I get it. It's a touchy subject. We were talking about my biological father, anyway, and I still don't see why he would care about me. My being a mere Halven and all. He returned to Tirnan to be with his *Fae* daughter. No one around here cares about the half-bloods."

"You are correct. We detest Fae-diluted offspring. They're a nuisance and defy everything we hold dear, weakening our abilities."

She clutched her chest in mock pain. "That hurts, Keen. But if it's true…" She paused for dramatic emphasis. "Why did they ask Elena for help? And why are they holding me here?"

He looked away. "Halven of nobility are—"

"Awesome-sauce. Kickass. Gorgeous specimens of perfect—"

"Unusual," he said.

Reese glanced at the ceiling and shrugged. "I'll take it. In other words, I'm *extra special*. I still don't see how that makes a difference. My father is a Fae with noble blood. They think I'll have powers…" Reese's voice drifted off. The emotions she'd picked up from her seamstresses and Ulric came back to her. Emotions she'd read without physical cues. She didn't want to believe that could be her power, because it seemed weird, and to tell the truth, kind of weak. But what if it was?

"What's wrong?" Keen asked.

She shook her head. "Nothing." Reese never read Keen's emotions, and she didn't think the abilities Halven possessed were choosy that way. What she'd experienced couldn't be her power. "If Halven are so universally detested, why would my father want anything to do with me, powers or not?"

Keen stepped back and opened a door across the hall. "Elena saved our people. It left a lasting impression. They may want to keep you in Tirnan for your abilities, something we prize. A few believe Halven of noble blood could be of use—never for procreation, but for other purposes."

Reese rolled her eyes. "Right—never for *sex*. Except, that's how we got here," she said, circling back to the argument she most enjoyed.

Keen frowned. "Enough." He waved her inside a room that looked different from the others she'd seen thus far. This one was—insignificant. Kind of plain. With gym equipment. "The queen and I have come to an agreement, and I've been given access to the training rooms. We will train, and attempt to prepare as best we can for what lies ahead."

Sure, because *that* didn't sound ominous.

SIX

It was a good thing Reese had asked Ulric to convince the seamstress to give her something comfortable to wear, because Keen was bent on breaking her ass in training.

"Again," Keen said, after Reese had performed twenty perfect roundhouse kicks.

"I told you"—she started another set—"I'm a black belt in tae kwon do. It was the one extracurricular my mom allowed me to choose. I won best in my weight class senior year of high school."

"That may be, but you are short and you weigh less than my sword."

"I'm not short, I'm five foot six!"

"Exactly. *Short.*"

She gave up arguing, because she *was* small compared to the six- and seven-foot Fae.

"During a fight with a female," he continued, pacing annoyingly behind her, "you might be evenly matched, even with the Fae's taller stature, but not against a male.

And not against either male or female if they possess weapons or use magic."

Reese could fight a six-foot opponent and kick his ass, as long as she accounted for his longer reach, but not a seven-foot opponent. And Keen was right. If they had weapons or magical abilities, she was screwed.

"You also use your legs too much," he pointed out. "That alone will not save you in a fight. You must practice arm strikes."

She nailed the bag with an axe kick. "Punching didn't earn me points in competitions."

"There are no rules when fighting Fae. The first to kill wins."

Reese faltered, and her next kick landed off. She grabbed the bag and caught her breath, letting his words sink in.

"We will focus on full-body battle tactics," he said, and walked to the center of the mat. He got into ready position. "Perform overhand rights, and uppercuts."

She let go of the bag and moved closer. "You want me to hit you?"

He sneered. "If you can."

Oh, she could. She'd been waiting for the opportunity to strike that smug look off his face. *Bring. It.*

Reese enjoyed hammering Keen with kicks and punches, but the darn Fae was fast. She didn't hit him nearly as often as she would have liked.

She made one last uppercut attempt—and found herself twisted around, her arm locked across her stomach and her back to Keen's chest.

His breath swept over her ear and the side of her face, as though his head had dipped closer. "You will need to work harder if you wish to best one of us." His words came out more sexy than threatening.

Her throat suddenly went dry, her heart hammering. "I need rest."

Keen released her as quickly as he'd disarmed her.

She limped toward the door. "And I could use another one of those trays of pastries and fruit. And cheese. I need lots of cheese. Please don't tell me what kind of animal it comes from. I'm afraid to ask after sampling the meat in the sandwich I ate this afternoon. It tasted gamey."

He hooked the kicking bag off to the side. "The animals in Tirnan are different from those on Earth."

She closed her eyes and held up her hand. "Shhh, no more. Your food tastes good; that's all I need to know."

He shrugged and walked her to her room, stopping outside the door. "You are a better fighter than I assumed."

"Why, thank you." She smiled broadly. It was one of the best compliments he could have given her.

"Tomorrow, we will focus on weapons."

Whoa, what? "But weapons kill."

"It is very difficult to kill a Fae, and highly unlikely you will accomplish it. If you should find yourself in a fight, having the ability to maim might allow you time to escape."

So he wanted her to run and hide? That wasn't her style. Though… "Weapons. Even if your kind can't die from them, I'm not a big fan of guns and such."

"You must get used to them if you are to survive. I cannot watch your every move." Keen glanced away. "There is one more thing. Portia is hosting a celebration in a week. She wishes you to be there. You will wear one of the gowns the servants made you."

"Yeah, what's with all those dresses?" She glanced down at the stretchy black pants, sleek boots, and the comfortable black tunic she wore. "This is way more my style while we're here. And, hey, it's better for training."

"Agreed. You will wear the uniform when we train. The dresses are for formal events. During your stay here, you're considered a part of the New Kingdom court. You must dress as the nobles do. I convinced Portia that if the Fae see you as a friend to the nobility, it might prevent them from attacking you."

"Awesome." She shook her head. "Not like I don't stand out anyway. I'm fair like the rest of you, but I'm still short, as you've so graciously pointed out."

"This is true. Anyone paying attention to your energy level can also tell you're Halven. Not to mention, the entire palace is aware of your presence."

"Exactly. So why do I need to wear those giant dresses?"

Keen's mouth quirked up on one side. "Because they are appropriate." He nodded at a guard outside her room, gesturing for the man to open the heavy wooden door.

"Those monstrosities are what you find appropriate?" she called after him as he walked away.

"At the palace? Yes. Anywhere else?" He looked over his shoulder and down her body. "What you have on would do."

"Because it covers every inch of me?"

"Precisely."

Grrr. She'd show him "appropriate."

CHAPTER

SEVEN

Reese's week was filled with fittings and training and eating. And boredom. How long would she be stuck in this place? What was happening back home? Was Elena okay? It was killing her not knowing.

She plopped onto the giant bed in her room. It was gorgeous and so comfortable it felt like she was lying on a cloud. Regardless of the luxury she came from, Reese was no delicate flower. But being catered to like a princess? Not such a bad thing.

She leafed through one of the books the younger seamstress had pilfered for her. Most of the books in this place were written in a strange language Reese couldn't identify, let alone read, but this one was a children's book and written in English. It described how Tirnan had been created. Kind of fascinating stuff, actually.

If Keen knew she was reading children's books, it would give him more ammunition to mock her.

He'd busted her ass all week in training, and he was right about one thing: she'd never stand up to a Fae. They were faster, stronger, and much, much taller. It was time to admit the truth.

In Tirnan, Reese was short.

She sighed. Keen wanted her to train with a sword, and she'd been arguing against it. The last thing she wanted was to truly injure someone. She considered the Fae a bunch of uptight assholes, but she didn't want to kill them. Was he crazy? But Keen had been adamant. And she couldn't ignore the truth. If it came down to a fight with one of them, she'd be quickly overtaken.

Reese flipped through the pages of the children's book and tried to learn something that might give her an edge.

And the land Tír na nÓg (Tirnan) was created to sustain the children conceived between angel and human, and blessed with powers. Three sons, the angels Gabriel, Zachariel, and Tobias, brought their fair children to live in the land of everlasting youth, beauty, and joy. There they prospered in harmony. Then one day, a Fallen emerged from the center of Tirnan, at the heart of the Land of Ice, and soiled their perfect world.

Reese tapped the page. No wonder the Fae were such vicious bastards. Some fallen angel had deflowered their Garden of Eden.

There were castles and swords, and Keen often spoke of battle in Tirnan. Whatever peace had once existed had died a long time ago. Tirnan wasn't what it was designed to be, and Reese suspected whoever created this place wouldn't approve of the Fae's treatment of humans or Halven. Fae were obsessed with their angelic bloodlines and precious traditions, and they used it as an excuse for all kinds of foul treatment.

She tossed the book aside and stood. The gilded cage they kept her in was getting old. She couldn't remain here forever. It had been almost two weeks since she'd left her and Elena's apartment in their college town. Someone besides Elena had to have noticed she was gone. Granted, her parents were often wrapped up in their own lives, but what about a professor? The next time Reese saw Keen, she'd grill him on what was happening back home.

The sound of the door bursting open startled her. She spun around. And a stream of blinding colors swept into her room. Not just any colors—fabrics—yards and yards of fabrics.

"My lady, your dresses are ready," Enid said happily. Enid was the young seamstress who'd brought her the book. "And look how lovely they are." She petted the red silk. "Do humans truly wear this style?"

Reese walked over and held up the cap-sleeved, off-the-shoulder gown she'd designed, with a sweetheart neckline, cinched waist, and column skirt that brushed the floor. The details were in the cut and fabric, but otherwise it was a very simple dress that accentuated her curves.

More dresses filled the arms of Enid's helpers, modest compared to the one Reese held. "For formal occasions, they wear dresses like this," Reese said, answering Enid's question. "Only with more skin showing. I held back. Didn't want to cause a Fae heart attack."

"A heart attack?" Enid's forehead furrowed. "How can a dress attack one's heart?"

Reese stared. And then remembered that Fae didn't get sick. "A figure of speech. Never mind." The Fae were a tad too literal.

Reese had bargained with the head seamstress to get the red dress made by agreeing to wear one or two of the throat-suffocating gowns, but it had been worth it. She hoped to give Keen the Fae equivalent of a heart attack when he saw her in it. It would serve him right after he'd punished her through training torture all week. He'd said it was for her own good, but he didn't need to work her so hard. She could barely move after each session, the jerk.

"Help me try this one on, Enid?"

"Miss Reese, the celebration begins soon. We must bathe you, and do your hair and makeup."

The celebration was four hours away, but Reese chose to pick her battles. The ladies liked to keep busy, and it looked like spending an afternoon primping Reese was how they planned to accomplish it.

She lifted another dress from the bed where a seamstress had laid it out. This one was a beaded green gown, and it wasn't half bad. It didn't look like the Victorian monstrosities the head seamstress had brought in—more like something the current princess of England would wear. In other words, proper, but very beautiful.

"What is this celebration for, anyway?" As far as Reese was concerned, inviting her to one of their events was a Fae political move she wanted nothing to do with. These people had nearly killed her in the dungeon and still held her hostage. She just wanted out.

Enid set out a robe and soap and a jar of the pretty-smelling shampoo she'd been washing Reese's hair with. "You have not heard? There is a new master of the guard. He will proclaim his fealty to our queen this evening."

Reese's fingers stilled on the green beaded fabric as a chill swept down her spine. When Keen wasn't training with her, he'd been busy. *Really busy* for a guy who wasn't from here; Keen was no more an ally of New Kingdom than Reese.

"But you already know him, miss," Enid said, and looked up. "It is the soldier, Keen of the Albrechts."

Reese's mind raced, her heart dropping to her belly.

Keen was aligning himself with Portia? Had he been behind Reese's abduction all along? No, that didn't make sense. He'd saved her.

Unless he'd pretended to save her in order to get close? But why would he do that?

"Strange, is it not?" Enid went on. "Keen is from Old Kingdom. A handsome male. I do not mind having him around, despite his origins." Her pretty cheeks pinkened.

Enid took the red dress from Reese's hands and laid it along the bottom of the bed next to the green one. "Keen comes from an old family. Having him on our queen's side is a great advantage." Her brow puckered. "Though our queen is not original to our land, either. She too is an Oldlander."

"Does that worry you? The Oldlanders being in charge?" Reese sensed concern from the girl. But she wasn't simply reading it on Enid's face; Reese *felt* the emotion grasp her chest and dip into her gut, as if it were her own, only not her own. Because the emotion had shot from Enid across space, hitting Reese in soft waves.

Okay, this was getting stranger. She needed to talk to Keen about sensing people's feelings. But whose side was he on? Why would he pledge himself to Portia, the woman who'd had Reese kidnapped?

Enid bustled across the room. "We mustn't speak of such things—'tis treason. A powerful leader is a blessing from the angels, no matter the leader's origins. That is all that matters."

No it wasn't. Reese could tell the girl wasn't saying everything. Enid was worried.

Something was happening. Inside this palace; inside Reese's body. She sensed people's true feelings, with or without physical signs. Everyone's except for Keen's.

She considered what Marlon had said about powers presenting. They called her Halven, but how could she be like Elena? Elena's ability to manipulate the elements was powerful, the way a magical ability should be, not to mention way cooler. This emotion thing wasn't what Reese had envisioned when they'd first spoken of abilities, but it was definitely odd.

Tangled in her thoughts, she didn't realize someone had entered until Ulric was halfway across the room.

"You almost caught me undressing again," she said. "I see Fae men have the same impeccable timing as human men."

His mouth twitched, which Reese took for a smile. "Please excuse the interruption. I'm taking over this shift and I wanted to make sure all was well."

"Just peachy—you know, being held captive. Don't you guys have television or computers to make the time pass?"

"Television?"

"That's a no, then? We really need to introduce the palace to electronics."

"The Halven, *Marlon*"—condescension oozed from Ulric's tone—"has a box that he punches his fingers on." Ulric framed his hands to show the size.

"A computer? So only one computer in this entire place?"

"I believe so, Miss Reese." He shifted awkwardly. "The room is to your liking? You are comfortable?"

"I'm perfectly fine." And she was. Ever since Keen had found her, she'd been very well cared for—even spoiled to an extent, with the flower-scented baths and beautiful clothes.

Somehow Reese didn't think that would last. And she worried about Keen's role in all of it.

No longer would she be a passive spectator in this abduction. Mingling with the Fae this evening would be the first test. Time to find out what was really going on.

~

OKAY, so maybe Reese shouldn't have requested a light corset for the red gown. Part of her air supply was being cut off, but the dress looked incredible.

Suffering for fashion even in the Fae realm—that was a new one.

She turned and gazed at the back of the gown in the mirror.

"You are stunning!" Enid exclaimed. "The dress is very —uh—revealing, but such a pretty color. Are you certain you feel comfortable wearing it outside the room? It isn't too late to switch to one of the other dresses. You have many beautiful ones to choose from."

Hell to the no. First of all, the red dress was pretty, and by Earth standards, not at all daring. Second, Reese was tired of being closeted away in this room. She wasn't the most patient person under normal circumstances, and right now someone was trying to decide her fate. She had a right to be a part of that decision-making, and what better way to get attention than to create an entrance no one could ignore? "Nope, this is the one. I'm ready when you are."

"Oh, no, miss. I am not attending. None of the servants are. One of the guards will escort you."

Seconds later, a knock sounded at the door—and Keen entered.

Keen often looked angry; it was a part of his charm. Other times he gave her a sultry look she tried to ignore.

Too darn confusing. But right now, he stopped in mid-stride and stared at her in stunned silence.

Bull's-eye.

Reese spun in a slow circle. "You like?"

His jaw clenched and he glared at Enid, who scurried away. "Remove it."

"Remove it?" Reese *tsk*ed. "I intended to make a splash, but I don't think walking out naked would draw the right attention. Besides, contrary to what some may think"—she cleared her throat pointedly—"I don't like to reveal all the goods."

He stepped forward, and yep—fury filled his features. But she still couldn't sense his emotions the way she could the others'. Which was annoying. If there was anyone whose emotions she'd like to read, it was Keen.

His face contorted. "You cannot possibly wear that."

"I absolutely can, you overbearing Fae. Who are you to tell me what to do?"

"Well, let's see now," he said in a deceptively calm voice, given his body vibrated, hands balled at his sides. "I am the one who saved you. I am the one who keeps you alive in enemy territory. And I am the one with the power to get you out."

"If you have so much power, get me out now."

He ground his molars. "I cannot. Yet."

"Right, so not as much power as you'd like. Which reminds me—*you can't tell me what to wear!*"

A deep sound of annoyance came from his throat. She should be afraid. He was big, and kind of scary when he was angry, but for some reason, Reese wasn't afraid of Keen. He'd never hurt her. She didn't know how she knew that, but she did. And she wasn't reading it on his face, or from some emotion she picked up. She just knew.

"I can't believe you're pledging loyalty to the crazy bitch who kidnapped me," she said, relaying Enid's news. Not because Keen had confided in her, or anything.

He looked away. "We all must make sacrifices."

"Doesn't seem like much of a sacrifice if you're given a promotion."

His hard gaze landed on her. "And how do you know it is a promotion?"

She shrugged. "Isn't it?"

"Things are not as they seem."

"Then tell me how they are."

"It's time; we must leave. Are you going to change?"

Awesome—no answer to her question. "Nope."

Keen looked to the ceiling, then spun toward the door. He strode across the room, and Reese hurried after him, silently cursing the corset.

EIGHT

Keen exited Reese's room and scanned the guards. He shot each of them a look, saying without words what he'd do to them if they stared too long at Reese, or in a manner he thought disrespectful.

What was the small human trying to do? Every male in the palace wouldn't be able to keep his eyes off her.

Keen's fists would be busy tonight.

He glanced back as Reese attempted to keep up in that ridiculous gown.

Ridiculous was a strong word. She was unimaginably beautiful—so beautiful she'd stolen his breath the moment he'd entered the room and caught sight of her.

Humans possessed beauty, he reminded himself. They could charm, and had done so for centuries. It was why Halven existed. Keen had believed, like all Fae, that the offspring of a Fae and human union were without value. At best, Halven were a nuisance, diluting the angel blood. But Keen's charge, Elena Rosales, had proven magically powerful. As powerful as many Fae, or more so, and that was something even Keen couldn't ignore.

That did not mean he supported matings between Fae and humans, or Halven.

It didn't matter how beautiful Reese was; a union between the two of them would never be. Not that he had considered it—he would never consider something so preposterous.

Keen waited near the door as Reese swept out. Ulric took in her outfit, as did the other guards. All of them quickly turned away at Keen's quelling glance. The only guard who didn't was Ulric. He scanned Reese's figure and shot Keen a worried look.

After Reese had described Ulric's suggestive words to her in the dungeon, Keen had immediately sought out the guard and made it clear to him that he was to keep his attentions off her. By breaking the guard's nose. And his arm. And his leg. Fae healed quickly; it was but a minor scratch. Had Ulric touched Reese, he would be growing a new arm right now.

After that was sorted, Keen had ordered Ulric to check on Reese. Reese was protected under the crown of New Kingdom, as long as Keen gave his loyalty to Portia. She was safe, but it was good to know another Fae watched out for the small human while Keen juggled his new duties inside the palace.

Most Fae treated Reese indifferently. Ulric's brotherly concern for the girl was intriguing. If Keen had sensed anything remotely sensual from the guard, he would have had him removed from duty. Thus far, Ulric appeared protective, which Keen approved of. He would allow Ulric to continue looking out for her.

The others—the ones whose eyes nearly popped out of their heads at the sight of Reese's creamy skin revealed by the red gown—would be dealt with later.

She finally reached his side. "Walk more quickly," he said. "I haven't got all night."

Her pert nose tilted up. "Worried you'll miss the celebration of your defection from the kingdom that raised and cared for you?"

He turned down the hallway, glancing back to be sure that she was following him. "Derek's father murdered my family. I don't feel loyalty to the Oldlander crown, even if Derek now rules."

"What about to the people? Your friends?"

"I have no friends in Old Kingdom."

"Why am I not surprised?" she muttered.

"I have been an Emain guard on Earth for a long time—since before you were born. My companions reside there."

Her shoes stopped clicking on the floor beside him. Keen halted and looked back. She stood staring at him.

"What do you mean since before I was born? You're my age, or you look my age. How old *are* you?"

He lifted one shoulder. "Approximately your age—physically. Chronologically, I am one hundred and twenty-seven years old. Give or take. The Tirnan-Earth continuum varies by season, year—it is difficult to predict with certainty."

"A hundred and... What the hell, Keen!"

She glanced at the guards, a good distance behind them now. At her look, they turned their heads quickly. They'd been observing her walk down the hall, the heathens.

"Are all of you that old?"

"No," he said, and waited for her to reach his side before he walked on. They'd never make it to the ballroom at this pace. "Most are older."

The heels she wore clacked quickly as she attempted to

match his pace. "So you're trying to tell me you're one of the young ones?"

"I am not suggesting anything; I *am* young. But don't mistake that for inexperience." He shot her a cocky grin.

Reese rolled her eyes, impertinent as ever. "I guess it doesn't matter. You're immortal. Of course you and the rest of your kind look younger longer... Hey, will I look younger too? Because that would be awesome."

"We know very little of Halven sired by royal Fae. A Halven with no abilities lives longer than the average human."

"I suppose that's something," she said, her gown swishing sensually against her delicate curves as she walked beside him. All the while, Keen caught every male, female, servant, and nobleman they passed, gawking at her.

The men's looks were licentious, the women's jealous. Reese would not make allies if she continued to ignore their customs.

The guards at the entrance to the celebration stood at attention as Keen and Reese approached, the sound of strings and flutes and deep bass floating out.

"My lord," the head guard said, and nodded at Keen.

"*My lord,*" Reese mouthed, her expression taunting.

Keen had been given back his title after he agreed to Portia's terms. He'd been born a nobleman, but his status had been stripped from him when he gave up his right to the throne.

They entered the ballroom to the sound of traditional Fae music. A symphony of what could best be described as a Viking-Gaelic fusion.

Reese gaped. "Wow. This makes the Oscars after-party my parents took me to last year pale in comparison. Is that champagne flowing from a waterfall?"

"That is *brune,* fermented allon leaves, and much stronger than champagne. Do not drink it."

Reese nodded absently as she took in the diamond and sapphire chandeliers overhead. She appeared to scan the ornate woodwork and beveled mirrored walls that made what was a grand room appear even larger.

Keen sighed. She was completely distracted. He'd be lucky to get her out of here alive. "Do not leave my side, little one."

"Sure," she said, staring at the women walking past.

He'd given her two direct orders, and she'd offered no backlash. Which could only mean she wasn't paying attention to a word he said.

A Fae ball was likely different than anything she'd been to before. Fae finery often included a blend of styles from centuries past, with beading and embroidery on the dresses, and embroidered sleeves on the tunics for the men. *Brune* literally flowing from the ceiling ensured everyone enjoyed themselves, and mounds of colorful fruit and finger foods were offered throughout the room as refreshments. In a few hours, a more formal dinner would also be served in a room furnished for dining, and just as elegant as this one. The dinner would consist of multiple courses, an array of desserts, and enough *brune* to have the guests slouching in their seats.

Keen didn't bother with the nonsense of formal court dress. He was a soldier. He wore his uniform—black pants tucked into Fae military boots, and a black long-sleeved shirt that magically protected against extreme weather.

The dress Keen had provided for Reese when she'd first arrived was a servant's gown—it was also the most modest of the palace attire. He'd known it would enrage her, given how little she wore in the Earth realm, but he couldn't help himself. Though he wouldn't admit it if asked, he enjoyed riling the small human. She was most entertaining.

Little did he know she would retaliate with the red dress.

Reese had never backed down from him—a situation he found as infuriating as it was intriguing.

He sighed. If he made it out of New Kingdom with the girl safely, it would be a miracle.

Keen spotted Portia and Marlon at the head of the ballroom, dressed in full noble regalia. He placed his hand lightly on Reese's lower back and guided her over.

Portia took in each of them as they approached, her eyes narrowing on Reese's gown.

Keen quickly tipped his head in a shallow bow. "It is an honor to be here." He nodded to Marlon, who never seemed to stray far from Portia's side.

Smart Halven. Regardless of Marlon's current alliance, Keen's people despised him. Should he leave his protector, he would find himself at the end of a sword.

"Yes, an honor," Portia said absently, still staring at Reese's dress. "She does clean up nicely, does she not, Marlon? Quite beautiful, this one."

Portia's thoughts were a jumble, cleverly hidden from Keen's abilities, but Marlon's mind was more transparent.

Marlon's gaze flickered to Reese, then drifted off. He felt no familial connection or care for his half-sister.

Considering Marlon had had Reese thrown in the New Kingdom dungeon, Keen wasn't surprised. Nor would he ever forget what Marlon St. Just had done to her, or his people. If it hadn't been for Portia's protection, Marlon would have been a dead man the moment Keen set foot on Tirnan soil.

"Our guest this evening will arrive soon," Portia said,

searching beyond them. Her gaze drifted to Keen. "I believe your association with her will prove most fruitful. I am eager for the two of you to be reunited."

He nodded, not allowing his surprise to show. He had no knowledge of a special guest tonight.

Reese glanced between him and Portia. She seemed to concentrate particularly hard on the queen. Her attention was so acute that he looked down to study her face. If only he could read her thoughts.

"May I have this dance?"

Keen had been so focused on Reese he hadn't noticed another Fae approach. He glared at the man standing behind her, waiting for her reply. Wearing slim chartreuse pants and a deep navy tunic with flounces at the wrists, the man was clearly a dandy, with dark blond hair slicked to the side and jeweled rings on several of his digits. Not noble, but higher in the ranks than most.

Keen rolled his eyes, but Reese smiled over her shoulder. She opened her mouth to speak.

"No, you may not," Keen said before she could reply.

She shot him a look of annoyance.

"Now, Keen," Portia said, "if the girl wishes to dance, she may dance. We want her happy."

Since when did Portia care about Reese's happiness? Portia kept the girl alive because she wanted to use Reese in some way Keen hadn't yet figured out.

Reese seemed confused by Portia's sudden change of heart as well, because she looked at the queen in the same concentrated manner she had a moment ago.

"Shoo," Portia said, and waved Reese away. "Dance. Be merry." With a shallow smile, she peered out over the dancers, searching again. For the surprise guest?

Perhaps a dance would not harm the girl. It was early

yet. A single glass of *brune* would make a human pass out, but it took much more before his kind became intoxicated. As long as the dandy kept his hands to himself, all would be fine.

Reese accepted the Fae's outstretched arm, and Keen watched them walk off.

"She is safe," Portia said, eyeing him. "Now, about our guest. It has been a while, but I'm certain you will remember her. Ah"—Portia stared past him, smiling—"here she is now."

Keeping a close eye on Reese as she whirled about the room in the arms of another, Keen paused to glance at the entrance.

And met the gaze of an Old Kingdom companion from his youth.

"Illa Radnor," Portia said in greeting once Illa had made her way over. "I assume you remember Keen of the now deceased Albrechts?"

Interesting that Portia chose to point out Keen's solitude in Tirnan—no family, few he'd call friends. A situation similar to hers.

The only true ally Portia had was her daughter, Beatrice, who'd made few appearances these last several days. Portia's old friends had been the New Kingdom royal family, Elena's ancestors—and the first people Portia had murdered in order to rule New Kingdom.

"Greetings." Illa smiled brightly.

Keen nodded. "It has been many years."

"It has." She blushed and looked at Portia.

Portia stepped closer and linked Illa's arm through Keen's. "Far be it from me to intrude on a wonderful reunion. You must dance. Go, go—" She waved them off the way she'd done with Reese and the Fae courtier Keen was still keeping an eye on.

Reese and the Fae dandy had finished their dance and stood off to the side talking, Reese smiling at something he'd said.

Keen frowned. He took Illa's hand and led her to the dance floor. They danced for a moment before he asked the obvious. "Why did Portia bring you here?"

Illa looked out at the crowd, a smile on her face. "I don't know what you mean."

Her mind was filled with New Kingdom guards twirling in pirouettes like ballerinas, but something else he couldn't quite piece together flashed in the background. She was attempting to block her thoughts. Most weren't as adept at blocking their minds as Portia. Given enough time, he'd figure out what Illa was keeping from him, but he wanted to know now. "You could not have changed this much in the quarter of a century since we last spoke. You were a bright girl—world-wise in the ways of the royal families. So I'll ask again: why are you here?"

"Such a charmer." She cut him an irritated, but playful glance. "I see nothing has changed."

He snorted. "I am still the masterful warrior Niall predicted I would be. And still irresistible."

"Still arrogant."

He grinned. "It is good to see you too, Illa, though I must insist on an answer to my question."

She peered in the direction of Reese and the dandy. "Who is the girl?" The question was light, curious. And a direct attempt at avoidance.

Keen nodded at a passing soldier. "What girl?"

"The one you can't keep your gaze off—the Halven, if

my senses are correct. Even in Old Kingdom we've heard of her capture."

Keen's back tensed. "I am here to ensure her safety while she resides in New Kingdom. Nothing more."

"Truly?"

Illa had known him well when they were younger. It seemed she still knew him. "Of course."

She made a sound in the back of her throat. "Very well. Keep your feelings for the girl to yourself. They are of no concern to me. As for why I'm here... I'm to become your bride."

CHAPTER

NINE

Keen might be a soldier, but he'd grown up in the Old Kingdom court. Old Kingdom rarely held soirees and social gatherings the way New Kingdom did, but he was still expected to know how to dance. Despite his skills on the dance floor, he nearly stumbled at Illa's words. "My bride? Were we promised without my knowledge?"

Illa smiled at Portia, who was watching them from afar. "Of course not. Your new queen wishes the union. We are of royal blood and full Fae, unlike the current ruler of Old Kingdom."

Derek. Portia wanted to take control of Old Kingdom from Niall's son, the Halven. And it seemed this alliance would make her quest easier.

Keen had known there had to be more to his bargain with Portia. She'd been too eager to allow him to stay and care for Reese. She'd ordered his fealty, and it seemed she wished to control his personal alliances as well.

He glanced down. Illa was a beautiful woman with light brown hair and dark blue eyes, and a flawless oval face. She didn't possess a dimpled chin, golden hair, and a full, obstinate mouth that told him what he could do with his orders.

Any Fae would wish for an alliance with Illa, given her beauty and lineage. She was calm and obliging. She didn't take Keen too seriously, which was to her credit. But he felt nothing romantic for her. She did not set his blood on fire. That the small Halven did was most vexing, and something he refused to give in to. He'd not make the mistake his weaker brethren had by succumbing to the allure of a pretty human face. Keen was considered one of the strongest soldiers in any of the realms. He was the last of his family line, and he would not disgrace himself or his name with a human or Halven dalliance.

He looked over at Reese and found her gaze on the woman in his arms, a frown on her face.

Despite Keen's decision never to be with Reese, her unhappiness had a most unsettling effect on his temperament. He didn't like to see her upset. "I will speak to Portia," Keen said. "There is no need for us to marry if neither of us wishes it."

"You may try, but my father sent me."

Keen studied her. "Does he know…?" He must not give away too much.

"That the Halven held captive wears his emblem? Yes, he knows."

Keen let out a deep sigh. Portia and Illa's father, Hakon Radnor, must already be negotiating for Reese if Illa was here speaking of marriage. But what was the ultimate goal?

An alliance between Keen and Illa would smooth the way for Portia to gain power in Old Kingdom, though Keen didn't know how much power he could possibly wield after having been gone so long. Portia handing over Reese into Radnor's care must be the price she was willing to pay in order to gain the union between Illa and Keen.

Surely Reese's own father would not hurt her? He seemed devoted to Illa, and he'd been more forgiving of his Halven son, Marlon, than any human or Fae could have expected him to be.

Keen glanced at Reese again—and halted in the middle of the dance floor. Four men surrounded her. She was smiling, but that was no reassurance. The men were circling her like the predators they were.

"Where are you going?" Illa called from behind as Keen stormed across the ballroom.

"This old thing?" he heard Reese say as he approached. "Oh, it's just something the palace ladies put together for me." She whirled in a circle and her gown billowed out, showing off her flawless figure.

The guards and courtiers leered at the glimpse of Reese's legs, then caught sight of Keen. They slowly moved away from her. Probably due to the lethal look he leveled at them.

Taking in the expressions on her admirers' faces, Reese turned around. "Is there a problem?" she asked Keen.

He stared at the backs of the retreating cads. "You will remain at my side from now on."

"Excuse me?" she said. "Pretty sure I'm safe in a ball-room with my guards surrounding me, including you. Or is it the other men who worry you? They're very friendly. This party was just getting fun."

Keen grabbed her hand to drag her back to her bedroom, when Illa, whom he hadn't noticed following him, spoke up.

"Keen," she said in her gentle voice. "Will you introduce me to my sister?"

Illa smiled at Reese as Keen said, "This is Illa Radnor, your half-sister."

"It is a pleasure to meet you. Please excuse my fiancé's behavior. He's being unpardonably rude."

Reese's jaw dropped. Her gaze landed on Keen with the force of a tumbling boulder. "Fiancé?"

"Well." Illa blushed. "Soon to be. Isn't that so, Keen?"

"No."

Illa shook her head. "You may speak to my father, but there is no way around it."

Reese hadn't tried to pull out of Keen's grip, so he began to drag her away again. "We shall see."

Out of the corner of his eye, he caught Portia sweeping across the room, her expression stiff with anger.

"What is the meaning of this?" She glared at Keen's hand clasped around Reese's.

He slowly let go of the girl and pulled his shoulders back. "It isn't safe for Halven among our kind. There is no reason for her to be here tonight."

"Oh, but there is. I wish everyone in the palace to witness your declaration to me. In fact, I see no reason to wait any longer." She turned and clapped her hands. "Begin the ceremony," she called.

The ballroom was crowded—dozens of conversations going on at once, music floating out—but at the queen's order, the music stopped and the room went silent.

Reese stood beside Keen, staring at the ground, which concerned Keen more than the angry look she'd leveled at him moments ago.

Servants entered the grand ballroom and rolled out a narrow red carpet with golden embroidered vines climbing the edges. The crowd parted down the middle, giving them space.

Portia strode the carpet and swept her gown forward to sit upon the massive gilt chair at the head of the room. Marlon slithered up and stood beside her.

Portia flicked her fingers for Keen to approach.

He hesitated. Catching Ulric's eye several feet away, Keen tilted his chin up, signaling for the guard.

Ulric walked over.

"Stay with her," Keen said, and Ulric nodded, moving closer to Reese.

"Wait." Reese grabbed Keen's arm, pulling him aside. She swallowed, her breaths shaky. "Don't do it. Her emotions—the queen's—they're a storm. So much anger. I can't explain it, but no one has emotions like hers."

"What are you talking about?"

"You can't trust the queen."

"Of course I can't. But what is this about her emotions?"

Reese shook her head. "They said I would have powers. I don't know if this is a part of it. If it's a precursor, or just something weird among Halven and Fae, but...I can tell what someone's feeling. Except for you; I've never been able to tell what you're feeling. That's why I wasn't sure if it was a magical ability or something else." She glanced at the dais. "But with Portia, there's no question. I know her emotions like I know my own."

Keen stared at her. "It is not a Fae or Halven thing. There is no such intrinsic ability, but I've heard of others possessing this power. We call them empaths." He let out a deep breath. "It makes sense—your not being able to read my emotions. I've never been able to read what you're thinking either."

She shook her head quickly, as if to clear it. "What are you talking about?"

He glanced at Portia, who spoke quietly into Marlon's

ear as he leaned toward her. "There is no time. We'll discuss it later."

Reese rubbed her temples. "Look, all I know is that you can't bind yourself to that woman. She's evil."

Keen had known this moment would come. That he'd officially pledge himself to Portia in front of noblemen and kingdom—and he no more wished for it than Reese did. Once he pledged himself, he could not betray Portia—without dying. But tonight's oath was a formality. The deal had already been struck inside the queen's chambers days ago.

He touched Reese's shoulder. "It is the only way."

"The only way to what?" she called as he walked off.

To keep you safe.

CHAPTER

TEN

Reese stood helplessly as Portia's personal guards divested Keen of his weapons and he knelt at the bottom of the steps to the throne.

The red gemstones of the gold circlet on Portia's head winked in the ballroom candlelight. She peered out as though ensuring she held everyone's attention. "Keen Albrecht, last of the Albrecht line, do you swear loyalty to me, your lady and mistress, to protect above all others?"

Keen was the decisive sort, but he seemed to hesitate.

Portia's gaze dropped to the top of his head, anger, thick and ropy like sap, stretching off her. But there was no need for such emotion, because in the next moment, Keen's beautiful, deep voice rang out.

He said the words Reese had begged him not to. The words that sealed his fate...

"I do."

For a moment, it seemed the floor had dropped from beneath Reese's feet. Bad enough she found herself irritated watching Keen dance with a beautiful woman—her *sister*. But this? Pledging himself to someone Reese could only describe as pure evil? So wrong. How could it be the only way? She couldn't stand by and watch.

Everyone in the room stared, fixated on the proceedings. Reese quietly and very slowly slipped toward the back of the room. Not even Ulric noticed her leave his side. Like many, he seemed distracted, a storm of emotions whirling through him—banked frustration and anger, mixed with resignation.

Reese watched as Portia touched a golden sword to Keen's head, her own frustration rising. Finally at the back, she spun around and exited, alone for the first time since she'd arrived. The guards at the door gave her a passing glance, but they didn't stop her. And why would they? She was one Halven among hundreds of Fae nearly twice her size. And Reese's special power?

Fireball creator? Nope.

Massive, inhuman strength? Not that either.

She was an empath.

Awesome. Just great. She could read emotions. What good was that?

Reese walked without knowing where she was going. Anywhere but her room, where she'd been kept under lock and key. Trying to escape the palace, castle—whatever they called this place—was foolish. She didn't know Tirnan, or how to return home, so she wandered aimlessly, attempting to make sense of what she'd learned.

Keen was engaged. Maybe. He didn't admit to it, but the woman had been pretty adamant. And not just any woman, but Reese's own *sister*.

Her entire life, Reese had wanted a sibling. She'd even gone so far as to negotiate with her parents for one at the tender age of eight. She'd offered up her prized possession —her first-place martial arts crystal trophy. Having a sister would have been the ultimate coup, but Reese would have settled for a brother.

Her parents had stared at her blankly, then gone back to what they were doing. Her father packing for a trip that would take him to another continent for the shooting of a film he'd written, and her mother discussing the next evening's dinner party with the housekeeper.

But Reese hadn't needed to get through to her absent parents. Turned out she'd already had a sister, *and* a brother—one Fae sister and a Halven brother who was the psychopath behind the disease created to murder Fae. Both of her siblings were decades, if not centuries, older than she was, though her sister looked Reese's age.

Illa was beautiful, her features far more refined and polished than Reese's dimpled chin and thick, dark blond hair that had a tendency to fall in her face. When Illa had called Keen her fiancé, Reese's heart had constricted. It made no sense for Keen to pledge himself to Portia, but his having a beautiful fiancée made sense. He was powerful, and as handsome as a prince. They made a stunning couple. And Reese was incredibly jealous. Which was ridiculous.

Reese shouldn't care whom Keen married. They were nothing to each other. He was arrogant and prejudiced toward humans and Halven, and a total prig when it came to women's fashion. If Reese could have captured his expression when he saw her in the red gown, she would have framed it. He'd been utterly appalled. It was a beautiful moment.

So why was she bothered by this supposed engagement?

Her heart was being stupid.

She swatted at the sound of a fly buzzing near her head.

Were there flies in Tirnan? She stopped in the middle of the hallway.

That was no insect. The strange buzzing grew louder.

And then a voice spoke near Reese's ear and she nearly jumped out of her skin.

Reese, this is Elena's mother, Theda. We are taking back New Kingdom and returning you home. Prepare for a battle—hide if you must—but tell no one. We will find you.

Reese grabbed her head.

No way—just, *no way.*

The corridor was empty with everyone at the ball, but Reese had heard the voice, no question about it.

Keen had said something about hearing another's thoughts, though he wouldn't clarify what he'd meant at the time. And he'd confirmed it was possible for Reese to sense emotion. Either she had more than one ability, or this was Theda's ability and Elena's way of calling out to Reese in the Fae realm.

Prepare for a battle?

Reese loved a good physical fight, but the ones she participated in back home had been scored, with an audience cheering her on—and they didn't involve death. Fae couldn't be killed, but humans could.

This was bad. Reese grabbed the skirts of her dress and rushed back in the direction of the ballroom.

Keen was right about the weapons training. If some Fae shitstorm was brewing, she needed to learn how to use a sword. Maiming a few of the Vikings in order to help Elena and her mother, and to get the heck out of this gilded prison, didn't sound so bad anymore. Maybe the training with Keen would come in handy after all.

She had to tell him right away... But Keen had pledged himself to Portia.

She stopped abruptly. What if she told Keen about the message...and he turned around and notified the queen?

It could get Elena killed.

Elena had become one of Reese's closest friends, calling Reese out on her crap and never blowing smoke up her ass the way her LA friends did. They were complete opposites, from two different worlds. Reese dressed on the sexy side, while Elena considered hoodies fashionable going-out wear. Elena's nose was always in a book that had more chemical symbols than it did text, while Reese would rather spend time at a party and socialize. They were night and day, but Reese trusted Elena. It was the trust and genuine affection she felt from her friend that made the relationship more special than any she'd had in her life.

Before she could decide what to do, one of the Fae she'd spoken to earlier, until Keen had scared him off, exited a door in the hallway. His eyes had a mischievous glint that sent a zing of warning down her spine.

She glanced behind her and saw no one.

Not good. But Reese had never been the wilting type. The men she spoke with at the ball were flirty, but nothing she couldn't handle.

"You are unescorted?" he said in a saccharine voice. "Please, allow me to take you wherever you wish to go."

"No need." She smiled sweetly. "I was just heading back to the celebration." She'd left the party because she couldn't handle watching Keen promise himself to that evil woman—and because she couldn't handle watching Keen with Illa. But as soon as Keen figured out she'd left, he'd have a Fae coronary—if he hadn't already. He was as uptight as the corset cinching off Reese's air supply.

"It is no hardship." The man stepped closer. "I enjoy your company."

He grabbed her hand, slipping it through the crook of his elbow and bringing their bodies close until her side touched his.

Too close. She enjoyed the attention the Fae men showered on her, but this didn't feel right.

She tried to pull her arm free, but the Fae held her still.

"You need to let go of me. *Now*."

"Do I?" he said, leaning down. "I don't think so." He grinned and wrapped his hand around her waist, pulling her flush against him.

Bastard. He was holding her in a vise grip.

Attempting to pull away wasn't going to get her anywhere; he was as solid as a bear. A very tall bear.

Reese ran through her options, because 1) this jackass needed to be taught a lesson, and 2) she was at a disadvantage in a ball gown with a built-in bustier cutting off her mobility along with her oxygen.

Point one to Keen. Fashion could be a bitch.

The one advantage she had, coincidentally, was that this jerk had brought her in so close he was within easy striking distance.

She dropped the elbow of the arm he wasn't holding, and struck him in the nose with the heel of her hand.

He loosened his grip slightly and she twisted away from him, twitching her gown to the side before delivering a side kick to his knee with her pointy heel.

A *pop* sounded, like that of a bone breaking, and her unwanted suitor stumbled and cursed.

Reese kicked off her shoes to run—and felt a breeze as something dark sped past her.

Keen barreled into the Fae, taking both of them down. And then he was punching the living crap out of the guy.

"Stop!" Reese yelled.

He didn't stop, not even when the man beneath him ceased moving.

She rushed over and tried to speak calmly. "Keen, you have to stop." She placed her hand on his shoulder.

He finally stilled and looked at her, his chest rising and falling. He sprang to his feet, scanning her body. "Did he hurt you?"

"Are you kidding?" She sniffed. "I totally had that under control."

An angry groan erupted from his chest and he ran stiff fingers through his hair. "You were in a physical fight with one of my kind. You did *not* have it under control."

"What part of my asskicking did you miss?"

He looked past her. "Take him to the dungeon."

Ulric ran toward them and grabbed the Fae Keen had beaten to a pulp, but who was now stumbling to his feet, blood no longer streaming from his nose and mouth.

How did the man heal so fast?

"She slipped out of the ball," Ulric said, panting, partly from the speed at which he'd raced over, and partly from the panic Reese sensed rising within. He wrenched the Fae's arms behind his back and began moving his prisoner down the hall, still looking at Keen. "I turned and she was gone."

Keen grumbled something that sounded like *incompetent*, and paced the hallway as Ulric dragged the Fae away.

"This was totally unnecessary," she said. "I was about to ditch that guy. You didn't need to beat him. I'm pretty sure I broke his leg."

Keen paused and pinned her with his gaze. "And you see how little that does when a Fae heals from such wounds within seconds?"

True. Fae healing was incredibly fast. Faster than she'd ever imagined.

"All you managed was to create another enemy within the palace."

She narrowed her eyes. "He was out of line. I had to do something."

Keen stalked forward and wrapped his arm around her waist. Air whooshed from her already constricted lungs as he picked her up and pushed her against the wall, her feet dangling. His arm dropped beneath her rear, holding her up and allowing air back into her chest. "You are no match for my kind. When will you get that through your thick skull, little one?"

Her heart pounded, but not in fear. Keen's body pressed flush against hers and his beautiful eyes were filled with such worry. Worry for *her*. Not because he was ordered to protect her, or because he was doing it out of some sense of obligation to Elena. This was different. Reese couldn't sense Keen's emotions magically, but she felt them just the same.

What had she done? Was he right?

She'd only meant to take a walk and clear her head after learning of Keen's maybe-sort-of engagement to her half-sister. She'd told herself that it didn't matter if he married another. But it mattered. It mattered a lot. Because she liked the arrogant Fae with his body pressed to hers.

"They could grab you and do unspeakable things without anyone knowing," he continued, his emerald eyes bright with heat. "Fae are brutal and ruthless."

"And what are you?"

"I am the same."

No, he wasn't. He'd done something no man had before —not even her father. He'd made her feel valued and protected.

At first, she thought it was for duty. Keen certainly wasn't doing things for her in order to get laid like every other man she'd encountered. He'd made it clear how foolish he thought it was for Fae and humans to *couple*, as he'd called it. He'd even gone so far as to tell her not to touch him. But he had a hard time following his own rules. Case in point, as he held her against the wall with his body pressed to hers.

Before he could say another word, she dropped her head and bit his lip, tugging it and lightly licking the edge. Not hard, just enough to show him she knew why he was here, holding her so close. And it wasn't to display how quick and strong Fae were, or how much danger she was in. Oh, it might have been for those reasons, but there were other reasons as well.

Important chemical reasons that involved sparks and energy—and the electricity that had simmered between them since the moment they'd met.

CHAPTER

ELEVEN

She bit him—actually *bit* his lip. And then her impertinent tongue darted out and swiped lightly across the flesh of his bottom lip before she released him.

Reese's floral scent, which didn't come from any bottle, filled his nose. Her soft curves pressed to his hard chest, and he stared into stunning green eyes filled with laughter and fire. Keen's body shook, his chest rising and falling.

Placing a hand on her small waist, he eased her to the ground and backed away, distancing himself.

Keen wasn't afraid of the tiny human. He was a deadly warrior and he would fight this—whatever this was—as if it were the most dangerous battle of his life.

He scrubbed a hand down his face, watching her warily.

Then his head snapped to the side. Illa was coming; he could hear her thoughts as she searched the corridor.

Is it right or left? This palace is too large by half. Leave it to the Newlanders to build a castle the size of a small city. Great Zadkiel, is that a tear in my hem? I'm going to kill Keen once I find him for making me search this blighted palace.

In two seconds, Illa would be upon them.

Keen took several more steps back, right as Illa rounded the corner.

"There you are." She looked relieved as she glanced between Keen and Reese, but it didn't last. A fine vee formed between her light brown eyebrows as she stared questioningly at Keen. "Portia is looking for you. You must return."

He nodded. "Just as soon as I escort Reese to her room."

Illa glanced once more at Reese, but nodded with a smile before walking off.

Keen grabbed Reese's arm lightly. She would not escape this time. She would not touch him again with her mouth… His body shook just from remembering it.

"Keen—" Reese started.

"Do not speak."

"Oh, good Lord. You're not going to be an ass over this, are you?"

"I thought I asked you not to speak."

"You *told* me, and I chose to ignore it."

"I also told you not to touch me."

She stared at his hand on her arm, and he dropped it. "You still doing the double-standard thing?"

He made a frustrated sound, but she was correct. He'd touched, held, warmed her with his body. But those were things *he'd* controlled. For the most part. He hadn't anticipated falling asleep and waking to her nearly naked body pressed to his. That had been the best and worst morning of his life.

The girl was a menace to his peace of mind. "I won't promise not to touch you. There may be times when I need to in order to protect you."

She pursed her pretty lips. "Fair enough. Then I retain

the right to touch *you* when I need to show you with my fist, or my *mouth,* when you're being a stubborn ass."

"Reese—" His voice came out gutturally, with a fine edge, before she cut him off.

"Don't give me any crap. You're hiding a lot inside that pretty Fae head of yours. No one beats a guy nearly to death for getting handsy."

Her mouth was turned down in a frown. She didn't seem to expect him to respond, and he had no intention of doing so. Nothing he felt was relevant. He was here to do his duty. One decision—one major decision—had him promising something that could be construed as *not* his duty.

He'd pledged himself to Portia in order to protect Reese.

Keen hadn't decided if that choice had been driven by his loyalty to Emain and the task to return Reese home, or something else. He couldn't take Reese home immediately, so he'd stayed to keep her safe. But pledging himself to Portia… He wasn't even certain the leaders of Emain would have asked that of him.

Keen stopped in front of the door to Reese's room. Ulric had returned and was standing there with another guard. "Are you capable of making certain she does not *slip out* this time?" he asked dryly.

"Yes, sir," Ulric murmured. "Won't happen again."

Reese pushed her way into the room. "This won't work, you know." She tossed her shoes on the floor, which Keen belatedly realized she'd been holding the entire way back.

He searched the room, looking in the wardrobe and a few other nooks to ensure all was well. "What won't work?"

"Holding me here. Assuming I'll sit by and be your patient damsel in distress. I know you're trying to help me, and I do appreciate it. You saved my life…" She closed her eyes briefly. "But I'm not that girl. I may have grown up with money and privilege, but my parents weren't... Well, let's just say I've had to fight to keep my head above water amongst a bunch of vultures. I don't know how to sit by and do nothing."

"I cannot allow harm to come to you," he said, his voice firmer than he'd intended.

"I understand, I just—Teach me how to use a sword. You said you would, and you're right. I need to know." She smiled lightly. "Did you hear that? I just admitted that you were right. Relish it, because it won't happen again."

His mouth twitched. "I will show you how to use weapons, on the condition that you will only use them if your life is in danger."

She nodded eagerly, and his chest warmed.

Lord save him from pretty females who enjoyed a good fight. Reese would be his downfall.

KEEN RETURNED to the ball and discovered that the *brune* was working its magic. Bodies were closer together in dance, some couples paired off in corners, and the volume of laughter was louder. All the while, Portia oversaw the proceedings from her throne at the front of the room, a scowl on her face.

He thought again how simple it would be to best her if he could read her thoughts. But she blocked him while others never learned how. She was clever that way—clever in many ways. If only she'd put it to good use instead of evil.

While Portia reigned over the room from the dais, Illa mingled with Newlander courtiers off to the side.

Her presence this evening had been a surprise. Not an unwelcome one, aside from the proposed engagement, to which Keen had no intention of agreeing. However, he remembered Illa with fondness, and he feared Portia's twisted machinations and plans for Radnor's Fae daughter.

Illa caught sight of Keen and whispered something to the courtiers before slipping away to join him.

"She is waiting," Illa said, her back to the throne.

Keen nodded, and the queen watched as he made his way to the dais.

Portia's gaze flickered around the room. "It's time to put your fealty to the test. Theda lives."

She studied him. Gauging his reaction?

He gave her none.

"She reached out to me, attempting to use our history together to bring peace. But she wants my kingdom." Portia snorted and smoothed her skirts. "Never." She watched him. "Theda will attack, but does she have the military power to back her? What condition is Emain in after the skirmish with my men?"

Keen rattled off numbers of soldiers in Emain. Meanwhile, he pondered his dilemma. He was beholden to Portia after his declaration this evening. But to go against the soldiers he'd fought and trained with in Emain for decades would not be pleasant.

"What of the abilities in Emain among those who remain?" Portia asked. "They have the Halven, Elena. Should have destroyed that child when we found her." Portia shook her head. "I wasn't in the right position at the time, but mark my words, I will not make the same mistake twice. She wouldn't have her powers if she hadn't come to our realm. Does she still pose a threat to us?"

Elena was always powerful. The Ancient Allon tea she'd

drunk in Tirnan had simply made her more so, but Keen didn't feel it prudent to point that out.

"Elena can manipulate natural elements into anything, as long as she understands its design."

Portia glanced at Marlon. A muscle in his jaw twitched. The male Halven was never far from Portia's side, yet he wasn't treated as an equal. It was a most unusual alliance. And Beatrice was nowhere in sight, likely implementing some other deadly scheme of Portia's.

"If Theda's Halven shows herself, we will be prepared. As for the rest, we can hold our kingdom—with your leadership of the soldiers, of course," Portia said. "However, to be safe, it wouldn't hurt to appeal to Old Kingdom for assistance."

Keen's brow furrowed. "Old Kingdom?"

Portia smiled. "You didn't think I'd let go of our homeland, did you? Rest assured, our precious Old Kingdom will be mine once more, as it was intended before that madman Niall took over. The only good to come from Derek O'Brien's devotion to Elena was his following her into Tirnan and putting an end to Niall's rule. And now I've formed a deal with Hakon Radnor, the next in line to the throne." Portia smiled across the ballroom at Illa standing in the corner with a group of courtiers. "He and his daughter will help complete the alliance."

"What alliance?" But Keen feared he already knew.

Portia's eyes widened, as though Keen were dense. "Between you and his daughter. You will marry Illa and help rule Old Kingdom—on my behalf, of course. I cannot be in two places at once, now can I? I need someone to gain the Oldlanders' acceptance of me as their rightful queen."

CHAPTER

TWELVE

All week Reese had tried to sense Keen's emotions, and bumped up against a brick wall. Much like the man himself.

"How come I can't sense what you're feeling?" she asked as she practiced the sword maneuvers he'd taught her that morning.

Reese had been reading her maids' emotions all week. Who would have thought such a complex storm of feelings existed beneath their stoic beauty? So far she detected steamy feelings from Enid toward Reese's guard Joseph, which he seemed oblivious to. And even the men had become an emotionally open book. Joseph resented Ulric. Reese hadn't figured out why, because she couldn't tell his thoughts, only his feelings. Meanwhile, Ulric had conflicted affections for Reese's sister Illa, who'd come to visit Reese a couple of times.

And damn, was *that* awkward.

Illa had no ulterior motives—at least, none Reese could detect—but Illa was super uncomfortable and anxious around Reese. Still, it was wonderful to get to know a sister she'd never known she had.

Keen paused briefly in the pull-ups he was doing—out of boredom, it seemed—and Reese had to admit the sight was hot-guy mesmerizing as his biceps bulged with every lift to the bar. She pretty much had to ignore what was going on off to the side, so she didn't accidentally cut off her arm.

"I've come to the conclusion we are blocking each other," he said. "Sometimes abilities between Oldlanders are so similar that they can block one another. It doesn't happen often, but it does happen."

She set the tip of her sword on the ground. "Please tell me we're not related."

His eyebrows pulled together. "Of course not. The Radnor and Albrecht families come from different angelic lines."

Oh, thank God. It would be extremely creepy to have... the sort of thoughts she'd been having about Keen if he was related to her. "You never explained your ability. I assumed you had none."

"A common misconception, and one I use to full advantage." He grinned devilishly, then dropped to the ground below the bar. He took a sip of water. "I read minds. And you read emotions—a distinction, but a subtle one. It is logical that the neurological and magical pathways we both use are conflicted in some way, and that is why we block each other."

She stared at him. "You people live in this historic building, give up the tech world—and you can come to that neuroscience conclusion? I'm impressed, Keen. That's the most modern thing you've ever said."

He seemed disgruntled with her comment, and Reese

smiled. Would have been more satisfying if she'd *sensed* his annoyance, but she'd settle for the sour look on his face.

He leapt up and grabbed the bar, returning to his pull-ups. Reese twisted away. She really couldn't watch him while he did that. "So how should we use my ability? Want me to read the emotions of Portia's advisors? See if any of them are unhappy or disgusted by her?"

She heard Keen thump to the ground again. "You will do no such thing. With my ability, I can keep track of what is going on."

Reese sheathed her sword, which she was growing fond of. Keen had even let her pick the pretty one with a lapis azure pommel. She set it aside and sank onto the exercise mat. "So what's going on? What does Portia want?"

She had yet to confide in Keen about the message Theda had sent. The more she thought about it, the more nervous it made her. He'd sworn loyalty to Portia, and he'd told her very clearly that Fae couldn't lie. Which meant he truly was committed to protecting Portia.

The information Reese had put Portia at risk. In the wrong hands, that information could get Elena and the others killed. She wanted to trust Keen, but she couldn't risk her friends' lives. Not after his declaration to Portia at the ball.

He wiped a towel over his face, but as far as Reese could tell, he wasn't sweating. Meanwhile, her training uniform was stuck to her back and wisps of her hair were plastered to her temples.

Keen tossed her a towel. Apparently, she wasn't the only one who'd noticed how sweaty she was. "You will remain in your room when you aren't training with me. I will handle the rest."

Reese stopped patting her face with the towel. "Um,

excuse me? First of all, that's what I've been doing, and I'm about to lose my mind from cabin fever. Second, why am I training if I'm not to take part in my own rescue efforts?"

Keen picked up Reese's sword and locked it away in a cabinet, which meant he was getting to know her too well. She'd gotten used to the deadly weapon and was no longer afraid of it; she wouldn't mind keeping her pretty sword at her side. He walked toward the door. "I did not save your life only to throw you into the middle of danger. Leave the negotiating and fighting to me and my men."

Reese followed him out. "Sexist much?"

"It is our way," he said, without looking back.

She scrambled to keep up with his long stride down the hall. "But women here fight. I've seen female guards, and Illa said she trained with swords."

He glanced over. "Illa?"

She parted her mouth in a silent *what?* "She visits me. We're getting acquainted."

Keen seemed to consider this. "I suppose that is all right."

"Like you have a say. Anyway, let's get back to this sexist treatment."

Ulric nodded as they approached Reese's gilded cage and opened the door to her room.

Keen kept on walking. "Goodbye, Reese. Ulric will ensure you are comfortable until we see each other again."

The hell she'd stay pent up in this place. It was dangerous, she got that. She might enjoy pretty dresses and colorful nail polish, but she also liked a good fight—physical or mental. Holding her out of the fray was like locking up shoppers in front of a Black Friday sale.

Ulric was beginning to feel uncomfortable, according to what she was picking up from his emotions. She considered yelling at Keen, but changed her mind because *brick wall*. Instead she turned to Ulric. "Why does he keep me locked away? I'm a prisoner, I suppose, though Portia didn't exactly treat me like that at the ball. I have guards protecting me day and night. Why do I need to stay in this room? It's not like Fae lock away their females."

Ulric scratched his jaw and shifted his feet. "Depends on the female."

"What's that supposed to mean?"

Now Ulric was tilting his head from side to side, popping his neck. Definitely uncomfortable. "We can be overprotective of our female family members, or…"

She rolled her hand, motioning for him to continue.

"Or when we feel—attached."

"Attached? As in, when you love someone?"

He looked away and sighed. "Or when we want them," he finally mumbled.

Reese couldn't read Keen, but she knew he was hiding his feelings from her. She thought she had a pretty good idea what those feelings were after he'd lost his shit and beaten the crap out of the groping Fae outside the ball.

Did she recognize male possessiveness from past experience? Hell no. But she'd watched plenty of it play out on the big and small screens, thanks to her parents' built-in movie theater. She knew what jealousy and possessiveness looked like.

No guy had ever defended her virtue without some ulterior motive. Until Keen.

And now Ulric was telling her Keen wanted her, which she'd already suspected. But that was the thing—Keen refused to give in to his attraction to her. As long as she had guards, she was safe inside the palace, yet he insisted on locking her away. Because this was about more than his desire for her physically. He cared, even if he never admitted it.

And that was how Halven came into existence. The angels made their Fae offspring far too beautiful and heroic.

Reese entered her room and stormed to the window. She looked out at the darkening sky, the strange red stars beginning to flicker. She had to put Keen out of her mind. He might want her, might even care about her, but it wasn't enough. Because he would never allow himself to do anything about it.

Regardless of whether Keen wished to lock her away to keep her safe, the battle Theda had warned her about was looming. There was no way Reese would hide.

She took a quick shower and was dressed and pulling a comb through her damp hair—when a hand clamped over her mouth. And the hand didn't have a body.

Reese screamed and screamed, her voice muffled by large fingers.

Then Derek appeared over her shoulder—his arm attached to the hand that covered her mouth.

"Quiet," he urged, and removed his palm. "The doors inside the palace are thick, but Theda says we need to keep our voices down. Fae hearing is powerful."

Reese spun and punched him in the stomach to make sure he was really there. And because he deserved it for scaring her so badly. "What the hell, Derek?" she whispered. "Why couldn't I see you?"

He didn't even flinch at the punch. Maybe because his abs were like granite. And because he was distracted. By Elena stumbling through thin air and landing in a heap on Reese's bedroom floor.

Along with a beautiful blond woman.

And another tall female—this one with black hair and fair skin.

"Elena?" Reese said. A burning sensation rose behind her eyes. It felt like months since she'd seen her roommate, not weeks. She'd never been so happy to see anyone in her life.

"No noise," Derek reminded her. "They know we're here, but they don't know where."

Elena climbed from the floor and ran into Reese's arms.

Reese hugged her friend so tightly she thought she might crush her.

Elena grabbed Reese by the shoulders and held her back a step, looking her over. "I was so worried when you didn't come home. You're okay?"

Reese nodded, unable to believe any of this. That after all this time, she was reunited with her friend. And that Elena had appeared out of nowhere.

"We searched high and low for you," Elena said. "As soon as Keen got word they had you in New Kingdom, we sent him and began planning a rescue."

How was Reese going to tell Elena about Keen?

"So much has happened..." Reese stepped away, trying to figure out how to explain Keen and his relationship with Portia—when she got a good look at her friend. Her gaze flew to Elena's heels to make sure she wasn't missing something. Elena had always had a few inches on Reese, but this was different. "Why do you look taller?"

Elena tucked her dark, wavy hair behind her ear and glanced at Derek. "It's a long story, but basically—*Tirnan*. We traveled here after you didn't return home, and it changed us."

Reese's forehead furrowed. "Keen said you came to Tirnan to create the cure."

Elena nodded. "And Derek was with me." She gave Reese the CliffsNotes version of what had happened in Old Kingdom with Derek's biological father, the ruler, and how Derek had been forced to kill him in order to save Elena. "The only way I could create a cure was to enhance my powers by drinking a tea made of leaves from the Ancient Allon, this giant tree that grows through the center of Old Kingdom's castle. It enhanced my abilities, but it also enhanced other things: my height, strength, speed. Derek drank it too."

This time Reese took in Derek, and really *looked*, not just because he'd scared the crap out of her.

He hadn't only grown in height, he'd become huge— bulky and strong-looking. "Wow." She shook her head. She thought she'd had a busy few weeks, but Elena and Derek hadn't only changed magically, they'd changed physically.

"How come I couldn't see you?" she asked Derek again. Because understanding his ability to float body parts seemed important.

He explained his power to Blend with air, water— whatever he wanted. He could become the elements around him. He hadn't sent his hand through the air; he'd been there all along. He'd simply allowed his hand to become corporeal while the rest of him remained a part of the elements.

Keen had told her that Derek's father had been a noble Fae and the ruler of Old Kingdom. It made sense that Derek would have an ability, but this was wild. Not to mention her friends had just stormed her room through an invisible door.

While Reese mentally grappled with everything, Elena grabbed her shoulders and twisted her in the direction of the two women who'd arrived with them. "Reese, I want to introduce you to my mother and her friend Camille. Camille has the ability to create small portals. That's how we got here. The portal is...well, actually, I don't know what it is physically. I just know what it does. It allows us to travel from one place to another, but it takes a lot of Camille's energy. She needs to rest in order to do it again."

Camille had long, dark hair—almost black—and bright blue eyes. "You're Fae?" Reese had never seen a dark-haired Fae before. There was something delicate about Camille, even though she was as tall as Elena.

"I'm from Sunland," she said. "It's the third kingdom in Tirnan."

"Camille is here to help," the other woman added.

"And this is my mom, Theda," Elena said, smiling at the other woman. "Can you believe I found her?"

Reese shook her head. "To be honest, I can't believe any of this."

There were four people standing in her bedroom—two Halven and two Fae—who hadn't been there minutes ago. But there was no doubt the woman named Theda was her roommate's mother. The love and devotion pouring off Theda when she looked at Elena wasn't like anything Reese had ever witnessed. Granted, Reese was new to sensing people's emotions, but Theda's seemed particularly strong —a true mother-daughter bond.

Camille walked to the bedroom door and touched the wood. "Four guards outside," she whispered.

"I can also sense Fae power better than others," Camille explained in answer to the question that must have been written on Reese's face. "It allows me to detect when and how many of our kind are near. We must be quiet and plan quickly." She looked at Theda. "I sense groups gathering in strategic places inside the palace. They are searching for us."

Reese held up her hand. "I swear I didn't tell anyone you were coming, not even Keen." She glanced at Theda. "Scared the bejesus out of me when you sent that message. How did you do it?"

Theda smiled. "That is my gift—to communicate with all animals across vast space. I've been in the Tirnan forests in hiding, along with one of my soldiers. The challenge was coordinating a plan with Elena on Earth. Sending messages between realms gets tricky, even with my ability."

Reese nodded, having only a general sense of what she or the others were talking about in reference to their powers. "What do we do now?"

Derek stalked around the bedroom, opening the wooden wardrobe, then a chest of drawers. Then he did the freakiest thing she'd ever seen and stuck his head through one of the walls.

He pulled his head back out. "We can hide in the adjacent room. Unless New Kingdom has others with Camille's ability that detect energy levels the way she can?"

"Not likely," Theda said.

"Good, then I can Blend us in and out of these rooms to keep us hidden when they come searching."

They'd all been careful to keep their voices down, so… "How does the palace know you're here if you snuck in through my bedroom?"

"Presence Charm," Theda answered, checking the weapons on her person. And holy hell, she was covered in them. A covert knife here, a sword secretly stashed on her back there. "All of the kingdoms use Presence Charms. They inform the palace when an intruder has entered the land, but they're not very accurate as to where the intruder is located. That provides us some time."

Reese glanced at Elena, who wore the same black pants and boots the palace seamstresses had made for Reese. "What *is* the plan?"

Elena grew a determined look. "To take back our kingdom."

THIRTEEN

Reese watched as Derek stuffed his backpack into the wall. "Umm, what are you doing?"

"There's a hollow behind a cabinet on the other side," he said. "The furniture is curved there. No one will find my pack behind it, but I can grab it any time I want through this wall."

"Do I want to know what's inside your backpack?"

"Just some weapons my talented girlfriend concocted." He smiled proudly at Elena.

Reese raised her eyebrow. "Girlfriend?" And yep, the love and sense of togetherness between Elena and their hot neighbor from back home hadn't escaped Reese. She'd simply been waiting for Elena to say something.

Elena glanced nervously at her mother, who had pulled Camille aside for a private conversation. "Well, you see," she said, "we grew close working on the virus and—things happened."

"I knew it!" Reese stage-whispered. "I called that the first day Derek came over."

Derek leaned down and kissed Elena on the head, because if Elena was over six feet after visiting Tirnan, Derek was closer to seven now. He joined Theda and Camille off to the side.

Elena smiled shyly. "Aside from Fae drama and you going missing—which had me so stressed, I can't even tell you—things have been good. With Derek, that is."

Reese tugged on one of Elena's dark curls, which bounced back as soon as Reese released it. "I knew what you meant. I always liked Derek." She gave her friend a side hug. "I'm happy for you. He's a good one."

"He is," Elena said, a sappy smile on her face. "It's complicated with my mom being heir to New Kingdom and Derek running Old Kingdom, but no one said they had to be sworn enemies, right?"

"Actually, isn't that exactly what they are?"

Elena's mouth pulled down into a frown. "I'm trying to think positive here. They are sworn enemies, but that doesn't mean Fae are incapable of forgiving and moving forward. At least, I hope not. Drives me nuts how traditional and stubborn the people in Emain can be."

Reese snorted. "Like Keen?"

She chuckled. "Keen is a prime example."

"I don't know what to do with him." Reese grimaced. "But I also don't know what I'd do without him."

Elena touched Reese's shoulder. "He promised he'd find you. He never gave up."

"He found me, all right. Now he's keeping me locked away in this room while he handles everything."

"That sounds like Keen. But now you have us, and we're here to kick ass and take names. Speaking of kicking asses"—Elena's pretty face brightened—"I made the coolest guns. They remove Fae powers. Isn't that awesome? Keen won't need to keep you locked away once we bust out these babies."

"You made *guns*?"

"Old Kingdom had them, and they were a huge pain in the ass." Elena's lip curled into a snarl, as though she was remembering. "Derek returned to Tirnan for a few days to take care of Old Kingdom business, and he grabbed me one. I made a bunch of replicas for the Emain Fae, and we brought some with us."

Keen used to be an Emain Fae. Now, Reese didn't know what he was. "Have you spoken to Keen lately?"

Elena shook her head. "No, he's been silent. But it's a huge challenge communicating between realms. We assumed everything was running according to plan. Why? Is something wrong?"

Reese bit her lip. "We might need a change of plans."

Concern wafted off Elena, at the same time Reese sensed apprehension from the others in the room. Theda, Camille, and Derek drew closer. They might have been talking off to the side, but it seemed they'd been paying attention to her and Elena's conversation.

Elena pulled Reese to the bed and they both sat on the edge of the mattress. "What's happened?"

Reese let out a deep breath, glad to have someone to confide in. "Keen promised to worship at Portia's feet, or whatever—I don't really understand the particulars, but it's not good. He told me he had to make a sacrifice. His pledge to Portia is the reason I haven't mentioned to him that I heard from you. I've sensed Portia's emotions, and she's horrible. I seriously think the woman is certifiably insane. And if Keen has to protect Portia...and he knows you're here...well, you can fill in the rest."

Theda hissed, hurt and anger rushing off her. Reese

sensed the betrayal, but she wasn't certain if Theda felt it in relation to Keen...or Portia. Portia had been Theda's companion once, so it could be either.

"Crap," Elena said. "Those *bastards*. Heads are gonna roll once we take this place back."

"Don't say that," Reese said, which was odd coming from her. She was typically more aggressive than Elena, but right now she felt vulnerable. "That could be a reality. Keen's been training me with a sword—a freaking *sword*, Elena. You know how much I love my martial arts, but this is intense, even for me."

Elena bumped Reese's shoulder with her own. "I know. And there's no harm if you choose to hide while everything goes down. We'll protect you."

Reese's eyes narrowed and she snarled, "Hell no. You think I'm sitting this out?"

Elena laughed silently. "No, I just like seeing you get feisty. I love you, Reese. I'm so glad you're okay."

"Even if I'm not about to skulk behind a chair, these guys are big. I had a run-in with one and I got away, but just barely. Keen stepped in and beat the crap out of him. At the time, I told Keen I had it under control, but as soon as my adrenaline died down, I realized he was right. I'm no match for these people. Nothing I could have done to that Fae, even with martial arts training, would have kept him down for long. They heal too quickly."

"We can gain the lead with the null guns," Elena said adamantly. "The Fae in New Kingdom don't have null technology. Though we'll still need to disable soldiers physically..."

That didn't sound good. "How do you plan to do that?"

"By imprisoning Portia and her advisors," Theda answered for Elena.

Theda stepped forward. She was tall, like all Fae, and willowy, with flaxen hair, an oval face, and stunning eyes that were more moss green than the emerald tone of Keen's. "We have reason to believe many, if not most in New Kingdom, are still loyal to my family. They are not pleased that Portia usurped control, along with her Halven advisor, Marlon. For reasons we haven't figured out, my loyalists haven't challenged Portia. Our plan is to reach out to a few influential Newlanders and get them on our side—prepare them for battle."

"How many people do you think you can convince to support you?" Reese asked. "Because there are a hell of a lot of soldiers in this place."

Theda glanced protectively at her daughter. "That remains to be seen, but I am confident."

Her emotions said as much. Theda believed she could take back control of her kingdom.

"Camille portaled a handful of our best Emain warriors to the woods moments before she brought us here," Theda continued. "But we'll need more if I am to wrest back my place on the throne."

Portaling so many bodies must have taken its toll on Camille, because she had moved across the room and was slumped in the fancy French chair Keen favored when he visited.

A knock sounded at the door, and Elena glanced at the others.

"Fae. Female," Camille said, suddenly alert.

It had been too long since anyone had come to primp or feed Reese. She was due a visitor.

"Shit," she said, and hopped up.

Elena scurried over to Derek, as did Theda and Camille. Elena held Derek's hand and her mother's, while Camille and Theda joined hands. And then they disappeared, just like that.

Creepy. And kind of cool.

"Who is it?" Reese called instead of answering the door like she normally would. She wanted to give Derek and the others a heads-up in case it was the guards searching for them.

"It is I, Illa," came a muffled, pretty voice from the other side of the thick door.

Reese glanced back to make sure her friends were still hidden, and walked over and opened the door. "Hi," she said a little too cheerily, her mouth spread in a wide smile.

She needed to simmer down and act normal.

"Greetings." Illa grinned back and entered, but she seemed to hesitate a couple of steps inside the doorway. Her head turned slightly, and Reese's heart thumped in her chest as Illa looked at the back corner—and the spot where Reese had last seen the others.

Illa couldn't know they were here, could she? Reese was beginning to enjoy her sister's visits, but she didn't trust any Fae—not even Illa. And if someone found out Reese was harboring fugitives who threatened the crown... She didn't even want to think about what would happen.

Illa turned and gave Reese a shaky smile.

Something was definitely up. "Everything okay?" she said, her mind racing. Maybe she was overreacting and Illa didn't know.

"Yes, of course. I just wanted to make sure you were well. There is a disturbance in the kingdom. Someone entered and the guards are searching for the intruders."

"Really?" Reese feigned disbelief. "Who do they think it is?"

"No one knows. And it concerns me." Illa walked over to a dresser and picked up a silver-handled mirror that looked like something out of old Hollywood. She set it down carefully. "My father is attempting to create diplomacy between the kingdoms." She turned back to Reese. "Something that hasn't been accomplished in several hundred years. And before that, it had been even longer. It's why I'm here. I fear this intrusion will put Newlanders on the defensive. You and I are not safe inside the palace with the military on alert."

Reese hadn't thought about what Elena and her mother's invasion would do to Illa, or anyone else in Portia's good graces.

"Can you leave? Return to Old Kingdom?"

"No," Illa said. "Not until the queen releases me. She is determined to see this marriage through. That is the only arrangement that will help bring a degree of peace between the lands."

Reese swallowed, attempting to control her breathing, which for some reason had grown choppy.

Illa had called Keen her fiancé, and Keen had denied their relationship. But if Keen didn't marry Illa, there would be no peace between the kingdoms. More was at stake than his personal freedom. Or the anguish that roiled through Reese at the thought of his marrying another.

No man had managed to get under her skin. Why Keen?

"Do you love him?" Reese asked, attempting to sound casual, but hearing the shaking in her voice.

Illa smiled. "He is a good Fae."

Not an answer to the question. "A bit bossy, if you ask me," Reese muttered.

Illa's smile grew. "That too."

Reese swallowed the ball lodged in the back of her throat. "Then you should marry him. He will protect you." She tried to grin, but it came out wobbly.

And then Reese felt Illa's sadness and concern.

"I will do what is best," she said. "But do not worry about me. I wish you to be safe, Reese. You are in more danger than I am. You must be careful. Stay with Keen, or Ulric—he seems to have your best interests in mind as well. But the others..."

Reese nodded. She'd grown to care for Illa—oh, not in the sisters-for-life way, but Illa was kind. Reese could see them becoming close, given enough time. Illa's emotions were filled with lightness...when she wasn't concerned, as she was now.

As she'd been when she first entered the bedroom.

"I must go," she said. "The queen wishes my presence at an induction ceremony. Keen isn't the only Fae whose fealty she is forcing. You understand we cannot lie?"

"I do."

Illa nodded. "Then you understand what she is asking of us."

"Has she asked for your fealty?"

"She cannot. I am an Oldlander. Keen is too, but he's been gone so long from our land they consider him from Emain now, a neutral zone. If I marry someone true to her..."

"You'll need to be true to her as well."

"Yes."

Reese stepped forward and squeezed Illa's hand. It was warm, her pale skin soft. "Stay on Portia's good side. I—I don't trust her."

Illa nodded and squeezed back. Then she walked to the

door. But she glanced at the back corner of the room before she exited.

As soon as the door was closed, Derek and the others emerged.

"She knew we were here," Derek said, voicing Reese's concerns.

"How?" she asked.

"Illa is an Oldlander." Derek rubbed his forehead. "I didn't realize it until it was too late. She might have seen the signs of us Blended. Oldlanders are better at detecting my ability when I'm in the elements. How much do you trust her?"

"Well, I can read her emotions, and—"

"Wait." Elena held up her hand. "Back up. You mentioned something about knowing Portia's feelings too. What do you mean, you can read Illa's emotions?"

"It's my ability. Keen calls me an empath. I can tell what someone's feeling."

"What are you talking about?"

"Elena," Camille said, "your friend is Halven like you."

Both Elena and Theda stared at Camille.

"You did not know?" Camille asked.

Elena shook her head slowly, then looked to Reese.

"Welcome to my crazy." Reese made a funny face. "You're not the only one with funky Fae-human relations in the family."

Elena sank onto Reese's bed. "This can't be a coincidence."

"Believe me, it's not," Reese said. "I wish it were, but Keen admitted that Emain arranged for us to room together on the Dawson campus. They anticipated one or both of us coming into powers."

Theda paced the room. "It is our way. To plan for every contingency. I am not surprised, though I didn't know about your roommate." She stopped and looked apologetically at her daughter. "I'm sorry, Elena. I wish I could have prepared you for all of this."

"You've done everything you could to protect me," Elena said. "The Emain Fae, on the other hand—they're going to get a piece of my mind as soon as we return."

She looked hesitantly at Reese. "Who do they think your Fae parent is?"

Reese laughed lightly and sat beside her friend. "Well, certainly not one of the people who raised me. It turns out that while my father was out philandering, my mom got it on with some guy named Hakon Radnor."

"*Radnor?*" Theda sounded shocked.

Camille shook her head, staring at the ground.

"You know him?" Reese asked.

"He is a noble Oldlander," Theda said. "He is also in line for the throne, should anything happen to Derek."

Derek's arms were crossed, his head bent, but at that, his head popped up. "And that means what?"

Theda barely raised her shoulder, but it was enough to indicate a shrug. And while the gesture was casual, her emotions were all anxiety. "That you might be challenged. Last I heard, Hakon did not have the backing to make an attempt at the throne, but much has changed in the last few weeks. Anything is possible."

"Awesome," Derek said without feeling. He tapped his finger against his thigh. "This doesn't change anything. We still have a job to do. We'll worry about Old Kingdom later."

Theda nodded. "Agreed."

"So, Reese is Halven, like me," Elena said. She looked at her mother. "Have you heard of an empath before?"

"We don't have many in New Kingdom, but there are several in Old Kingdom. The ability can be very useful."

Camille glanced wearily toward the door. "We may need it."

FOURTEEN

Elena and the rest of her group slept in Reese's room, but otherwise, Reese had seen very little of them. They were too busy preparing an army outside the walls of the palace.

Reese had only seen Keen once since her friends had arrived. When he finally made an appearance, he approached her with a worried look on his face, which made her anxious. She didn't want him knowing Elena and the others were here.

"You are certain all is well?" Keen had peered around her room, his gaze overly alert. "No one else has sought you out?"

Now if Reese had been perfectly honest at the time, she would have mentioned her roommate was in town and crashing on her bedroom floor. But Keen seemed to be referring to other *Fae*—or at least that was how Reese chose to interpret it. "Nope. Not like people are getting past the guards you stationed outside my door." She'd smiled, but his eyes turned to slits, as though he didn't believe her.

Something was definitely up. Had Illa spoken to him?

Derek thought Illa might have detected his Blending when she visited Reese the night they'd arrived, but if that was the case, why wouldn't Keen have asked Reese if Derek or Elena were here?

Unless Keen didn't want to know? Was he still protecting her?

Elena and her mother were a direct threat to Portia. If Keen knew Elena was here, he might be forced to do something to protect the queen.

As if their communication wasn't bad enough, Keen's oath made things worse. Reese couldn't tell him what was really going on without risking her friends' safety, but she also wanted to know why he was acting so strangely.

He hadn't shown up for their regular training session today, which confirmed in her mind that something was wrong. Keen took perverse pleasure torturing her in the workout room; he'd never miss the opportunity to make her sweat. But today it was Ulric who came to teach her sword and knife maneuvers.

Ulric's sword slashed through the air and Reese ducked low to keep her head on her shoulders, where she preferred it.

She assumed Ulric wouldn't actually behead her, but could she be certain?

Hell to the no.

Ulric lowered his sword. "You cannot fend off a foe through defense only. You must attack."

"But what if I hurt you?"

He looked to the ceiling and sighed.

"Am I interrupting?" Illa entered the training room, a pleasant smile on her face that faltered slightly when she saw Ulric—and then her emotions went berserk. Surprise, anxiety, longing, confusion, more longing…

Hmmm.

"You're not interrupting," Reese said when Ulric just stood there, his attention no longer on the ceiling but on Reese's beautiful sister. "We were practicing, but apparently I'm not chopping off enough of Ulric's limbs."

Illa's face brightened. "Would you like some pointers, sister?"

Only among Fae could warfare be a pleasant pastime.

"On how to maim Ulric?" Reese stepped aside and handed Illa the sword she'd secretly named Ulga. "By all means. I'd love to see what the women around here can do."

A lot—and she meant *a lot*—of things had gone wrong since Reese had arrived in Tirnan and New Kingdom, but discovering she had a sister wasn't one of them.

"This isn't a good idea," Ulric said, his jaw firming.

Reese caught more funny emotions, this time coming off him. He watched Illa while she tested out the sharpness of the sword. Surprise, joy, and deep apprehension wafted from him.

Illa was wearing a pale pink beaded gown. Not exactly warlike attire, but that didn't stop her. She crouched in ready position, the sword close to her hip. "Afraid?"

Ulric snorted. "I'm simply concerned for your safety. You are no warrior."

"Ah shit," Reese said. "You've done it now, Ulric." *Some popcorn and a couch would make this moment perfect.*

"I think I should teach him a lesson, don't you agree, Reese?" Illa waved her sword in a flashing maneuver.

"Whoop his ass!"

Ulric rolled his eyes. He relaxed his stance, but didn't move to ready position. That didn't stop Illa from spinning in a circle and attacking him on the right.

Ulric blocked the blow with his blade, holding firm. "This is not necessary and will surely get you hurt."

"I'll heal," Illa responded. "*If* you manage a hit."

He blocked her next blow as well, and this time, he seemed to put a little more effort into it, because his immense Fae muscles were bulging beneath his black uniform.

"Lookin' good, Illa!" Reese called.

And then it was on. Illa and Ulric parried in a beautiful dance—which was the only way to describe it. Illa was graceful, and Ulric was all strength and resistance. He was on the defensive, and Reese sensed his caution. He didn't want to hurt Illa. But Illa was skilled with a sword and grinning as she went up against the tall warrior.

Reese was getting good pointers watching her sister stand off against a larger foe.

And then Illa slipped in her court heels.

Illa's arm dipped and suddenly that graceful ballet was just a fraction off, her sword not fully blocking Ulric's next counter. He accidentally slashed the side of her shoulder with his weapon, and Reese's heart stopped.

Illa didn't call out in pain, though her smile dropped and she looked down. But you would have thought she'd staggered and fallen, given Ulric's reaction.

He dropped his weapon and grabbed her arm, apparently to steady her.

Illa looked mildly intrigued at the injury, even though her dress was quickly turning red.

Reese jumped to her feet and ran over—while Ulric picked up Illa and cradled her in his arms.

Illa's eyebrows drew together. "It is only a cut. What are you doing?"

He brought her to a chair and set her down. Then tore

open the dress where she'd been slashed, revealing one elegant shoulder and a cut that even Reese could tell wouldn't affect Illa for long. The nasty gash was already stitching itself together before Reese's eyes.

Which was pretty insane. She'd noticed how quickly her attacker after the ball had healed, but she'd never seen Fae healing take place.

Ulric sat back on his heels and let out a stiff sigh.

He wasn't as stoic as Keen, but Reese was taken aback by his reaction. And not only his physical response of cradling Illa in his arms. He had panicked emotionally over her injury, though he knew as well as anyone how quickly she would heal.

The Fae were nonemotional on the surface, but that was all a mask. Beneath they were as capable of strong feelings as any human.

"Are you really okay?" Reese wanted to reassure herself as much as Ulric, whom she sensed needed it too.

"Of course." Illa pushed up her torn sleeve and stood. "Round two?" she said to Ulric, her dress still torn and bloody.

He simply stared at her. But underneath...oh, underneath lay something else. He was *angry*.

Ulric stood and turned on his heel. He collected Reese's sword and put it away. "Let us go, Reese. It is time we returned you to your room."

Reese scurried after him, glancing back apologetically at Illa, who seemed perfectly fine and not the least bit ruffled after sustaining a gash by a sword. "Thank you for the demonstration. It was really helpful, until—Well, anyway, thank you."

Illa waved her off. "My pleasure. I'll be sure to join you for the next round."

Ulric huffed out a disbelieving grunt and continued walking, never looking back.

LATER THAT NIGHT, Elena and the others returned to Reese's room, looking tired—each of them giving off vibes of deep apprehension.

"What's going on?" Reese said.

Derek stashed his backpack through the wall. "We need to talk."

Reese sat on the edge of the bed beside Elena, while Camille avoided the window. They'd been extra careful not to be seen since Illa had entered Reese's room while they were here.

Theda clasped her hands in front of her. She appeared only a handful of years older than Elena and Reese, though she was much older. Aside from her fair coloring, Theda looked much like her daughter, with strong cheekbones and full, bow-shaped lips. "We need your help," she said.

"You have it," Reese answered. They'd risked everything to find her after Marlon and Portia kidnapped her. She'd do whatever she could to help them.

"Don't agree without thinking it over," Elena said. "This is dangerous. Listen to what we're proposing first."

"Okay." Reese drew out the word. "You do understand that it's dangerous for me here no matter what, right? They almost killed me the first few days inside that dungeon. And then there was the attack in the abandoned hallway with the lecherous Fae. However you look at it, I'm not safe. It's why Keen has guards outside my door twenty-four-seven."

Elena closed her eyes briefly, as though pained. "I didn't know about the dungeon." She stared at Reese. "I'm sorry."

"Keen arrived here in time, thanks to all of you. You understand why I feel the need to help?"

Elena chewed the tip of her thumb. A nervous habit. "I understand, but this would make you even more vulnerable."

Reese stood and threw up her hands. "I'm tired of sitting back while everyone else takes risks. I need to do this."

Elena's emotions indicated she wasn't convinced, but she wasn't the one who spoke next.

"Your friend deserves to fight for her freedom and rights as much as the rest of us," Theda said. She stepped closer, her voice quieter than usual. "We've been meeting with leaders outside the palace. Influential Fae who are able to pull together a large army of loyalists, but...it is difficult to tell whom we can trust. We've had to reveal ourselves in order to speak with them. Some I've known all of my life and have no trepidation over. Others..."

"The Fae are crazy skilled at manipulation," Elena explained. "They'll say something in such a way that it won't be a lie, but it won't be the truth either."

Theda brushed a hand over the painted warrior scene on the wall across from Reese's bed. "It comes from millennia of getting around the truth when needed."

"Why can't Fae lie?" Reese had heard it said so many times. She wanted to know the reason. And to understand the depth of Keen's pledge to Portia.

Theda slowly lowered her hand to her side. "You understand we descend from angels?"

Reese nodded.

"The angel blood doesn't allow us to speak falsehoods.

To kill, certainly, for angels fought and killed those they deemed harmful, like the Fallen ones. But to lie breaks a code of honor by which our forefathers lived, dating back to before Fae came into existence. Should we speak an untruth, our bodies would perish. One could argue that Portia was deceitful when she attacked my people and took over our kingdom, but she never spoke a lie. She manipulated the truth, hid her intentions, but never lied. That is how one gets around the truth... And this is where you come in, if you agree to help us. Fae may manipulate or hide the truth, but they cannot hide emotion. And emotion speaks truth."

"Keen hides his emotions from me," Reese said.

Camille raised her head. "You cannot sense his feelings?"

"No. He says we block each other."

She looked at Theda. "He is telepathic."

Understanding filled Theda's eyes. "That happens sometimes when abilities are similar, or opposite—they may cancel each other out. It is possible you will run into other Fae where this is true, but it isn't common. And I don't believe it will happen among the group we plan to meet tonight. They are Newlanders who possess power over the elements, not the mind. Which is to our advantage. You can read their emotions, and they won't be looking for your ability."

"We'll be heading to a seedy part of the village," Derek said. "Leaving the palace poses a risk. As does returning."

"Why return at all?" Reese asked. "This is what we want. To get out of here with our lives."

"I understand your desire," Theda said. "You wish to leave, and you have every right. But I must fight for my kingdom. The woman who calls herself its leader is ruthless. I fear she will abuse my people and lead them to their deaths. It is how she gained power. I do not put it past her to do it again if she thinks it will gain her control over the realm."

Derek dropped his hand protectively on Elena's shoulder. "The only way to gain back the kingdom is from the inside. We have to return to the palace."

Reese thought about Keen. He'd sacrificed by pledging himself to that madwoman. To keep the peace. And possibly, in some twisted way, to protect Reese.

And she'd sat inside her room like a trapped bird, allowing everyone to make decisions for her.

She was no frail thing, no matter what Keen believed. She could help if given the chance.

Here was her chance.

"I'll do it," she said.

FIFTEEN

Reese stared at Elena's outfit, then down at her own. "We so look like Jedi right now, only cuter. These belts are figure flattering."

Elena tugged on a hat that was square on top, with flaps that covered her ears. She tied the leather strings below her chin. "Except for the hat."

"Yeah, the hat's not so cute." Reese glanced at Elena's boyfriend. "Why does Derek get the cool hooded cloak?"

Elena groaned. "Reese, don't start bitching about the clothes."

"No," Theda said. "Your friend is correct. She stands out among us with her shorter stature."

Reese straightened. "Why do people keep saying that? I'm beginning to get a complex. Five foot six isn't short."

"My mom's right—you're super short by Fae standards. And your Halven power level is totally obvious. Which is why you'll be in the middle of us at all times. Camille thinks that if we stand together, there's a chance your power level won't be noticed." She handed Reese a cloak. "Wear this, and hopefully anyone looking will assume you're a child."

Reese snatched the article. "I'll try to not find that insulting." She put the cloak on and pulled the hood over her head. The hem dragged like a wedding train when she walked. "I might trip in this thing."

Theda pursed her lips and Camille tilted her head.

"That won't do," Camille said.

"No," agreed Theda. "We must shorten it." She turned to her friend. "Do you know how to use thread and needle?"

Camille raised her eyebrows incredulously. "I wasn't taught those skills."

"Nor was I," Theda admitted. "Elena?"

"I cook. That's my one domestic skill."

They all turned to Derek.

"Don't look at me!" he whispered loudly. "I'm no seamstress."

"Everyone, simmer down," Reese said. She turned to Theda. "You're organizing followers, correct?"

"Yes," Theda said cautiously.

"Can we begin at the palace?"

"Too dangerous," Derek blurted.

Elena shook her head. "Derek's right. We considered it before we arrived. If something went wrong—if word got into the wrong hands—we'd be trapped. At least by beginning our search for loyalists outside the palace, there's always the possibility of escape. The palace, on the other hand, is fortified with soldiers at every turn. We'd never make it out before they caught us."

"The Presence Charm we triggered when we arrived has worn off by now," Camille added, "but they have not stopped searching for the intruders. It seems Portia isn't taking any chances."

Theda nodded. "And if what you said about Keen's oath

to Portia is true, we cannot be certain he won't betray us. We would be taking a large risk going to him."

Reese lifted the hem of her cloak and flung it over her arm to get it out of the way. "I wasn't thinking about Keen. I was thinking of someone whose emotions indicated she isn't happy about Portia's new position. I think there's a good chance she'd be on our side."

"Do you trust this person?" Theda asked.

"Enid is a palace servant, and she's been kind. She snuck me books. I don't think she'll betray us."

"It is all we have," Camille said. "Our trust in others. And your ability to tell when one's emotions conflict with their words. You will go to this girl, and she will help cover for you while you are gone."

Reese shook out the cloak. "Not only that—Enid knows how to sew."

Reese, Elena, Derek, and the two Fae escaped New Kingdom palace with a little help from Enid, who, with a conspiratorial look, asked no questions at their request to cover for Reese's absence. Enid also did a quick hem job on the overlong cloak.

Rubbing the shoulder she'd landed on—or fallen on, to be more accurate—Reese stood and hurried after Elena and the others, who'd already recovered from the unusual transportation and were making their way down a cobbled street. "So that was a portal?"

Elena looked back. "Well, one of *Camille*'s portals." Her booted feet sloshed through a puddle from what must have been a recent rain. The sky was dark, made darker with cloud cover—the only light came from the soft glow of gas lamps amid gray stone buildings straight out of another century. "Camille's portals are bumpier than the regular ones."

Reese chuckled quietly. "Right, because traveling through space is so normal. Do regular portals toss you around like the Zipper without a cage?"

"A zipper?"

"Not *a zipper,* but *the* Zipper. You know, the carnival ride?"

"Oh yeah, spinning is a part of all portals. So is the rainbow of lights. But Camille's portals are rougher for some reason."

"What about the sense of being shot from a cannon onto the ground?"

Elena laughed lightly. "That's specific to Camille's portals too."

Camille looked over and grinned.

Elena's face scrunched. "I've almost gotten to the point where I can land on my feet instead of my face. But I'm not as coordinated as you, Reese. With that cool tumble roll you did, you looked pretty good."

"I'll remember that when my shoulder is black and blue tomorrow."

Elena grinned and stopped behind her mother, who was standing outside a doorway with a sign above it that read *Lucifer's Larder*.

Broken wrought iron covered the single window on the building, and the sagging wooden overhang was one hard rain away from collapsing. "Classy. This place is safe, right?"

"Of course not," Theda said, and opened the door.

"Just making sure." Reese held her breath and stepped in after Elena, but before Camille and Derek. As they'd agreed beforehand, her friends surrounded her to make her Halven power level less noticeable.

Derek and Elena were Halven as well, but once they had drunk from the Ancient Allon to increase their powers—and as it turned out, their height and strength—their power levels became closer to that of Fae. Unless someone was paying close attention, they wouldn't notice a difference—which was deceptive, because Elena and Derek had more magical ability than most Fae. They came from strong angel lines, and it showed.

Inside the small, den-like room, round tables and wooden chairs crowded the space, and were filled with men. Mostly. The few women there looked odd, and it took Reese a second to figure out why.

The women inside Lucifer's Larder wore risqué clothing, something Reese thought she'd never see in Tirnan. Oh, these women weren't wearing anything like what a girl going out on the town back home would wear. But bared shoulders and arms, and billowing, gauzy gowns where Reese could detect the outline of legs? That was downright scandalous for Tirnan.

"What is this place?" she whispered to no one in particular.

Camille looked about. "Part pub. Part brothel."

Reese raised her eyebrow. "A brothel? In Tirnan? Among the blessed Fae? I thought you guys were pure and only procreated for heirs?"

Camille shrugged her dainty shoulder. "We are not perfect."

Reese grumbled an obscenity. If this went on in Keen's homeland, what was up with him being a bastard about her ball gown that revealed far less skin than what these ladies were wearing? Granted, these ladies were presumably offering up their bodies, but still.

"That is Amund." Theda nodded to a group across the room.

Reese followed the direction of Theda's gaze...to an extremely large, scary as hell Fae, sitting with about a dozen other men who looked like they could tear Reese apart with their pinky fingers.

"He's very...burly," she said, and noted that Amund was the only man in this land she'd seen rocking full-on beard stubble. His skin was slightly darker as well. *Swarthy.*

Theda seemed to consider him. "He is only reliable some of the time. Which is why I did not offer him a position on my guard. Otherwise, he's a ruthless warrior who's fought and won many battles. I would have liked to have had him at my side. Perhaps now is the time to take a chance."

"On this ruthless, unreliable warrior?" Reese wasn't exactly scared of the burly men, per se, but shit. Was this a good idea? Maybe there were others who were more trustworthy.

"He is the one person everyone claims holds the most influence," Derek explained. "Don't worry, Reese. Amund's already indicated his support of Theda. Remember, we just need you to make sure everything is on the up-and-up and that there isn't anything he's hiding."

"Okay, but I can't read minds. I'm not Keen."

"No," Camille said. "But you will be able to tell if he has ill feelings toward Theda or any of the rest of us."

Reese nodded. "I can do that. Right now I'm picking up on distinctly horny emotions from the Fae with the funny-looking beret in the corner, who's checking out Elena. And the redhead sitting on the man's lap to our left is worried for some reason, even though she's smiling."

Derek's mouth twisted and he dropped an arm over Elena's shoulders, glaring at the bereted Fae.

Reese studied the men Theda wanted to talk to. "I'm not sensing ill feelings from your group in the corner."

"Good." Theda started across the room.

Heads turned as Reese and the others passed through the pub. No vibes of surprise came from the customers, so she assumed they didn't notice her weaker power level while she was smashed in between Elena and Camille. They arrived safely at the table, and Reese let out the breath she'd been holding.

Theda stopped across from Amund. "Greetings. May we join you?"

Amund flicked his fingers toward one of the Fae on his right. The man stood and walked the perimeter of the group, standing sentry behind Camille.

"The glamour is intact. Our conversation will not be overheard," Amund said in a baritone that sent chills over Reese's skin. She wasn't sensing anything bad from the guy, but he was even bigger up close. Probably the most heavily muscled Fae she'd met, and they were all well built.

"What's he talking about?" she whispered to Elena.

Elena tipped her head closer. "He put a silence glamour on our group. No one outside this circle can hear us, but they can read lips, so be careful."

Theda took the only seat available, the one beside Amund, and Reese and the others stood, which was just as well. Reese was about as tall as the soldiers while seated, and that was just sad. She really must look like a child to them. At least from this position she could keep her hood drawn low without appearing rude.

Theda looked at Reese, a question on her face.

Reese gave her a subtle nod. So far, so good. The only sketchy vibes she was getting came from behind—from someone else in the room—but not these men.

Reese looked over her shoulder, but no one stood out. It didn't matter anyway. Amund and his men were the ones whose trust they needed.

Theda set an amulet in front of Amund. "We will take back the palace three days hence. Present this to my lead soldier and you will have his complete trust. Are your men ready?"

"My men are always prepared for a skirmish." He smirked devilishly.

"There can be no errors," Theda said. "You understand what is at stake?"

Amund leaned forward. "I understand, Your Majesty, but my men and I want to know how you will repay our efforts. We will take down the queen's puppet army, but only at a price."

Theda's mouth twisted into a frown. "Your payment is that you will have your *rightful* queen in power—a noblewoman born and bred for the position who will protect this land with her life."

Amund glanced at each of his men. "A good reason, to be sure, but my men and I have been left on the outside for far too long."

"Because you have been known to throw down your swords when the mood suits you."

Amund's battleax of a fist slammed down on the table, causing Reese to jump. She glanced at her friends, but they remained still, watching the heated conversation unfold.

Apparently, this was normal soldier negotiations?

"It was one battle three hundred years ago. I did not

fight with our kingdom because I was called to the Land of Ice."

Theda shook her head. "No one lives in the Land of Ice."

"So sayeth some." Amund drew his fist back to his side. "Be that as it may, I was not here when the Oldlanders"—he glanced at Derek—"ruthlessly attacked our people. Had I been present, we would not have lost so many lives."

Theda laid her hands on the table, one over the other. "I am prepared to trust you and your men again. If you pledge yourselves to me."

"We do," Amund said without reservation.

Theda glanced at the others with him. "I must hear it from all of you."

One by one, each warrior pledged his life and loyalty to Theda.

Reese understood why Theda demanded it. She couldn't risk someone turning on her in mid-battle, but Reese couldn't help remembering Keen's similar oath to Portia. Only in this case, Theda truly had her people's best interests in mind.

"And what of the rest of your warriors?" Theda asked. "For we will need an army of hundreds if we are to take back our kingdom."

"I give you my word on their loyalty." Amund grinned smugly. "You will have to trust me this time, my queen."

Theda twisted around to Reese.

Reese nodded. He was goading her, but Reese also read admiration and enthusiasm from him. Amund respected Theda. He and his men also seemed pretty excited to go to battle against Portia and her military, if Reese was interpreting it correctly.

He lifted his chin toward Derek. "What of the Halven leader? Whose side does he stand on?"

"Derek O'Brien is my daughter's consort, and the rightful heir to the Old Kingdom crown. He saved my daughter's life. The two of them are responsible for healing our people from the virus, your men included, as I'm sure you're aware. Derek can be trusted. In fact, anyone who causes harm to him or his Oldlander soldiers fighting alongside us will be severely dealt with. In this battle, the kingdoms are united. We can discuss how the kingdoms will move forward once I've regained my throne."

"I don't trust Oldlanders," Amund grumbled. "But no harm will come to the Halven king. He saved my family and the lives of some of my men. We are indebted to him and your daughter." Amund nodded to Elena, and she returned the gesture.

"And the cloaked one?" Amund's heavy gaze landed on Reese. "I see the pale hair, but not the face. Who is she?"

"A youth, here to ensure you tell the truth."

"Through mental abilities? Another Oldlander?"

"Yes. As is your man who created the silencing glamour."

He grinned boldly. "And her assessment of me and my men? Can we be trusted?"

All eyes turned to Reese, and it took everything in her power not to squirm.

Nevertheless, she nodded, because these Fae *could* be trusted. She didn't sense fear, envy, or anger from them. In fact—Reese looked over her shoulder again—the worst emotions from anyone in the room came from the man on whose lap the scantily clad redhead sat.

Reese had sensed it when they first walked in, and later as Theda negotiated with Amund, but she'd been more worried about the people Theda was aligning herself with. Now that she was certain Amund and his men wouldn't betray Theda, she couldn't help paying attention to the man at the entrance of the pub.

He was dressed all in black, and though he and the redhead were together, neither seemed focused on each other. The woman was still afraid, and the man had grown angrier the longer Reese and her friends lingered.

"We should go," Reese said quietly to Elena. Even with the din of noise in the pub, she was sure Amund heard her, as did Theda, because they both looked up. The New Kingdom guards might not hear their voices through the heavy wooden door of Reese's bedroom, but Fae had superior hearing, and even Reese had noticed an increase in her sensory abilities since she'd come into her Halven powers.

Theda stood, and so did every man at the table. "Samuel will be in touch. He is the leader of my soldiers. You will defer to him for further instruction."

Amund nodded and watched them walk toward the exit. And they almost made it too—out the door and safe from the dilapidated pub and its nearly all-male inhabitants.

Until a large arm hooked Reese's waist and dragged her onto a distinctly male lap.

"Little one," came the deep, lyrical voice, "what are you up to?"

CHAPTER
SIXTEEN

Only one person called Reese *little one.*

She twisted around and stared at the hooded Fae who'd grabbed her and continued to keep a determined hold on her waist atop his lap. "What are you doing here, Keen?"

He pushed back the hood of his cloak, and angry emerald eyes stared down at her. "I believe I asked you that question."

Elena had raised her hands when Keen first grabbed Reese—probably to singe his ass with her magic—but she dropped them now.

Reese wished she hadn't. Keen could use a little zapping.

How had he known she was here? She'd barely seen him in the last few days, and they'd been so careful when they left the palace this evening.

"We'll give you a moment to..." Elena trailed off, and she and the others went to stand near the door, glancing over every second or two.

Keen couldn't be trusted, and now he knew Elena and Derek were in Tirnan. "I can explain."

"Can you?" he asked, anger still in his tone. In fact, his arm around her waist had tightened. "I followed you when Illa came to me, concerned. She sensed a presence in your bedroom the other night, but thought twice before alerting the guards. It is good for your friends that she did not. Elena and her mother are enemies of the state. Had the guards been alerted, they would be imprisoned or dead right now."

"Only because Portia stole Theda's crown."

"Be that as it may, your friends would be executed if discovered."

"Which," she said, "is why I didn't tell you. How do I know you won't go to Portia and tell her about Theda after we leave this place?"

"I swore to be Portia's soldier and to protect her. Is she in danger?"

Reese studied his eyes, which seemed to be warning her. She said nothing.

"And if she is not in danger," he continued as though she'd answered, "there is no reason for me to bother her with this, correct?"

Reese nodded slowly. Keen couldn't have heard their conversation with Amund while the silence glamour was in place. But if she told him details of their plans to take back the palace, he would be obligated to tell Portia. And he seemed to be saying as much with his eyes.

She wasn't Fae. She could lie with the best of them and not suffer any ill fate, except to her conscience. But in this case, her conscience was clear, because Portia was an asshole and she needed to be knocked down a peg or two.

"Reese," Keen said with deep exasperation, "you cannot

roam Tirnan. I am trying to keep you alive, but you are making it very difficult."

"Locking me away in that room isn't keeping me alive. It's keeping me trapped."

"Is there a difference?"

"Yes, damn you!" Reese glanced to the side, realizing she was causing a scene.

She twisted so that she faced him more squarely, and lowered her voice. Belatedly, she realized how close that brought them—their chests nearly touching. "I'm not weak, Keen. And I'm not stupid, despite what my hair color indicates."

"You are blond. How does that make you stupid?" He seemed sincere.

"Human joke." Most Fae were blond. For all she knew, fair hair was probably the epitome of superiority and intelligence in Tirnan. "The point is, I can handle myself."

"You have never gone up against one of my kind."

"The hallway—"

"That was not a battle," he said. "That was one man attempting to force his attentions on you." He ground out the last words. "Had I not arrived when I did, he would have hurt you."

Keen's eyes were fierce, yet somehow deeply vulnerable. He didn't like the reality he'd painted with his words.

He was right, she knew it, but he was so very wrong about her. She appreciated Keen's concern, but as long as he saw her as something frail and to be protected, he'd never respect her. She wanted his respect as much as she wanted his desire.

"I've been underestimated, undervalued, and flat-out ignored by my family my entire life. My philandering parents might have succumbed to the seduction of money, power, and sex, but I'm not my parents," she said in a low tone. "It's why I trained to be a fighter. It's why I excelled in school. I don't need someone thinking for me. Regardless of how I look, I have principles, and I don't rely on my appearance to get me around in the world."

He shook his head and stared away, letting out a deep breath. When his gaze returned to hers, he said, "I do not believe you are weak. *I* am weak when it comes to you. I keep you guarded so that I don't have to fear anything happening to you."

If Reese hadn't been aware that she was sitting on Keen's strong thighs, nearly straddling him, as he held her and declared a weakness for her, she was aware of it now.

But his declaration wasn't enough. Men had wanted her before; they'd simply never loved her. And in the worst case—her father—there was a complete disregard for her. "You've done what you said you would. You saved me, and now my friends are here. You can wash your hands of me. Marry my sister, if that's what you wish." And if her voice choked on that last part, Reese played it off like it hadn't.

Keen tucked a lock of golden hair that had slipped forward back beneath the hood of her cloak. "I do not wish to marry your sister."

"Do you have a choice? Portia wants it. You're duty bound to do what she says."

His eyes grew intense. Angry. "For now I'm not committed to another."

But later he would be. And it wouldn't be Reese.

Why did she care whom he committed to? Yes, she was attracted to him, but that meant little in the scheme of things.

The problem was that she felt more than attraction for Keen; it had always been like that. The way he looked at her

—pissed off most of the time, and also protective and desirous—drove her crazy. But Keen would never be with a Halven. And Reese was Halven.

She squirmed to get off his lap, but he held her there. "Do not go," he said.

She sighed. What was his problem? "I thought you ordered me back to my cage?"

He raised his eyebrow. "Cage? You are in one of the finest guest rooms in the kingdom."

"And can I leave it freely?"

"I prefer that you do not."

"Then it's a cage." She glared at those beautiful eyes that often said one thing while his mouth said another.

And then his jewel-toned gaze darkened. And that mouth that irritated her with its words dropped—and caressed her lips.

Reese's breath caught. Keen would never kiss her—but he was.

Which could only mean one thing. He'd lost his damned mind.

She quickly recovered from her stupor and kissed him back, because the guy who caused her equal parts annoyance and lust was *kissing her*. Hell yes, she was gonna partake.

His lips were soft, startling in their gentleness. He pulled back the briefest amount, and then his fingers slid up the back of her neck, sending a shiver down her spine. He kissed her again, but this time his lips parted and his tongue entered her mouth, mimicking all sorts of naughty things he never voiced.

Reese slid her hands up his broad shoulders to his head, where she captured him and showed him what he'd been missing. But she never gained control of the kiss. The staunch Fae, who'd scoffed at her elegant red dress because it revealed her shoulders, slid his hand down past her waist and squeezed her ass, showing her without words that he was in control.

Reese's heart nearly punched out of her chest, and her stomach clenched.

She pulled back and stared at his half-lidded gaze, more to get a grip on herself than anything else. "What's gotten into you?"

He released her backside and looked away. "I apologize." He peered in the direction of their friends, who must be shocked, but Reese couldn't get herself to look away long enough to tell. She needed to know what had just happened.

"You should go," he said, his shoulders tense, as though he regretted the moment.

She gaped at him. How dare he kiss her like that, then act like it was a mistake? Was that all she was to him?

Oops, didn't mean to wake up naked with you pressed to my chest.

Sorry, didn't mean to nuzzle your hair in my sleep.

My bad—my mouth slipped and landed on yours.

She was *more*. In his world or hers.

Reese scrambled off Keen's lap, and this time he let her go. She didn't know if she wanted him to hold on to her or not, but the fact that he let her go just pissed her off more.

If she hadn't been so angry, she would have realized her hood had dropped back, revealing her face to the room. Revealing that she was no child. That she was Halven.

The angry man with the redhead on his lap pushed the girl away none too gently and stood. The girl scrambled across the room with her head bent, seemingly eager to get away.

Reese looked around. All eyes were on her. And the once-noisy room had gone silent.

Amund stood in the back, along with his warriors. Their eyes moved from the angry Fae to Reese.

She sensed Keen rising to his full height behind her.

"Walk out the door with your friends," he said lowly. "Go straight to the palace, and for once, listen to me."

But it was too late. The Fae who'd caught her attention earlier because of the anger she'd sensed rolling off him pulled a small sword from somewhere on his back and bore down on her.

A flash of lightning slammed into the man and he screamed. The sword in his hand clattered at Reese's feet.

Something or someone—she assumed Keen—pushed her hard in the direction of Elena and the others. And the room spun into full motion.

Chairs scraped, swords were drawn, and voices rose. The front door slammed shut in a gust of wind that came out of nowhere—or more likely from one of the magic wielders. All Fae possessed powers, some stronger than others. But the majority of the people in this room had control over nature's elements. Like wind. Like lightning.

If Reese made it out of the room alive, it would be a miracle.

She looked back at Keen. "You can't hold them off. There are too many." At that exact moment, wind whipped, papers flew past their heads, and glass shattered, muffling her voice. People covered their heads, and Reese glanced at the door to find Derek attempting to pry it open with both hands while Elena stood nearby with her eyes closed.

Her roommate had started a tornado.

Camille separated from the group and approached a

man who seemed to be concentrating on the door. He wore peasant clothes, like Reese and the others.

Camille pulled a blunt weapon from inside her top. The peasant glanced down, but it was too late. She clocked him on the side of his temple and he dropped like a sandbag.

A second later, the peasant shook his head and began to rise, but by that time Derek had the front door open.

Reese looked back. She couldn't leave Keen to fight everyone off, she just couldn't. His dagger was drawn, his gaze taking in the room. "I won't leave you here," she said.

He peered past her and threw the knife.

It landed in the chest of the angry Fae who'd been climbing to his feet, having recovered from the bolt of electricity Elena had hit him with.

"Amund is a friend." Keen pulled out what looked to be a machete he'd somehow had stashed in a side pocket. "I see he is a friend of yours now as well?" He raised his brow, but his gaze promptly returned to the number of men in the room who were looking less like friends and more like foes. "Amund and I will show the Fae who wishes to harm you and the others why that would be a foolish idea."

Her friends were calling for her to leave, but she couldn't. Not yet. "Do you support Theda?" she asked Keen.

"I know not what Theda has planned, and I don't wish to," he said pointedly. He threw off his cloak. "Leave!" he shouted, and dove at a group of men attempting to get to her.

"Reese!" Elena called. "Now!"

Keen was beating the crap out of four Fae at once. Then Amund, who kicked the guy in front of him out of the way, turned to help Keen.

Reese ran for her friends and Derek grabbed her hand. A tingling sensation washed over her.

They escaped the pub, all of them hand in hand to maintain the Blending, though when she looked down, she saw herself, the same as always. But that was how Derek's magic worked. She'd experienced it when they crept out of the palace earlier.

They ran down the cobblestoned street, and Derek tugged her and the others down one side alley, and then another. They stopped beneath a darkened overhang, and Derek broke the Blending. The tingling sensation that had been vibrating down her body disappeared.

"Why are we stopping?" Reese said.

"No one saw which direction we went; we don't need to Blend anymore. But we should keep going." Derek nodded to her hood. "Put that back on."

She did as he said and went to follow him and the others, but Elena grabbed her hand, holding her back.

"What in the fudge was that about, Reese? Since when are you and Keen hooking up?"

"*Fudge* isn't a curse word, Elena." Reese urged her friend forward, and they jogged to keep up with the others.

"My mom's in front of us. I don't want to make her uncomfortable with curses. She's already wary of Derek and me sleeping together on a blanket in your room. Which, when I think about it, is weird, because before her and my dad got married, they were... Well, anyway, that's another story. Let's get back to you and Keen." She glanced over while they maintained a steady pace behind the others. "Is there a you and Keen?"

Reese thought about the kiss that had shocked her—and at the same time had felt like it was a long time coming. And then she considered Keen's words afterward.

An apology. He'd even ordered her in the past not to touch him.

He might want her, but he didn't wish to be with her. Not really.

"There isn't anything going on. That was nothing. Just Keen improvising."

Elena snorted and nudged Reese toward an alley the others had turned down. "Didn't look like nothing. Seemed like a whole lot of something, if you ask me. Kind of hot, actually. Except, maybe not so much for the people in the pub, who thought you were a child. Until your hood fell, of course. Kind of hard to miss the woman beneath. And that you're Halven. You realize this will be all over the kingdom soon? Shit, it will be all over the realm. Portia will know what happened by the time we get back."

Reese pinched her eyes closed for a brief second. "You said *shit,*" she pointed out as a distraction. "So much for proper language in front of your mother."

The look Elena shot her said she knew what Reese was doing.

"It was stupid. The kiss." Reese shook her head. "I'm sorry."

They caught up with the others just outside the palace. "Not stupid," Elena said slowly. "Curious. Maybe even complicated, but not stupid. I love the guy, even if he is a stubborn Fae. But don't let him give you crap, Reese."

She chuckled. "Him, give me crap? Never."

Elena grinned. "That's my girl."

Derek looked past them, and Reese turned.

Keen was jogging their way. *How the hell?*

"You were just in a pub brawl with forty people," she said as he neared. "How did you get out so fast?"

He glanced at her briefly, but otherwise kept his gaze on the others. "Amund and his men have been looking forward to a good fight. They had it under control. I left soon after you did. But word will spread of Theda's presence and the Halven working with her." He glared at Reese. "The Halven who is supposed to be locked away in the palace."

"What about the Fae guard who crossed the line with the Halven?" she shot back. "Will they talk about him too?"

His gaze grew half-lidded, but no less threatening. "Doubtful. Fae have dabbled with humans and the like for millennia."

Reese swallowed back the rush of heat that filled her throat, blinking back the pressure behind her eyes. Of course she meant nothing to him. Never had, never would.

Only that wasn't what she'd felt in his kiss. He cared. It simply didn't matter, because he didn't *want* to care.

"We done?" Derek said, exasperated. "Let's get inside before Portia's military finds us here and picks us off one at a time."

Reese chewed her lip. "Is that the right thing to do? After what happened? Shouldn't we hide somewhere far away from the palace?"

"We cannot," Theda said. "They will be searching the area for us. We are better off beneath their noses. Ironically, it will be harder for them to find us inside, among the hundreds that live and protect the palace, than out here on our own, where our energy levels will signal our presence like a beacon."

Camille created a portal in front of a large tree that looked like a pine, but with a squat, wide base. One by one, they leapt through it and landed inside the training room.

Elena brushed off her legs where she'd skidded across the floor like she was stealing a base. She really needed to work on her portal landings. Camille's portals were bumpy, but once you got the hang of it, not as difficult as Elena made them out to be.

"There are guards inside your room," Camille said, looking up, as though she could see through the ceiling.

Derek reached for Elena's hand. "I'll Blend us. We can hide out while Keen and Reese..."

"I'll take care of it from here," Keen said, a silent acknowledgment passing between them.

A second later, Derek, Elena, Theda, and Camille were gone.

Reese rounded on him. "What do you mean you'll take care of it? I knew we should have escaped while we could and gotten as far from the palace as possible. What does Derek expect us to do now?"

Keen removed his shirt and kicked off his boots in answer.

"What. Are. You. *Doing?*"

He brushed back his hair and sauntered over.

Reese backed up, her stupid heart racing. For some reason, it hadn't gotten the memo that this hot guy wasn't boyfriend material. "Oh, hell no," she said. "I don't like that look in your eye. Reminds me of the deceptive way you looked at me in the pub."

He drew closer. "And what way was that?"

"Like you wanted me."

"I don't want you," he said, but his body language, his eyes—they spoke differently.

Her jaw shifted and she let out a sigh. "No shit, so stop looking at me like you're trying to melt off my panties with your gaze. And for the love of God, put your shirt back on!" Despite her words, she couldn't take her eyes off his chest.

Keen stopped inches away. "We need a cover." He grabbed her hooded cloak and removed it, tossing it in a far corner. "This is the only way... Will you cooperate?"

"With what?" she asked faintly, too distracted by the muscles of his chest to concentrate.

He drew closer. So close she smelled his clean scent. "The ruse," he murmured before he took her mouth and picked her up, his arms crossed beneath her ass. "Play along with me?" he said before his mouth covered hers again.

He'd asked her to pretend, but this didn't feel fake. The heat of his body scorched hers, his lips feverishly trailing from her mouth down her throat, as if he could consume every inch of her.

In the dark recesses of her mind, Reese detected footsteps down the hall. But Keen had found a spot at the top of her breast that was particularly sensitive. He'd pushed her unisex commoner outfit aside and licked her there, then lightly bit her while his hand reached up and squeezed her other breast above her clothes.

She gasped and clamped her arms around his head. Then dug her fingers in his silky hair, kissing his brow.

Keen lowered her to the mat and braced himself over her, his hips slipping between her thighs as she angled up to kiss him. His hand slid up her top until it grazed the bottom of one of her breasts.

Her breath caught. She was really liking this new position, as his body was pressing down on all the fun spots, but... "Is this necessary?"

"No." He kissed her again and palmed her breast.

He was lucky she liked everything he was doing, or he'd be in a world of hurt right now. From her knee.

Using their situation to cop a feel? Extremely naughty.

Which she liked.

And two could play this game.

Reese reached around and squeezed Keen's ass. And, oh God, was it a perfect ass.

She arched against him, losing all train of thought as she wrapped her ankles around the back of his legs, feeling him everywhere.

She didn't hear the door open.

Or hear the soldiers walk in.

"What is the meaning of this?" came an angry female voice.

Keen lifted his head.

Reese started and scrambled to the side, realizing, belatedly, that now wasn't the time to teach Keen a lesson. Or to enjoy making out—*pretend* making out—with him. She and her friends were within seconds of being thrown in the dungeon. This wasn't a game.

Portia stood several feet inside the doorway, an array of guards surrounding her.

"I was just given word that Theda Rainer is in the village," she said to Keen, who was leaning in leisurely fashion on his side, "along with a Fae who goes by the name of Camille, Theda's daughter, Elena, and that Halven, Derek O'Brien." She stared at Reese. "I'm told *our* Halven was there as well."

Our Halven? As though Portia owned her? *I don't think so.*

Keen reached out and covered Reese's bared midriff possessively with his warm palm. "As you can see, we are here."

Reese pushed his hand away and tugged her top down, but Keen discreetly held her shoulder when she tried to sit up.

"I see that," Portia spat. "Why are you with *this*"—she waved vaguely at Reese—"when you have Illa as fiancée?"

"I am not promised to Illa."

"But you will be. In fact, I order it." Portia's emotions

were all over the board. Rage, disgust—and elation. Portia seemed to get some perverse pleasure out of pushing around the chess pieces and controlling everyone.

"You ordered my fealty as a soldier. You cannot order whom I marry," Keen said casually.

"And you choose this Halven?" Portia said in disgust.

He hesitated. "Of course not."

"Then what is the problem? If it is power you wish, let me assure you, you will have it. An entire kingdom's worth, for I wish for you and Illa to rule Old Kingdom in my stead." She cut Reese a sharp look. "Trifle with the girl all you want, but bind yourself to Illa."

Portia spun and stormed toward the door, the guards at her heels. She paused sharply on the threshold. "The girl is banned from training, henceforth. I felt it harmless in the beginning while we needed her out of the way; she couldn't hurt one of us if she tried. But she's proven more cunning than I assumed. She needs no further fighting skills, even if you believe her in danger from our kind inside the palace. She has you at her side," Portia said saccharinely. "What more protection could she require? In the meantime, find Theda. I want her head."

CHAPTER

SEVENTEEN

Portia and most of her soldiers left. Two stayed behind and stood outside the doorway, presumably to ensure Reese was taken directly to her room.

She rolled away from Keen and sat facing him with her arms wrapped around her knees. "What now?" she asked.

He stood and pulled on his shirt. "You do nothing."

"Bullshit!" She leapt to her feet.

One of the guards glanced back, but otherwise remained with his back to them.

"Not now," Keen said quietly. "Later, my love, we can continue what we started."

Reese rolled her eyes. "You wish," she muttered, so that only he heard.

Keen escorted her to her bedroom, but instead of leaving, he walked inside. He went to close the door behind him, but one of the guards stopped him.

"The queen wishes it to remain open."

Keen tilted his head, power radiating off him. "Jacob, have you forgotten who your new master of the guards is?"

"No, sir." Jacob glanced nervously at Reese. "But the queen—"

"Put me in charge," Keen said. "And as you witnessed earlier, I have the Halven well in hand." He grinned licentiously, and Reese fought to not roll her eyes again. "Now, if you don't mind, we'd like some privacy. You may tell the queen that Reese's ability presented, and that she is an empath. Such an innocuous power. She cannot create fireballs or paralyze the body with a touch. We are safe from her mundane Halven ability." Keen closed the door in the guard's face.

He'd downplayed her ability, but he also spoke truth. Reese wished her Halven powers were stronger, though they *had* been useful tonight. She had identified a Fae who wished them harm, and she'd confirmed that Theda's trust in Amund wasn't misplaced. That was something.

Keen tilted his head, as though listening. "Jacob departs to speak with the queen. The other three guards wait outside, but they believe we are…"

"Getting it on?"

He shrugged.

She paced the room. "You can't stay here. I need to talk to Elena, and you can't be around when I do."

He moved closer. "You must not interfere in Theda's plans, whatever they are. Stay clear of Elena and her mother, and whoever else they have helping them."

She shook her head and laughed bitterly. "I'm not sure why you care whether I'm harmed or not; you've managed to thoroughly confuse me as far as how you feel. But I can tell you one thing. There is no way I'm not getting involved. I will. I am."

His face tensed with anger. He spun on his heel, strode

to the door, and opened it. "She is yours to protect," he told the men outside, then stormed away.

Reese turned her back and flattened her hands to her face.

They weren't good for one another. He didn't want to be attracted to her, and she didn't want to be with someone who didn't respect her.

"Reese?"

Reese wiped her hands down her face, closeting away the emotions that threatened to overtake her. She turned to find Illa standing in the doorway. Concern filled her sister's face and mind.

Illa moved inside. "I came to tell you that...our father arrives tomorrow. There will be a dinner to discuss an alliance between the two kingdoms."

Reese wagged her head slowly. She remembered what Portia had said in the workout room about wanting Keen to rule Old Kingdom. "How can there be an alliance without the Oldlander king involved? Derek O'Brien rules Old Kingdom."

Illa looked sad. "Yes, but there are few who feel he is worthy."

Her Fae sister had been kind, but Reese was on her last nerve. "Derek *not worthy*? He and Elena saved this entire realm. You'd all be dead if it weren't for them."

Illa swallowed, her emotions filled with shame and frustration. "I don't hold the same beliefs others do when it comes to Halven. Many in Tirnan have changed their opinions about offspring between Fae and humans since your friend cured the virus. But there are also those who believe Derek is not capable of leading a kingdom about which he knows little."

She was right. But for the wrong reasons.

"Derek might not know much about Fae customs, but that's because we've been kept separate from your kind our entire lives and treated as outcasts. Not knowing who our sisters and brothers are."

Illa's face crumpled. "I am sorry, Reese. It was not my choice to have been kept from you. If it makes a difference, I didn't know you existed until recently. My father never spoke of you."

And somehow, amidst everything that had happened this night—nearly having a sword speared through her in the pub, facing off with Portia, being kissed by Keen and rejected, then kissed again by Keen and rejected *again*—this thing, this knowledge that not even her biological father cared one whit about her, sank to her core, slicing her open.

She wrapped an arm around her middle and covered her face with her hand, turning her back to Illa. "Please leave."

"Reese, you must understand. It is not our way. Our father...he isn't a bad man. He's the best of fathers."

Reese's shoulders shook. "I wouldn't know. Now, if you don't mind?" She wouldn't look at her sister. Couldn't.

Reese heard Illa's soft footfalls grow faint as she left the room and moved down the hallway. And that was when the tears began to pour down Reese's cheeks.

She crawled onto her giant, plush bed that held no warmth, no sense of home, and let out all of her pain.

Enid helped Reese into the beaded green gown. "This one is stunning, Miss Reese. You will be the prettiest woman there."

"Don't you mean I'll be the only woman?"

Enid grinned. "The only Halven woman. But also the prettiest of Fae women as well."

"Thank you. I highly doubt it, given the glowing celestial beauty all of you possess, but it's kind of you to say."

"It is truth. We never—"

"Lie." Reese smiled, and so did Enid.

Reese looked down at the gown that clung to her curves, while also remaining modest. "I do like this one, only—" She looked toward the door the guards had allowed her to close while she dressed with the servant. "It needs something."

Enid scanned Reese's figure. "Any adornment would take away from the beading, and the color is so striking on its own."

"Not that. I was thinking of something along the lines of...my pretty sword?" Reese grinned sheepishly. "Will that fit?"

Enid's eyes grew wide.

Reese had received a message from Theda last night. It started like the buzzing of the last communication she'd sent with her powers.

We are in hiding inside the dungeon, where few venture. The attack takes place tomorrow evening. Be prepared.

All Reese knew was that things were going down tonight. The same evening she was supposed to meet her Fae father.

"No, I suppose my sword wouldn't fit. Besides, after Portia banned me from training, they may have confiscated it." Reese's mouth twisted. "What about a dagger?"

Enid glanced at the door and nodded. She reached beneath her prim gray gown—hers of the matronly variety that went up to her neck—and pulled out a double-bladed short knife with a star design on the hilt.

"Jesus, Enid." Reese gawked. "How long have you been hiding that thing beneath your skirts?"

"This is only my short knife. The long one is strapped to my thigh. Would you prefer that one?"

"No, no." Reese held up her hands. "You keep it. In fact, maybe you should consider stashing it close tonight. Just to be safe. Do you understand what I mean?"

"I believe so, miss." Enid's eyes narrowed, and she lowered her voice. "The palace is aware of her highness's presence in the kingdom."

"Portia?"

"No." Enid shook her head and looked around, though they were the only ones in the room. "Our true queen," she whispered, barely audible. "But the kingdom fears rumors about a secret weapon the current queen hides. They dare not make a move against her. Not to mention, many have been made beholden to her."

A secret weapon? They couldn't afford another problem.

"Portia and her pledges of fealty," Reese muttered in irritation. "She's forced it on so many? Is that normal?"

"No, miss. Among high-ranking guards, yes, but not noblemen and servants. It's never been needed before... well, before there was a change in authority. The kingdoms hold their nobility in high regard, protecting them to the death. They are our rulers, but they are also most holy. It is typically our honor to protect them."

"Holy..." Reese said, considering. "What exactly happened to the angels who created your race?"

"Gone. To the holy realm, never to return. No one alive has ever seen them. They left millennia ago. It is said they wished for us to live prosperously without them, and we have lived in peace ever since."

"Wait, aren't you guys always warring with each other? Old Kingdom and New Kingdom fighting to the death?"

"Oh, yes, but only because Oldlanders are vicious beasts known to murder for power." She blushed. "No offense, miss."

Reese didn't bother to point out that Newlanders could be a bloodthirsty lot as well, because she figured it would fall on deaf ears. Fae seemed blind to their prejudices. "None taken," she said instead. "And it's not like I'm a true Oldlander. My father is, but I've never met him."

Enid winced. "He is here. Your father."

"I know." Reese took a deep breath. "Illa told me."

"Well, he cannot find fault in you tonight. You will be the most beautiful woman there."

Beautiful, but not valued—not respected. Not even in this land. Reese tried to smile, but her mouth couldn't quite form one. She held up the blade instead. "You have some way for me to hide this beneath my dress?"

CHAPTER

EIGHTEEN

Keen didn't escort Reese to dinner. She hadn't seen him since she told him she would fight alongside Elena and Theda. He'd been furious. Obviously, he'd written her off.

She swallowed, her throat raw.

"This way, miss," Ulric said, guiding her toward a massive parlor.

She paused at the entrance. There had to be four hundred people drinking what looked to be *brune*, the liquid Keen had told her not to touch. They stood in pairs or groups, chatting amongst themselves, all of them as elaborately dressed as she was tonight.

Enid had been kind when she complimented Reese's appearance. Reese wasn't the most beautiful this evening— Fae outmatched her in beauty, height, and strength. But not intelligence or sheer will.

She entered the room alongside Ulric. Somehow her guard caught sight of Illa within seconds and led Reese to her and the handsome older Fae standing beside her.

"Greetings," Illa said brightly. She was incredibly

nervous. So nervous, Reese thought *she* would break out in a sweat from the emotions spilling off her sister. "This is my father, Hakon Radnor."

And suddenly Reese understood the cause of Illa's nerves. She should have suspected this. She'd been warned he'd be here tonight.

Illa's anxiety jumped to Reese, because the man in front of her was *her* father too. The Fae sperm donor, at least, not the man who'd claimed to be her father.

She shouldn't care what this man thought, but she did. Her own father had paid her little attention. Would this man be the same?

Illa stepped to the side with Ulric almost immediately. They spoke in soft, low tones, totally ditching Reese.

"Illa tells me you are brave and headstrong," Hakon said, forcing Reese to stop shooting her sister the evil eye for abandoning her.

Illa finally glanced over. She must have overheard Hakon, because she shrugged unapologetically.

"I have my moments," she said.

Hakon—*her father*—was very handsome. Tall, of course, though not the tallest among the male Fae. And she resembled him, which was most surprising of all. Reese had his nose and his full lips. And the same eye color.

Her father back home had brown eyes, and her mother's were blue. Reese had assumed her green eyes were a mix of the two, but she was wrong. Hakon had extremely pale green eyes, just like Reese.

"So, you knocked up my mother." She wouldn't let this man know how much it mattered that he hadn't cared to meet her until now.

Hakon's brow furrowed. "Knocked up?"

"Had an affair—you got my mother pregnant while she was married to my father."

He compressed his mouth. "*I* am your father. And, yes, I suppose you would see it that way."

"Not my father." Reese's face grew hot with anger. She took a deep breath—and felt a large, warm hand touch her lower back.

Keen. She knew who it was before he moved to her side.

"Radnor," Keen said.

"Albrecht." Hakon nodded in greeting. "I'm told you have aligned yourself with New Kingdom." He brushed his hand down his embroidered tunic, as though clearing away the unpleasant topic of Reese's birth. "Why should I agree to a marriage between you and my daughter if you are in traitor territory?"

For a moment Reese stood stunned. And then she realized Hakon wasn't speaking of her, but of his Fae daughter —*Illa.*

Keen's palm dropped from Reese's back, and an instant chill swept up her spine. He didn't look at her when he said, "There is no understanding between your daughter and me."

Reese glanced at Illa, who was standing nervously off to the side and staring at the ground. Ulric watched her, his jaw taut.

"That is not what I'm told," Hakon said. "The queen wishes a union between you and my daughter. It is why I am here tonight. This union would prevent the need for an internal battle among my people. I'm told the Halven ruler will submit when you marry my daughter. That you will rule Old Kingdom with Illa at your side."

"He will not submit," Reese snapped, and everyone

turned to her. "What idiot told you that? Derek rules Old Kingdom. Neither you nor Keen have a right to it."

"Daughter—"

"Don't call me that." Her voice came out clipped, but what did he expect? "You haven't earned it. You haven't been there for me."

Hakon flinched, and she sensed his pain.

Reese had ignored the man's emotions since she and Ulric approached, but she couldn't ignore them now. He cared for her, even if he'd never been around.

Had her father back home felt the same all these years and she'd missed it?

Hakon pasted on a bland smile and looked at Illa. "I see what you meant about her being headstrong. As I was saying," Hakon continued, "our line—*your* family line—is next to rule Old Kingdom. Had this Halven not shown up, we would be in power."

"Have you lost your mind?" Whether or not he cared about her, this man was spouting nonsense, and Reese wouldn't sit back and listen. "It was Derek's power that saved you. His power that took down the previous king. You've had hundreds of years to do it yourself and you didn't. *Derek* did."

"Reese," Keen said in warning.

She turned to him. "Don't *Reese* me. It's the truth. Everyone in this backward realm refuses to see it."

Keen pinched the bridge of his nose.

"Daughter," Hakon said, "be careful what you say, or you will suffer the wrath of the angels."

Reese speared him with a look. "Do you mean the angels who've been gone for thousands of years? I'm not worried about them; I hear they'll never return. I'm worried about my friends who have a right to their land and thrones you all prize so much. I'm worried about the revolution that brews under your noses, with my people caught in the middle. The machinations of the Fae are unbelievable. You have no right to take the throne from Derek, and if you try—"

"Careful," Keen said.

She closed her eyes and took a deep breath.

Keen was right. She'd been locked up too long, every pent-up emotion unleashing itself tonight. And she was taking it out on Hakon, because he'd abandoned her.

The room had moved into motion while they spoke, hordes of people moving toward the back.

"Perhaps we should adjourn to the dining room?" Keen said. "It seems it is time."

Hakon nodded, and Illa joined him at his side. But once they entered the dining room—inside of which Reese's Hollywood mansion could have fit—Keen escorted Reese to one end of the table with Ulric, then joined Illa and her father at the other end, distancing himself from her.

It was no surprise that Keen didn't believe her worthy of his presence in a formal setting when he wasn't protecting her. And it seemed Hakon saw her as beneath him as well.

She squared her shoulders and sat primly, hiding her disappointment. For a moment, Reese had wondered if this father might be different, but of course he wouldn't be. Fae were far less tolerant toward those of mixed race than humans.

The last person entered the room—the queen. And she was draped in a red silk cloak, with a full diamond-encrusted skirt beneath. It was over-the-top wealth and power. Portia had the balls to steal what she did and abuse power this way.

Beside her stood a pretty younger Fae with pale red hair pulled back into an elaborately braided ponytail. She appeared to be a young high noblewoman, but Reese had never seen her before.

On Portia's other side was Marlon, in midnight clothing nearly as fine as Portia's. He looked out at the room smugly. He seemed pleased to be standing at the head of the Fae table.

"Good evening, my people," Portia said. "My daughter Princess Beatrice and I are pleased to welcome you." She smiled at the pretty redhead beside her. "As many of you know, Princess Beatrice is a New Kingdom diplomat, passing between the realms of Emain and Tirnan to solidify a truce. I am also ever so pleased to acknowledge another diplomatic achievement—a celebration of a most joyous union between one of our own and an Oldlander noblewoman."

Portia looked at Keen and Illa, and it was then that Reese began to shake. Gone was her fake composure. Because she finally understood what this evening was about.

She stared at Keen, who looked straight ahead.

He wouldn't...or would he? Portia had said it would happen. Illa had said so too.

Somehow in the back of her mind, she'd hoped that Keen would find a way out of marrying her sister.

But it wasn't all Keen's fault. Reese didn't even know if Keen had a say in whether or not he married Illa. It was all such a mess.

"Our two kingdoms, Old Kingdom"—Portia gestured to Hakon—"and New Kingdom have been divided for nearly as long as Tirnan has been in existence. This rift started long ago with our forefathers. We shared their alliances, and we shared their foes. But it need not continue to be so." She grinned, and Reese felt the ambition rolling off her. This woman didn't give two shits about the kingdoms uniting; she wanted power.

"We can bridge this distance, just as the Bridge of Fates unites our kingdoms physically," Portia continued. "We possess equal power and strength, merely in different areas of the magic inherent within all of us. Imagine if we brought those abilities together? United. How powerful would we be as a people?"

There were murmurings around the room. All seemed to agree, or were at least open to her words.

"An alliance between the kingdoms cannot occur overnight. That would be asking what not even our holy forefathers were able to achieve. However, we could place one of our own—an Oldlander of noble lineage now pledged to me, who was wronged by his homeland as an infant—back in his land of Old Kingdom. For diplomacy. To mate with one of theirs. To rule with one of theirs, while also being loyal to our land."

Reese hadn't eaten the bread and cheese set before her, but she thought she might be sick.

Portia gestured to Keen and Illa. "If they would stand—"

Whatever Portia was about to say got cut off.

Because the number of people in the room instantly doubled.

Shouts erupted. Footsteps thundered. And screams filled the room.

Theda and her army had arrived.

CHAPTER

NINETEEN

Theda and her army appeared out of thin air, surrounding Reese and the hundreds of Newlanders sitting at the massive dining table.

Derek and Elena stood beside Theda near one of the doors, their soldiers gathered around them. They were dressed in black and armed with multiple weapons, including the null gun Elena had shown Reese. Derek must have Blended all of them into the palace.

The doors to the large dining room slammed shut of their own accord.

Chairs scraped back from the massive table. People stood and weapons were drawn from secret pockets and beneath skirts, the emerging metal flickering from the candlelight and illuminated sconces on the walls.

And then Keen stormed across the room like a Viking on a rampage. He was one of the first to make a move, and he was at Reese's side in seconds.

He grabbed her arm and shoved her toward Ulric. "Get her out of here!"

Ulric maneuvered Reese toward one of the closed-off exits, while Keen returned to Hakon and Illa.

She tugged to get her arm free. "Stop it, Ulric. I need to be here."

He ignored her and continued pulling her to one of the doors. It was locked from the outside and didn't seem to budge under his impressive strength. He dropped her arm and used both hands on the door.

Reese quietly backed away.

"What is the meaning of this?" Portia screamed from her position at the head of the table, glaring daggers at Theda.

Beatrice held a sword, her pretty face dark with rage as well.

Theda lifted her chin regally. "You stole the throne you sit upon, Portia. You and your partner, Marlon St. Just, murdered our people. You deserve punishment, not absolute control, the way you've plotted with this marriage of Keen Albrecht to Illa Radnor."

Portia looked heavenward, and Reese sensed her annoyance. "St. Just is not my partner. Unlike you, I would never lower myself to an inferior consort."

Marlon's gaze shot to Portia. He looked longingly past her at Beatrice, who wouldn't meet his eyes. "We have an agreement," he said, loud enough for the room to hear.

"Oh, that." Portia held out her arm, admiring the diamonds that winked along her red cloak. "Yes, well, it seems Princess Beatrice wishes a *Fae* union."

Marlon's face turned a mottled red, and he looked across the room toward Hakon Radnor.

"Do not look to me, child," Hakon said. "You put my life and that of your sister in danger by releasing the virus in our land. Many suffered. Many died. I cannot protect you."

Marlon took a step back, seemingly realizing for the first time how everyone looked at him. With hatred. With loathing. He had no allies. And he was in enemy territory, not the land of his dreams.

Reese's presence might be undesired in New Kingdom, but Marlon was Halven enemy number one. He'd created the only disease able to affect Fae. Under Portia's protection, he was safe, but she was turning her back on him.

Portia gave a subtle nod to Beatrice.

The strawberry blonde with the beautifully braided ponytail and deadly sword stepped back. She swung around her mother, and cut down Marlon where he stood.

Reese closed her eyes.

Marlon was a weasel. He'd captured her and sent her to this place. But he was also her half-brother. Portia had betrayed Marlon just as she'd betrayed Elena's mother and so many others. Marlon should have stood trial, not been slaughtered before them.

Reese looked across the room to Hakon. He held his daughter's hand, his expression stoic. His emotions were less so.

True sorrow rolled off the older Fae.

Beatrice used a cloth napkin from the table and wiped off her sword, dripping with Marlon's blood. She returned to her mother's side.

"You see, Theda," Portia said, "I accede. St. Just's methods were barbaric, and now he's been dealt with."

"He was not the only one who acted unjustly," Theda said. "You supported and assisted him in releasing the virus into our land. Without your help, St. Just could not have accomplished all he did to weaken our people."

"You dare speak against your queen?" Portia growled.

"*I* am queen." Theda's voice resonated strong and

proud. The woman knew her place, and she wasn't backing down.

Portia's gaze swept over the palace soldiers, her manner the tiniest bit flustered. "Take her! She is a traitor and a betrayer of her people. Lying with a human and siring Halven is a sin. And this from a noble Fae? Utter hypocrisy."

For a split second, no one moved. Perhaps because Portia had inadvertently confirmed Theda's rightful place on the throne by acknowledging her royal blood.

Reese wasn't all that big on the noble blood thing. Seemed to her that if a Halven like her roommate Elena could wield great power and save Fae from disease, Fae shouldn't be so picky about little things like bloodlines. All Reese knew—and what she sensed everyone in the room silently acknowledged—was that Theda should rule New Kingdom, not Portia. But Fae, with their verbal pledges, couldn't go against their word, and they'd pledged their honor to Portia.

Keen, the head of Portia's guard, drew his sword first. He attacked the soldier closest to Derek. The rest of the New Kingdom soldiers attacked as well, making their way to Elena's mother, who had her fiercest warriors protecting her while she fought to reach Portia.

Ulric must have given up on the door, because he stepped closer to Reese and stretched out his large arm, blocking her. She sensed his indecision, which had Reese puzzled. He must not have been one of the guards who'd sworn fealty to Portia if he was protecting Reese on Keen's orders.

Ulric couldn't take Reese out of the room while the doors were sealed, and he couldn't fight and leave her defenseless either. So there they stood, neither of them moving, while all hell broke loose around them.

If Reese thought watching Marlon cut down was bad, the scene in front of her was nearly as grisly. Metal clashed and weapons impaled. No one fell the way Marlon had—he was Halven and couldn't survive the physical attack from Beatrice—but blood poured everywhere. And that was before magic entered the mix.

Elena shot hail the size of baseballs at a group of Portia's guards, knocking them into a wall.

The floor rumbled and darts of fire whirled toward Derek and his men.

An Oldlander soldier snuck up and touched the heads of New Kingdom guards, and their bodies froze where they stood.

All around her, battle took place, and it wasn't just the soldiers—it was *everyone:* courtiers, guards, older Fae in elegant dress.

Ulric had backed Reese against a wall, blocking her body with his own and fighting off an Oldlander. She caught a look from Elena and thought she heard her friend yell at the soldier attacking Ulric, but she couldn't be sure with the level of noise filling the room. Either way, the soldier didn't stop his assault.

Ulric fought off one of Derek's men, and was kicking some serious ass, until his head turned sharply.

Reese hadn't heard anything over the commotion, but she looked in the direction he peered, and saw Hakon fighting alongside Derek and Elena. And Illa slumped against the wall, blood and singe marks crisscrossing the pale blue satin of her gown.

A roar erupted from Ulric. In two swift moves, he confiscated the sword from his attacker and broke the guy's neck. Not a deathblow for Fae, but not something the guy would recover from anytime soon.

Ulric had been holding back—defending but not attacking—until he caught sight of Illa injured. The emotion rolling off him now was like a hundred-foot wave of rage and determination, crashing down and taking out everything in its path.

He shoved Reese forward. "Get under the table." And bulldozed his way across the room toward Illa, who looked to be recovering somewhat, her face no longer pale.

Reese had stood there like a defenseless lamb while her friends fought and her sister bled. If she didn't do some-thing soon, she was no better than what everyone pegged her to be.

Weak. Useless.

Still, she got under the damn table and considered her next move.

Elena had pulled out that crazy null gun she'd made and was targeting magic users, shooting them one by one. Derek stood beside her, fighting off Portia's supporters and inching closer to where Portia and Beatrice were.

Beatrice fought Derek and Theda's men, while Portia glowered and shouted at her subjects, "Imprison the trai-tors!" over and over like a madwoman.

Keen battled the soldiers loyal to Theda as well, but never Derek or Elena. Yet he was still protecting Portia, honoring his promise, though he was using a loose inter-pretation.

Reese had witnessed what Keen could do in training, and this wasn't him unleashing his full potential. He was holding back the way Ulric had. He fought Derek's men and the men from the village that supported Theda, but he was herding them away from Portia, not fatally injuring them.

Keen glowered at Ulric, who was over by Illa and her

father now. "Why are you not following my order?" he shouted over the din.

There was no acknowledgment that Ulric had heard Keen, even though Reese had and she was under the table. Ulric was wholly focused on Illa.

He picked her up and stormed toward one of the exits. To do what, Reese didn't know. If they couldn't escape out the door earlier, she wasn't sure how he'd accomplish it now.

But the door that wouldn't budge a moment ago exploded into a thousand pieces of wood, splintering out in every direction—lodging into wall and flesh on both sides of the battle.

Because of Ulric? Why hadn't he used that ability earlier?

He exited with Illa in his arms. A few Fae who appeared less enthusiastic about fighting followed him out, particularly the fancy courtiers of the palace.

Hakon stayed behind, but like Keen and Ulric, he seemed to be choosing whom he bloodied and whom he did not. He never touched Keen, though they stood nearly back to back. And he never touched Theda.

This was some politically touchy business.

Portia was in power and people had to follow her orders, but they could also choose which one of their enemies they fought. No matter how many times Portia screamed for people to kill or take Theda, the soldiers in her power deflected the order by fighting the person in front of them, as though they couldn't quite reach Theda. They were protecting Portia, but never harming their true queen.

Keen looked at Reese again, and began hacking his way through the fighters, seemingly toward her.

Reese maneuvered out from beneath the table, the dagger she'd hidden in a strap at her calf gripped in her hand. She focused on the emotions of Portia and Beatrice and attempted to find an angle from which to help the others. Until an ice ball punched her in the chest.

She rocked back and fell against the table, the knife flying from her hand.

Across from her, a Fae grinned.

She clutched her chest, breathing shallowly until the pain and stinging subsided, and stumbled back under the table for shelter.

Theda was making her way to the front of the room—to Portia—while Elena and the others fought off the New Kingdom guards.

From beneath the table, Reese closed her eyes and tuned out all of the emotion hammering her senses. She focused on Portia. If she could use the woman's emotions to predict her next move, it might help.

Too much fear, anticipation, and anger filled the room. Reese couldn't distinguish from which point the emotions came. She needed to get closer to Portia.

Reese crawled along the perimeter of the table toward the front of the room, dragging her pale green gown with her, careful to not make herself a target for another A-hole Fae who thought she needed a hole in her chest.

She made it a few feet from Portia and her guards, and peered through the damask tablecloth. The queen whispered something to Beatrice, and her daughter nodded.

Beatrice slowly made her way to Elena and the others, along with one of Portia's men.

Inflamed. Eager. Hateful. And the deepest, rawest resentment slammed into Reese. And it wasn't coming from Portia. It came from Beatrice, who angled around Theda and seemed to be heading for Derek and Elena. But her eyes were on Elena.

Hell. No. Reese saw murder in the girl's emotions, and there was no way she'd let anyone take down her best friend.

She looked desperately toward Keen and the others, but none of them were paying attention. Theda was still fighting off New Kingdom soldiers and keeping an eye on Portia. Keen was fighting to reach Reese, though he was still too far away. And Derek and Elena were fending off a circle of guards who'd swarmed them. No one was watching Beatrice's steady movement forward. The guards knew to put extra protection around Theda and, of course, Derek, their king, but not Elena.

If Reese shouted, she'd call attention to herself—making herself another target. She had to be sure she was right about Beatrice's intentions. That it was Elena and not Derek they were after.

And then Keen looked directly at Beatrice. His brows pinched and he glanced worriedly at Elena.

He knew. Was reading their thoughts.

Reese climbed from beneath the table, grabbed the heaviest object she could find—a crystal goblet—and threw it at Beatrice's head. "Elena!" she shouted.

The goblet hit the back of Beatrice's skull. A glancing blow that barely slowed the girl, but it was enough to catch Elena's attention. She turned at Reese's voice.

"Beatrice!" Reese screamed, but by that time, she'd drawn the attention of Beatrice and several of her soldiers.

Elena attempted to turn in Beatrice's direction, but it was too late. Beatrice was directly behind Elena, a dagger in her hand.

Call it a mother's sixth sense, or whatever, but Theda, who'd been standing close enough, broke Beatrice before the girl had a chance to touch her daughter. That was the only way to describe what had happened.

One moment, Beatrice was standing with a dagger aimed at Elena's back where her heart would be, and the next Beatrice was coughing up her own blood.

Theda knocked the dagger from the girl's hand and gently eased her to the ground at the same time Portia let out a high-pitched shriek like that of an injured animal.

Multiple soldiers swarmed Theda, swords slashing at her arms, her midriff, her throat. Reese lost sight of Theda as she fell to the ground.

"No!" Reese screamed.

After what seemed like minutes, though it was probably only seconds, the soldiers attacking Theda slowly stepped away, their faces expressionless.

And then Reese heard Elena's screams, her voice raw, as if she'd been doing it the entire time. Which she probably had been.

Elena stumbled for her mother and Reese ran toward both of them, heedless of the swords and magic flying by her head—but someone grabbed her around the waist, stopping her.

"We must go," Keen said.

This was all wrong. Theda wasn't supposed to be harmed. "We have to help them!"

His eyes flickered with some strong emotion she couldn't read. "It is done. If you remain, they will murder you the way they've murdered Theda."

CHAPTER

TWENTY

Reese kicked, but Keen was being a bastard and holding her tight. He carried her from the room of fighting Fae. "Let me go!"

"We must get you out of here," he said, his voice strained with what sounded like fear and a bit of desperation. "After the outburst that got her daughter killed, Portia will have your head."

"Theda is queen. Or she will be as soon as this is all over."

"Theda is dead."

That was what he'd said earlier. Reese squirmed some more to get out of his hold. "She can't die. She's Fae; Theda will heal."

He set her on the ground in one of the corridors inside the palace and grabbed her shoulders. "Theda is dead. Fae are almost immortal, unless the injury or abuse is severe."

Reese couldn't read Keen's feelings the way she could everyone else, but that didn't mean he was without any signs of emotion. She'd heard the fear and strain in his voice, but now she saw it in his eyes—and that undid her.

"No, no, it can't be..." She went numb.

She didn't object when he grabbed her hand and urged her to run with him down the hallway, up two flights of stairs, and to the end of another hallway. And then they were rushing through a door and past flashing light—spinning and whirling through what could only be a portal.

Reese fell on her butt, and Keen would have landed on top of her if it hadn't been for his quick reflexes that had him dodging her at the last moment.

They were outside. In the town she'd traveled to with her friends. The cobblestones, the gas lamps... "What are we doing here?"

"Hiding you." At some point during their mad dash through the palace, Keen must have grabbed a cloak, because he threw it at her. "Put it on and do not show your face."

The air outside was cool, and Reese shivered. She'd shaken for days when she first arrived in Tirnan. Keen had told her it was a part of her gaining her magic. This shaking wasn't from magic, though; it was from adrenaline, from worry over her friends, and from the fear that what Keen had said was true. Theda was dead.

What would happen to Elena? Who would rule New Kingdom? Leaving Portia in charge was unacceptable. The woman was using the Fae code of honor against them.

Keen helped her with the cloak, pulling it down low over her eyes and covering her hair. He grabbed her hand. "You are my pet, should anyone ask."

"Your *pet*?"

He stopped and turned to her, squeezing her hand. "Your position at the palace was precarious. Theda murdered Portia's daughter tonight. Portia will have you all slain, do you understand? I need you to do as I say. I cannot fight you and save you at the same time."

"I don't need a man to save me."

He sighed. "Here, in Tirnan, you do. But I must also help Elena. Will you cooperate so that I may help your friend?"

She hated that he was right. "Yes. Of course. Where are we going?"

"To Lucifer's Larder."

"The brothel? Is that why you want me to tell people I'm your pet?"

"Lucifer's Larder has lodging. You will be safe there. No one will touch you if they believe you are with me."

"But they saw me last time. They know I'm Halven."

"It was not a Halven who killed Beatrice. By the time the details are worked out, I'll have moved you somewhere safe."

"There's just one problem. Why are you helping me at all, when you should be helping Elena? Or, better yet, Portia? You know, that lady you've pledged to protect?"

"Elena has Derek. He will get her out of the kingdom."

"And Portia? You're supposed to be protecting *your queen*."

He sidestepped a muddy puddle and guided her around it. "Portia isn't in danger at the moment. The fighting has ceased."

"How do you know?"

He cut her a look. "I'm listening."

His ability.

"We're here." Keen opened the door to the tavern and ushered her across the room. It wasn't as busy tonight. In fact, only a couple of patrons occupied the space. Which made sense, because Reese could swear she'd recognized several people fighting for Theda from her previous visit to the tavern.

A proprietress with light brown hair pulled into a tight bun came out from behind the counter. She was wearing a sturdy gown similar to what Reese's seamstresses wore. Kind of conservative for a brothel owner.

"We need a room," Keen said.

"Certainly." The woman tapped a bell on the counter, and a young man scurried out. "Watch the customers," she told him.

The proprietress led them to a back hallway and up a narrow staircase. She pulled out a large key ring and unlocked a door at the end. The room was simple, with a large bed, a small chest of drawers, and what looked like a toilet curtained off. "Will you be needing food?"

Reese shook her head.

"Nothing for now," Keen said.

He gave the woman some sort of token or tip, Reese wasn't sure, but as soon as the woman pocketed it, she quickly left the room and closed the door behind her.

Reese pulled off the cloak and covered her face with her hands. Everything had gone so horribly wrong.

She looked up at Keen, who was staring at her, concern on his face. "We have to help Elena. You need to go after her —find them. Help them with Theda..."

He walked over and very slowly pulled her into his arms. She closed her eyes and sank into his warmth. They shouldn't be touching like this, but she didn't care about *should* or *should not* right now.

Even if she scoffed at the notion of needing it, she always felt so safe and protected with Keen.

Why him? The one she could never have.

He pulled back. "I will find the others and bring them here."

She nodded and watched him walk to the door.

"Lock it behind me." He pointed to an extra key on a side table.

And then he was gone.

AFTER ABOUT AN HOUR of moderate silence, in which Reese paced the room and picked off the last of the red nail polish she'd applied weeks ago in the Earth realm, she heard crying. A muffled, keening crying—and multiple footsteps coming up the stairs.

She pressed her ear to the door. Voices of men, women—and not just any women. She heard *Elena*.

Reese threw open the door to find her friend walking beside a soldier...who was carrying her mother's still body.

It was real. Theda was gone.

Elena looked up, tears streaming down her cheeks. The magnitude of sorrow pouring off her best friend had Reese's chest aching.

She crossed the hall and wrapped Elena in her arms, squeezing her tightly. There was nothing she could say. Nothing she could do to make it better.

"This way." Keen motioned to a room down from Reese's. He must have gotten a second set of keys from the proprietress.

He unlocked the door, and the handsome soldier holding Theda strode inside and gently sat on the bed with Theda in his arms. Reese had seen the man fighting alongside Theda earlier. And the way he was looking at her now—the mix of emotions... He loved her. Reese wasn't certain what kind of love, but she suspected the everlasting, unrequited kind.

The soldier brushed a lock of pale blond hair off Theda's forehead. She was covered in blood—from the stab wounds in her torso.

Reese swallowed and turned to Derek. "What happened?"

Elena sat beside the soldier and leaned down, touching her forehead to her mother's.

Camille had entered silently behind them and now faced the wall, her arms wrapped around her chest. Anguish, despair, confusion—all rolled off her the way they did everyone else in the room.

Derek stepped back, bringing Reese with him. "Theda saved Elena, but the girl she subdued... She didn't survive. And neither did—" He looked at Theda.

Reese pressed a fist to her mouth. "It's my fault. I read Beatrice's emotions before she acted." She turned to Elena. "I thought I was helping..."

Elena looked up, but she appeared to be in shock, her face expressionless.

Tears filled Reese's eyes. "I'm so sorry."

"I heard Beatrice's thoughts at the last minute as well," Keen said. "You and Theda saved Elena. Theda knew what she was risking by attacking Beatrice, and she chose to save her daughter."

Derek rubbed his forehead. "The attack on Theda happened so fast, as if a switch had been flipped. Once the guards turned on her, she had no hope. Too fast—it all happened too fast. I couldn't get to her in time."

Elena bent over her mother, her arms trembling. But she glanced up, some of the daze cleared from her eyes. "It wasn't your fault, Derek. Or yours, Reese." She stared down at her mother and cradled the queen's head. "There was always risk—to all of us."

Reese walked over and sat beside Elena.

Elena looked up at the soldier holding her mother. "What do we do now?"

He finally pulled his gaze from Theda and looked out at the room. "We give her a proper burial." His voice choked on the last word.

Elena leaned over her mother again and kissed her forehead, her hands shaking. After a moment, she stood and peered around the room, looking panicked. "Keen? I don't know what to do. With my mother gone..."

Though Elena's expression was panicked, her emotions were subdued. Depressed.

Keen was leaning his shoulder against the wall with his head bent. He looked at her now. "You know what to do, Elena."

She swallowed and rubbed her eyes. "I can't go through with it."

He eased away from the wall. "I am loyal to her majesty, but you have a claim to the throne, just as Derek took over Old Kingdom once his father passed."

Derek muttered an oath. "Are you saying Elena and I could be ruling opposing kingdoms?"

"Has it ever been any different?" Keen asked. "You were the Halven prince of Old Kingdom, and now you are king. Elena was a princess to the rightful queen, and now she is queen—should anything happen to Portia."

Derek paced the room. "I'll give up the kingdom—I'll stay and help Elena."

"Derek," Elena said, "that's crazy."

"She must win it back first," Keen pointed out. "And this

is where I leave. I cannot help you and be true to the present queen."

Reese had been listening to the back-and-forth, but at this she stood. "You're leaving?"

His lips were stiff, and he wouldn't look her in the eye. "An agreement has been arranged. As soon as I return to the palace, my engagement becomes official."

"You said you didn't want it. And after everything that's happened tonight... Why?"

"The queen insists." He gave her a hard, unfathomable look. "Without the betrothal, tensions between the kingdoms will rise. If I marry Radnor's Fae daughter, the queen feels she can negotiate with Old Kingdom."

"What do you mean, negotiate?" Derek said. "As far as I know, I'm still in charge. The only person she should be negotiating with is me."

"Reese's father is also of noble blood and next in line to the throne," Keen said. "He will challenge your rule unless I marry his daughter. After losing Beatrice, Portia is bereaved—grasping. She believes I can convince you to renounce your claim to the throne and bring peace between the kingdoms."

"You mean let you rule," Derek said. "And if I don't want to play nice with you or Portia?"

"I must kill you."

"No!" Elena yelled. "You're still my bodyguard."

"I am not," Keen said darkly. "I work for her majesty."

"If that's true, why are you helping us?" Elena asked bitterly.

He glanced at Reese, and so did everyone else. "It is time I leave."

"I don't understand." Elena looked between Keen and Reese. "Who is he supposed to marry?"

Reese's heart felt heavy as she waited for Keen to walk away. This time for good.

He would marry another. Wouldn't be there for her anymore. She'd told him she didn't need him to protect her, but she *wanted* him at her side. Wanted to argue with him, and kiss him, and...

Reese straightened her back, answering the question Keen wouldn't. "He's to marry my sister, Illa Radnor."

TWENTY-ONE

"I will walk Reese to her room," Keen said, surprising Reese. She figured he'd leave, and she would stay to console her friend.

But Elena turned and wrapped her arms around Derek, who was glaring at Keen.

Portia had destroyed so much, and now she was coming between the alliance Elena and Derek had formed with the Fae warrior.

Keen was marrying her sister to prevent all-out war between the two kingdoms. He was more likely to negotiate a truce with Derek than anyone, but if Derek didn't agree to the terms? He'd be forced to fight a friend.

Reese exited and walked with Keen down the hall. She entered her bedroom, and he did too. "You can't marry her. There's got to be another way."

He closed the door and let out a light sigh. "It would not be my first choice."

"So it's your second choice?"

He ran a hand down his face, then gave her a look. He

crossed the room and had her in his arms in seconds. His mouth came down on hers, hard and demanding.

She squeaked at the suddenness of it, and he gentled the kiss.

But she didn't want gentle. She wanted him. Reese pulled back and held his head between her hands. "Don't do it."

He set her down without letting her go. "There are whisperings that Portia has another form of the virus. One that Marlon created alongside the first that is just as powerful, but different enough that it would take time for Elena to cure. Whether or not the rumor is true, no one can be certain. But is it worth finding out?"

Reese took a step back and turned away. Enid had mentioned a secret weapon Portia held over their heads. This must be it.

She couldn't refute Keen's logic. But she also couldn't agree with him. Because to do so meant she'd lose him.

"I've searched for the second virus and I cannot find it. It would be easy enough to hide while Portia forces loyalty from people. And if the rumors are true... Our numbers were decimated with the last virus. Regardless of what I wish, Portia is in control at the moment. I cannot defy her."

All of his words made sense. Except to her heart.

She turned. "Can't you? Don't marry my sister."

He closed his eyes. When he opened them, pure determination lingered in their depths.

He stepped forward and swept her up and into his arms, kissing her as he carried her to the bed. He set her on the mattress and braced his body above hers. "I didn't want to like you." He kissed her throat. "I didn't want to desire you." He kissed her chin—square on the dimple in the middle. "But there was nothing that could keep me from you."

The things he was doing and saying had her head fuzzy, distracted, but not so distracted that she'd lost her mind. Reese shoved his chest. "Except the other woman you're marrying. I'm no cheater. And I'm not someone you can use."

He rolled to his side, his brow crinkled as he held her hip. "I don't wish to use you for my pleasure."

Very formal. And the way he worded his response had her wondering... "But you've used others?"

He raised his eyebrow. "Only with their full acquiescence."

Reese shook her head slowly. "Are all men alike? Even Fae?"

"Perhaps. But you are not like all women. Not to me."

He rolled back over her and kissed her lips gently. "This feeling that burns in my chest when I see you—that turns to murderous rage when you are in danger—it will not let me go. They search for you and your friends as we speak. They have not found the tavern, and the warriors who fought for Theda are hidden far away. But they will be discovered eventually. And so will you. I must do what I can, and agreeing to marry Illa buys us time."

Reese's lip quivered, dammit. "So you're saying it's as good as done. Why make the sacrifice? I can protect myself."

He brushed a lock of hair off her cheek. "You are strong, little one. So strong. You are my heart. I will do what I must to protect that frail thing inside my chest that can't handle the thought of anything happening to you."

A muffled cry erupted from her throat, and Reese grabbed his head and kissed him with everything she held inside. She didn't want him to leave her. Ever. And for the moment, he didn't seem inclined to.

She tugged at his shirt, pausing for a moment, remembering the times he'd told her not to touch him.

His large hand moved up and covered hers as he gazed into her eyes. Then he was kneeling back and tugging the thick knit shirt he wore over his head and tossing it behind him.

Reese sighed and ran her hands down his chest. "I love your skin."

His hand skimmed down her waist to her hips. "And I love your skin, your face when you are angry with me—or desirous."

"I am not—"

He pressed his finger to her lips. "Do not deny it."

She rolled her eyes. "Fine. I want you. Now will you please remove your pants?"

He raised his eyebrow again.

"What? You've teased me with your chest and I want to see the rest." She grinned. But her grin faltered. "Is that a problem? Because if you suggest in any way that I'm loose, I might injure you."

"I did not say that you are—*loose*—if I'm correct in interpreting your meaning."

"I beg to differ. You've said my clothing is too revealing on many an occasion."

He smiled. "That is because I do not wish for others to see what lies beneath."

"You were—jealous?" She smacked his shoulder. "You jerk. You made me think you thought I was some floozy."

"What is a floozy?"

"Someone free with her body."

A dark look crossed his eyes. "I do not wish to share

you. Ever." He dipped his head and nuzzled her neck. "Or hear of your past," he murmured near her ear.

She stretched her neck to give him better access. "But that was the problem with your jealous comments. The only guy I've ever been with scarred me something fierce with words like that."

Keen leaned back, his jaw tightening. He scanned her body. "Scarred you? Where? And who is this human who dared hurt you?"

"Not physically." She ran her hands down his chest again. "He was my first, but..."

He closed his eyes and let out a deep breath. "But?"

"He never called afterward. Which hurt, I'm not gonna lie, though what he told his friends and their friends was worse. He said I was easy. It didn't help that I dressed—Well—you've seen my style. I'm not ashamed of my body."

Keen looked off. "He used you, then made you feel that his actions were your fault."

She tilted her head, considering. "I internalized it more —but yeah, that about sums it up."

Keen's eyes grew intense. "That man will pay for what he did to you."

This conversation was going in the wrong direction. "He doesn't deserve more attention." She slipped her hands to Keen's stomach, where his body was taut with muscles that dipped and undulated in waves. She tugged at the waistband of his pants. "I want to move on, and I want it to be with you."

"Be that as it may, I will need a name."

Keen's attention was way too focused on her asshole ex. She just wanted him to understand why his words in the beginning had hit her hard.

She'd never wanted anything serious with anyone.

Avoided it, in fact. But with Keen, she wanted everything. Absolutely everything. And it scared her, but not enough to stop what they were doing. "You said you have to leave soon. Let's not waste time talking about the past."

"But—"

She cut off whatever he was about to say by pushing him back and sitting up. She unzipped her dress. The gown was elegant and modest, but not so much when it gaped around her breasts in the lacy bra Enid had given her to wear.

Keen watched her gown slip off her shoulders to her waist. He reached out and ran a hand along her arm to her wrist, where he twined their fingers and leaned over and kissed her. "Let me protect you. If it's the only thing I can give you, let me give you this."

His eyes were so intense, so fucking loving. What was he doing to her?

"What if I want more?" She ran her hand down the smooth skin of his back and squeezed his ass.

He growled. "You are breaking me."

"In a good way?"

He leaned down and took her mouth in answer.

She'd call that a *yes*.

Reese tucked her small fingers beneath his fitted black pants, and squeezed that firm backside. "These pants really need to go."

Keen kissed a trail down her neck to her breasts, where he seemed to get distracted, pushing them together inside of her bra with his large hands and kissing them one at a time. She wiggled her hips, and he moved farther down until he came to where her dress pooled at her waist. He slid the gown down her legs and over her satin heels, tossing it to the bottom of the bed.

His eyes never left her body. From her heeled shoes to her tiny bikini underwear to her push-up bra that gave the girls extra oomph—he took it all in. He settled his hand on her hip, where it shook above the thin panties. When his gaze locked with hers, his emerald eyes were so dark they looked black.

Her strong warrior's hands were shaking...because he wanted her. Wanted to protect her—wanted to touch her.

Reese reached up and squeezed his biceps and smiled in what she hoped was a clear invitation.

He scooted down, lifting one of her legs over his shoulder until his head was above the center of her.

"What are you—"

He kissed her *there*. Through her panties, which might as well have been made of organza, because she felt that kiss to her core.

Reese's head dipped back, an inarticulate sound escaping her mouth.

She looked back at him, and he grinned. "I thought you were conservative. What happened to *we only mate for offspring,* and all that business. You said it's not done for pleasure..." She trailed off as he linked his pinkies under the sides of her panties and pulled them down slowly, bending her knee to remove them.

"That is correct." He paused and licked her where he'd kissed her moments ago.

She panted. "Keep doing that, please. I promise I won't enjoy it."

He winked.

Forget that bullshit about Fae being sired from angels. Keen was the devil. Because he spread her legs wide and did it again—licked her over and over.

With his tongue on her pertinent parts, doing unholy,

pleasurable things to her, he slid his hand dexterously up her back and unhooked her bra.

She registered him pulling it down her arms, but mostly she was moaning. And rocking into his mouth.

"Your pants are still on," she said shakily—surprisingly lucidly, considering the havoc he was wreaking on her body. "I think they should be removed. But not for pleasure. For comfort... Don't you think you'll be more comfortable?"

She glanced down, and sweet Jesus, his mouth was still on her as he balanced on one hip and unsnapped his pants. And he wasn't wearing underwear.

Her eyes went wide.

There was large, and then there was Keen. "Maybe we should rethink this?"

He pulled off her heels and tossed them, his wet mouth sliding up her belly as he kicked off his boots and his pants. "You do not wish to be with me?"

His mouth encircled her nipple and he flicked it with his tongue, licking and sucking lightly.

She rubbed his shoulders, running her hands down his muscular arms. "I've never wanted anything more," she said before she could think.

That was the problem. She couldn't think when he was touching her. Or near her.

He lifted his head and studied her face. And then he slid up her body, the huge length of him resting between her thighs. But as distracting as that was, when he touched her temples with the tips of his fingers and looked into her eyes with what appeared to be something dangerously close to love, she could think of nothing but how deep her emotion went for this man.

He kissed her with lips and tongue, tasting and mimicking the rocking of their bodies pressed together. And then that part of him she thought would never fit was easing inside in slow measures, entering her and seducing as much as his mouth.

Reese felt stretched, and at the same time her body shook with arousal. In this moment, she was his and he was hers, and nothing else mattered. Not his species, or whether or not they were right for each other. Because in this moment no one in the world was righter for Reese than Keen, kissing her with such intensity and tenderness that he stole her breath.

His nose ran along her hairline, his soft lips pressing against her temple.

She kissed his jaw and felt his heart quicken. He was fully seated inside her now—by what she could only presume was some kind of Fae magic. Or her body being extremely turned on.

He shifted, entering at a slightly different angle, and she moaned.

"I swear I'm not feeling pleasure," she said, rocking her head back, because whatever he was doing was revving up something wild inside of her. "No need...to worry...about defying Fae rules for coupling."

She bit her lip. Something was building, and she wasn't sure she could keep it in much longer.

His breathing was ragged. "It is not only pleasure between us...it is more."

He kissed her deeply, and she lost her hold on that elusive building, exploding, sinking, then soaring above this room and the world. There was a good chance she cried out. She couldn't be sure, because a moment later her lover was moaning in her ear, setting off another rush of heat through her.

Keen's movements slowed and he dropped his head

above her shoulder, seemingly catching his breath. He lay above her, most of his weight on one arm, but that still left a lot of hot naked guy covering her. She smiled and closed her eyes. She might even have drifted off.

What felt like minutes later, Keen moved again. But this time he was pulling away.

Reese's eyes popped open. "Where are you going?"

Please don't leave me.

She told herself to simmer down. Some men could be depended on. Keen had proven how much he cared by being there for her, even when she didn't know she needed him. This wasn't the same as her first time. Keen wouldn't abandon her. He'd said men mated with one woman...or wait, women only mated with one man?

Shit.

She would not beg him to stay.

No matter how many times her father hadn't shown for graduations and birthday parties. Not even after that high school jerk started the rumors. She never begged—never let them see how much they'd let her down.

Reese pulled the covers over herself as Keen stood and slid on his pants. He didn't look at her until he was fully clothed. When he did, she saw regret in his eyes.

A stab of pain lanced through her chest. She read it all in that look.

He *was* leaving. Nothing had changed.

She turned away and reached for her dress. "Don't say anything. No excuses. I can't...I can't take it. Just leave."

Out of the corner of her eye, she sensed him standing there as she put on her bra and pulled the dress over her head. She couldn't help it. In a moment of weakness, she glanced over.

He was staring off, not looking at her, his arms stiff at

his sides. She couldn't tell what he was feeling. Could read any number of emotions from everyone else, but not Keen.

He stalked to the door and gripped the handle for a split second before he opened it and slammed it shut behind him.

Only then did Reese collapse and roll to her side. There were no tears. Not this time.

But inside, her heart was bleeding.

CHAPTER
TWENTY-TWO

What had he done?

Keen had mated with the girl. With Reese. A Halven. And nothing and no one could have stopped him. He tightened his hand into a fist and pressed the heel of it against his temple.

He'd defied his ruler by helping Reese tonight. Not outright, but through subterfuge so that he wasn't disobeying the queen. He'd fought off the invaders during the battle. Then he'd assured himself the queen was safe and left the palace. With *her*, the girl who filled his every thought.

Storming back inside the palace, Keen found his soldiers searching every nook and cranny for Elena and her supporters—exactly as Keen had commanded before he'd left. He hadn't mentioned that he knew where the others hid. But he hadn't been asked for that information.

Again, he'd defied his ruler by any means necessary to protect Reese. And he regretted none of it. He would do it all again. For her. Always for her.

When he'd left her room, the pressure in his chest to

return to her had weighed so heavily that he feared he might stumble down the stairs like a human. But he had to leave—had to deflect Portia's suspicions and follow through on his commitment to Illa and Hakon Radnor.

Keen made it to the queen's quarters, where no fewer than two dozen guards protected her surroundings. More would be inside.

He let himself in, and saw the queen braced against a chair across the room. Beside her, her daughter's body lay on a bed covered in dark purple velvet, hands crossed over her chest in the death pose.

Beatrice had been Keen's age, and young by Fae standards. She was also Portia's only child. Regardless of what Portia told the gathering tonight, Beatrice had been labeled a traitor weeks ago during the race for a cure to the first disease Marlon had created. Little did anyone know that her mother was the mastermind behind everything.

Keen suspected Portia had kept her daughter out of the public eye until she felt she had firm control over New Kingdom. That Beatrice had shown her face this evening spoke for Portia's confidence in her newfound power.

Keen moved closer, standing just beside Portia, who didn't take her eyes off her daughter. It was a shame Beatrice had lost her life for her mother's ambitions. Theda might have driven the deathblow, but Portia had given her no other choice.

Theda had killed Beatrice to save her own daughter—a Halven.

And Keen could find no fault in it.

He'd changed.

He no longer saw Halven as inferior, though he wasn't sure when the change had occurred. Probably around the time he'd discovered Reese in the dungeon close to death.

He'd wanted to slaughter every one of his kind for the atrocity.

Portia's head tilted up and she looked over, as though just now realizing he was there. "Where have you been?" Her speech slurred with emotion.

"Searching for the Halven."

"And did you find and destroy them?"

She'd ordered them found, not destroyed, thankfully, or he didn't know what he would have done. "They escaped via portal." *Not an untruth.* "According to Derek's thoughts, they are on their way to Old Kingdom."

Reese would be safe in the other land. She wouldn't be with him, but she would be safe.

For now, that was all that mattered.

Reese felt a nudge on her shoulder.

"Wake up. We need to hurry." Elena's voice was loud, and seemingly right next to Reese's ear.

She sat up, still wearing her dress from the night before, and rubbed her eyes. Elena was crouched beside the bed. And then Reese remembered where she was—smelled the clean cedar scent of Keen on her clothes—and her stomach cramped.

She wrapped her arms around her waist and leaned forward, trying to forget what had happened, and that Keen had left her when she thought this time he would stay. "Is everything okay?"

Elena stood. "Amund came by and said soldiers were on their way. They'll be here any minute. We have to leave."

Reese slipped on her shoes, and they hurried into the

bedroom where Derek and Camille stood. The guard and Theda's body were gone.

"Where's your..." How did you ask your best friend where her mother's body was?

Elena looked down. "Samuel, my mother's guard, is watching over her until we can bury her in the royal mausoleum."

Reese squeezed her hand.

"I just found my mom, and..." Her voice broke off on a light sob.

"I'm sorry—so sorry," Reese said, and hugged her.

After a second, Elena pulled back and squared her shoulders. "I can't think about what I've lost. We have to get out of here, or we'll lose much more."

Reese had to ask. "Did you hear from Keen?"

"No."

"But he can hear your thoughts, can't he? Not mine, for the same reason I can't sense his emotions, but he'd be able to hear yours."

"After you told us about his agreement with Portia, my mom taught us how to block him." Elena pressed her lips together, as though the mention of her mom was unbearable. "Instead, we've communicated what was safe."

"We're returning to Old Kingdom," Derek said. "We'll be secure in my castle until we come up with a new plan to get Elena's kingdom back. I let down my mental shield for a split second to shout the message to Keen. Felt I owed him that much after what he did for us here. And because..." He glanced at Reese, then shifted his feet and looked down, inspecting one of his knives. "He would have wanted to know we were safe."

Elena's expression firmed. "We don't need to come up

with a plan. I don't want my mother's kingdom. Not if she's not here."

Reese sensed the crushing sadness that filled her friend.

"You don't mean that," Derek said gently. "It's your birthright."

"Is it?" Elena stared blankly. "I think if you ask anyone inside this kingdom, they'd disagree."

Derek moved closer and wrapped his arm around Elena. "It's the last thing you have of your Fae family. It belongs to you."

She let out a tense breath and shut her eyes. "You might be right, but it isn't worth risking more lives."

He pulled her into his arms. "No one said anything about losing lives. We'll come up with a plan and it will be a good one."

"We must go." Camille ran her hands along the wooden wall of the tavern bedroom. "Guards have entered the building, and their energy levels are spiked. They seek to fight."

TWENTY-THREE

The Newlander soldiers were seconds behind Reese as she brought up the rear in the leap through the portal. Fortunately, along with being a bumpy ride, Camille's portals were also short-lived, and closed before the soldiers got there.

Elena caught the look on Reese's face as they entered the Old Kingdom castle and great hall. "Trust me. It was worse before Derek added new plumbing."

Old Kingdom, Reese's paternal birthplace, was...different. Hollow, all sharp angles, and dark. It looked like your typical stone castle from outside, with a moat at the entrance. They didn't use electricity, and shutters kept out the cold instead of windows, which explained the chill in the air. The place made New Kingdom, with its bedroom murals of bloody battles and statues of angels having sex with humans, appear downright elegant and modern.

Derek walked off to speak with some of his soldiers, and Camille approached the center of the great hall...where a massive tree with a trunk as thick as a semitruck grew through the middle. She stepped over the rope barrier and placed her hand on the trunk, resting her forehead against the tree.

"Umm?" Reese looked nervously at Elena. "She okay?"

"That's *the tree.*"

Reese nodded. "A tree, yes. A big one, too. Hey...did the leaves just do something? *Elena.*" She jabbed her friend in the arm with her elbow. "The leaves!"

"That's what I'm talking about. You're looking at the Ancient Allon. And yes, the leaves move. They hop from branch to branch."

Reese cut her friend a look. "Right, because *that's* not weird."

"I realize a lot has gone on, so I get it if your head's not all there, but keep up, will you? *That's the Ancient Allon.* They say the angels planted the tree a million years ago. Drinking tea from the leaves was how I increased my powers. Granted, it made me a little sick, but it was worth it."

"And that's how you got your height?" The tree's leaves were moving again. *So bizarre.* "And how Derek bulked up and got huge?"

"All of it. Allon trees grow everywhere in Tirnan, but the Ancient Allon has magical properties more powerful than any other magic in the realm, from what I understand."

"Another good reason to return to Old Kingdom," Camille said, and Reese jumped. She was jumpy. Sad. Scattered, like Elena suggested. But Camille could also be stealthy when she wanted to. Reese hadn't seen or heard her approach.

"Not only Halven abilities," Camille said, "but Fae abilities may also increase after drinking tea from the leaves of the Ancient Allon. I've never heard of Halven gaining as much power as you and Derek did, Elena, but then, they've never tested the effects on Halven with noble blood."

Elena's brows pinched. "Since when have they allowed Halven in Tirnan? I was told a Halven in this realm was as good as dead."

"I'm afraid, before you and Derek, the survival of Halven in our land was, indeed, low. And not simply because they couldn't withstand the nectar of the Ancient Allon."

"Because Halven were scorned and murdered?" Elena's tone was bitter.

Reese sensed Camille's sadness and shame at the words. "Elena, Camille is our friend. Without her, we wouldn't be here."

Elena closed her eyes and shook her head. "I'm sorry, Camille. I'm—not myself."

"Understandable," Camille said. "Theda and I suspected there could be Halven in our land after Marlon's alliance with Portia, but as far as I can tell—and I've cast my ability wide to read power levels in both kingdoms—the only true Halven in Tirnan are you, Derek, Reese, and Marlon when he was alive. After drinking the Ancient Allon tea, your and Derek's energy levels became closer to Fae. That leaves—" Her gaze landed on Reese.

"Me," Reese said.

Elena frowned. "I thought Marlon made some deal with Portia to allow Halven in the realm. Wasn't that why he agreed to work with her?"

"That is what we believed, but...it seems Portia did not hold up her end of the bargain."

"So, let me get this straight," Reese said, her anger rising to match Elena's. "The queen used Marlon to murder Fae—including Elena's royal family—in order to gain the crown, and planned to kill my half-brother all along?"

"Very likely. Who can say for certain?" Camille peered across the great hall. "And it seems she wishes to control Old Kingdom as well. That is what powermongers do, is it not? Seize control by any means? Portia is no fool. She cannot manage both kingdoms without true supporters. She is holding on to New Kingdom through forced fealty and a few misguided brethren. As for Old Kingdom, she plans to use Keen Albrecht to gain power. I'm told he swore fealty to her in order to keep Reese safe—"

"*He what?*" Reese stared at Camille. "You're wrong. He swore fealty to save his own skin."

"Yes...and yours. He is one of the best warriors in the land. He could have escaped. But not along with you. He did what he needed to keep you both safe."

Reese's breathing grew constricted and slow. He'd made that sacrifice for the same reason he had so many others. Because he cared about her. More than he let on. Every political move he'd made had tied him to Portia— and had given Reese and the others freedom. "*We all must make sacrifices,*" he'd once said.

"Keen is an Emain Fae with powerful Oldlander blood," Camille continued. "He is an ideal candidate to win Oldlander support."

"But he'd be working for Portia, potentially betraying the people here for Portia's gain," Elena pointed out.

"Yes. And if the Oldlanders discovered his perfidy, it would not go over well."

Reese had pushed the memory of last night to the back of her mind—had pushed her feelings for Keen away. At least for the past hour. But now her stomach dipped and her mouth tasted sour.

She'd lost him, resigned herself to it, but hope had bloomed when he'd come to her last night. Except that wasn't real, or at least it wasn't lasting, because he had to marry whether he wanted to or not. And if his sacrifices got him killed?

Not okay. She couldn't live with that.

Damn him. They weren't meant to be together, but that didn't mean she didn't love him.

No matter how hard she tried to place Keen next to the men in her life who'd let her down, he was different. He'd been there for her in ways no one else had. And now he was putting his life at risk for everyone.

She didn't regret last night. She simply ached for what she'd lost—or nearly had.

"Keen will marry Illa, Hakon's daughter." Reese attempted to keep her voice steady. "Will that protect him?"

"Possibly," Camille said. "The engagement is official. Hakon reported as much through a magical messenger. Keen returned to New Kingdom palace hours ago and announced his betrothal to Illa in front of queen and court."

Right after he made love to me.

Reese's legs weakened. She locked her knees and stared straight ahead, but her chest ached like a sledgehammer had hit it. "So it's...to take place." Her voice shook, and she had to clear her throat to get the sentence out.

Camille nodded, and Elena moved closer to Reese, their shoulders nearly touching. Reese wouldn't look at her, though. If she did, she'd fall to pieces in front of the entire castle guard, who all seemed to be congregated in the great hall.

"Does Portia think Derek will just hand over the kingdom?" Elena visibly bristled beside Reese. "What kind of fool is she? These are Derek's people, and he's determined to protect them from another ruthless ruler. Not that Keen would be ruthless, but he wouldn't be the one in charge. Portia would be."

Camille's bland expression didn't hide the distress Reese sensed from the Fae. "Derek has served the kingdom well, but he is at a disadvantage. He gained the respect of his men, but there are many in this land who do not approve of him—who wish him harm for daring to take leadership of our kind. Old Kingdom respects name and blood, both of which Hakon Radnor possesses in full measure."

"And so does Keen," Reese murmured, remembering how Keen had told her Derek's father murdered his family.

"Yes," Camille agreed. "The king had Keen's family eliminated when Keen was an infant, removing them from the succession. He forced an oath from Keen when Keen grew of age, that he would forfeit his birthright. But Osulf Niall hadn't planned on Keen outliving him, making that oath null and void. Keen is eligible again—if he manages to take control from Derek."

The situation was going from bad to worse. With Theda's death, they'd lost their best chance at regaining New Kingdom for Elena, and now it seemed Derek would have his birthright taken from him as well—by Keen.

They weren't safe in New Kingdom, and if Derek lost Old Kingdom, they wouldn't be safe here either. Reese would have to return to the Earth realm, which she'd always intended to do, but for some reason the notion felt off now. She wasn't the same girl she'd been when she arrived—not physically, and not emotionally. She was tied to this place and people. And she wasn't sure how she'd ever go back to her old life.

Reese had no reason to stay in Tirnan, but she would help her friends as long as they needed her, and then she'd leave. *And remain a commitmentphobe for the rest of my life,* she thought bitterly. Only now, she didn't want to be unattached. She wanted what she couldn't have—to be with the stubborn Fae who'd risked everything for her.

Derek crossed the room and joined them. "The soldiers are preparing for a full-out battle with New Kingdom."

"Isn't that what they did the last time?" Reese shook her head. "How can this one end any better?"

A chill seemed to rack Elena's body. "She's right, Derek. It wasn't enough. We had soldiers from Old Kingdom, from Emain, and the New Kingdom warriors my mother recruited. She thought..." Elena's face went blank. Reese squeezed her hand, and Elena blinked. She swallowed and cleared her throat. "My mother thought it would be more than enough. She knew Portia hated her, that Portia would make her the target. She didn't count on Beatrice attacking me. Portia is unpredictable, and now she's grieving and desperate. We can't go back. Not unless we have a better advantage."

"But we do..." Reese looked at the tree. "If we make a few changes." She turned to Camille. "You said Fae can increase their powers with the Ancient Allon just like Halven, correct?"

"Yes." Camille's eyes shimmered, as though she was thinking the same thing.

"Have all Old Kingdom soldiers drunk the tea of the Ancient Allon?" Reese asked Derek.

He scratched his head. "Probably, but I'll make sure."

Camille scanned the men in the room. "The Ancient Allon will not make Fae much stronger than they already are, but it will enhance our abilities slightly. Amund and his men have never drunk from the tree. In our history, Newlanders and Sunlanders have rarely been allowed here. And certainly not to gain powers. Until now. Amund and his soldiers, and anyone else on our side, will drink from the tea of the leaves, myself included."

"And I'll drink from it too," Reese said.

Elena's eyes widened. "No, Reese. It won't hurt a full Fae like Camille, but it could kill Halven. It *has* killed Halven. And humans don't stand a chance; they never survive. It's not worth the risk." She shook her head fervently, tears blooming in her eyes. "I can't lose you too."

Reese reached for her friend, holding her tight. She wasn't afraid of drinking the tea. Her biological father ensured she came from a royal Fae bloodline, but she understood Elena's fear. She'd just lost her mother. Even a slight risk of losing someone else close to her was too much right now.

Reese had nothing to lose and everything to gain by building her powers. If she could help her friends with a stronger ability and tip the balance in their favor, it would be worth a little illness. Even if she couldn't tell Elena her plans right away. The alternative was to return home, knowing she could have done more and hadn't.

Knowing the kingdoms would be ruled by a madwoman.

Knowing the one person she loved might lose his life because he'd sacrificed for her and everyone else.

TWENTY-FOUR

Reese waited in the room she'd been given. It was a simple space with stone walls, similar to the dungeon back at New Kingdom, but warmer and with a large, comfortable bed.

And this was one of the finer rooms in the castle.

A fireplace in the corner provided heat, and wooden chairs and a small table offered creature comforts. She'd already bathed—in a wooden tub. That was a new one. But whatever, she'd smelled Keen's scent on her skin and it had been making her crazy. She'd washed it off with the soap the maid gave her. But the moment it was gone, she regretted it. What if she never saw him again—never smelled that cedar scent mixed with man, and a hint of metal from the weapons he never seemed to be without?

Reese paced her room, and darned if this didn't feel like her time trapped in New Kingdom. She'd had a moment of doubt, when she considered doing as Elena asked and not taking the tea. The last thing she wanted was to make things harder for her friend. But this was bigger than the both of them. She couldn't sit by and wait for things to happen. There were no guards outside her door, no one in this castle waiting to attack her the way they were in New Kingdom.

A knock sounded, and her maid entered the room. "Your food, miss." The girl crossed quickly and set a tray of cheese, bread, and strange Tirnan fruit on the table.

Before they'd parted, Elena and Derek and the others had decided a quick meal and rest in their rooms was best for tonight. The Fae who'd never drunk the Ancient Allon tea were doing so this evening. They'd need rest, or so Elena and Camille had said. Even Fae needed to sleep and heal from the effects of the Ancient Allon.

The maid turned and clasped her hands in front of her, a mild but friendly smile on her face. "Is there anything else I can get you?"

"Yes. Tea from the Ancient Allon. I'll be drinking it this evening as well."

The girl's gaze dipped down Reese's body. "But miss, it is poison for one such as you."

Elena had said the tea was deadly to humans and could cause death to Halven. But the belief was that Halven with royal blood survived. Derek and Elena had, and they'd benefited from the magical properties of the leaves.

Reese had been a prisoner and a victim in this land, and she was done. She wanted to be strong. She wanted to do more.

"I am of noble Fae descent. I can drink the tea without harm, but"—Reese stepped forward—"do not tell anyone, do you understand?"

"Miss, I cannot help you. I must do as my king commands."

"And what were his commands?"

The girl studied her warily. "To provide the tea of the Ancient Allon to any warrior who requests it."

"And I am a warrior."

～

REESE WAS NO DUMMY. She made sure her maid agreed not to tell anyone that she was taking the tea, by binding the girl with a promise. And now Reese lay on her bed, her stomach cramping, her head throbbing, wondering what the hell she'd done to herself.

She moaned and curled into the fetal position. It would be all right. Everything would be okay. She'd survive this. She had to. Because she wasn't leaving this land until she helped her friends ensure their people would be safe from Portia. Reese couldn't bring Elena's mother back, but she could help her regain the right to protect her people. And she could make sure Keen wasn't a slave to Portia, even if he was married to another.

A stab of pain shot through her midsection and she cried out. Her eyes teared up from the throbbing of her head. She leaned over the bed and expelled the contents of her stomach, too weak to get up and find a bowl.

She breathed shallowly, her hands tightening and curling after the loss of fluids. The room winked...and then faded entirely.

～

REESE HEARD SHOUTS, a female voice—anxious, distraught...

Moments, or hours, later, she woke without opening her eyes to a warm pressure on her arm. And sensed terror from the person touching her.

"Sister, what have you done?"

Illa.

"What is the meaning of this? What has happened to my daughter?"

Radnor? And he, too, was frightened. She'd been sick after drinking the tea. So sick. She still felt like death.

Reese managed to blink. Radnor was staring down at her, a look of terror in his gaze.

He turned to a soldier behind him. "Get the castle alchemists."

A few moments later, Reese woke to the prodding of a man in monk's robes—except this man had golden hair, rosy lips, and he was beautiful, like all Fae. He placed a hand on Reese's forehead.

"Well?" Radnor said.

"I cannot predict whether she will live or die. Only the leaves determine such things."

"You imbecile!" Radnor shouted. "Heal her."

The alchemist lifted Reese from behind with his strong arm, and she moaned, the movement making her head swim and throb simultaneously. He brought a bowl to her lips. "It isn't much, but the broth of the sibel flower strengthens the blood."

She tried to sip it, got some down, and then coughed nearly all of it back up.

Radnor gripped the bedpost, his eyes wide, an avalanche of emotion pouring off him. And then Ulric entered.

Along with Keen.

Despite her poor physical state, Reese's heart managed a weak lurch.

And then she gagged and expelled the precious drops of liquid the alchemist had managed to get down her throat.

The alchemist handed her a cloth and helped her lie back. When she caught her breath and opened her eyes again, Keen was standing over her, looking angrier than she'd ever seen him. And then she passed out.

"WHY WOULD you give her the tea?" Keen shouted. Reese would know his voice anywhere.

Her stomach rioted, her head pounding so hard that when she opened her eyes she couldn't see anything for several seconds. Her vision cleared—to Keen squaring off with Derek.

"She is small! What were you thinking?"

"I didn't give it to her," Derek bit out. "She suckered one of the maids into getting the tea. And Reese may be small, but she's strong."

Not small—five foot six, Reese would have said if she could.

Keen punched Derek in the face.

"Keen!" That was Elena.

Derek touched his bloody lip, then tackled Keen.

"Damn you both," Elena shouted. "We don't need this right now!"

Off to the side, Hakon pressed his fingers to his forehead and shook his head.

"Stop," Reese said, so weakly she feared no one would hear her. "Please."

Keen's head whipped around. He rolled to his feet and strode over, his nostrils flaring. "Reese." The word came out like a prayer, so soft and full of longing.

She closed her eyes, taking in the sound. Was there anything in the world more comforting?

"Don't fight," she whispered.

"No, little one. Not until you are better and I can punish you thoroughly."

Her eyes were closed, but her mouth curled up at the edges. It was a hollow threat, and they both knew it.

Someone grabbed her hand, but it wasn't Keen. Reese opened her eyes and found Illa at her side. Elena stood in the background, biting her thumb, worry rolling off her as Derek wrapped his arm around her shoulders, his bloody lip nearly healed.

Illa brought a bowl forward. "Sister, please drink more of the alchemist's broth."

Reese tried to sit up, and this time it was Ulric who helped her. She sipped the broth and twisted her mouth away from the bowl when she couldn't get any more down.

Ulric set the broth on the nightstand and went to stand behind Illa. He placed a hand on her shoulder, and Illa absently reached for it.

Reese's brow furrowed. "Shouldn't you be holding Keen's hand?"

Shame and confusion tossed around inside Illa. Her hand fell to her lap.

Ulric shot a glare at Keen, irritation and jealousy cutting through him.

Being ill made the emotion storm around her more nauseating. She was too weak to block it.

Keen didn't seem aware of the tension coming off Illa and Ulric, or he just didn't care. He was staring at Reese with utter mortification, his chest heaving.

"Everyone out." His tone was deadly calm.

"But—" Elena started.

"Now!"

They left the room one by one, except for Hakon, who lingered near the door. "You will let me know if…"

"She will be fine," Keen said over his shoulder. "But if… I will let you know."

Hakon closed the door behind him.

Keen moved closer and gently set his large arm over her chest, cradling the side of her face. "You cannot die, little one."

Stubborn man. As if she had a say in these things.

She turned into his warm palm and swallowed the ball that had knotted in the back of her throat. "I don't plan to. Strong…"

"Yes." His voice was strangled. "You are strong. Remember, it is I who am weak when it comes to you. You must not leave me."

"You…left me."

"Never. I'll never leave you."

She shook her head. "They won't let us be together." Her forehead scrunched. "Not sure who they are…maybe the universe. We're not meant to be together."

He pressed his hand to her chest above her heart. "We are together in here," he said softly, and touched his forehead to hers.

Warmth spread through Reese's body, and the pounding in her head eased slightly. She breathed deeply and fell asleep.

CHAPTER
TWENTY-FIVE

Reese woke with a head that no longer pounded like the devil. And found herself being spooned by Keen.

For just a second, she lay there with his arms wrapped around her and pretended they were of the same world, and that this was how she would wake every morning. In his arms.

But they weren't of the same world. And this wasn't how things could be. Keen would marry her sister, and Reese would return home. To school. To her messed-up parents. To a life that meant little after everything she'd experienced in Tirnan.

She wanted more. More with Keen. More with Halven and Fae and her powers, and learning what her ancestors meant to this world and the Earth realm. They had to exist for a reason. *She* had to be here for a reason. She'd survived the Ancient Allon leaves. That must mean something.

Reese reluctantly rolled to her back, and Keen stirred.

He rubbed a hand down his face and sat upright. He took in her expression. "How do you feel?"

"Better."

He let out a deep breath, his eyes soft for only a moment before they hardened. "Good… Now I must kill you for what you put me through. What were you thinking, drinking the tea?"

She rolled her eyes. This man did not scare her. Not one bit. She sat up and pressed her face to his neck, breathing in his scent, because he was still in bed with her and she could lap it up all she wanted right now. "I was thinking I'd like to kick some ass in the realm of my ancestors, and that I needed a little extra power to do it."

"That is a terrible reason to put your life at risk."

Tough words, but his heartbeat kicked up a notch as her lips pressed against his throat. "Sure."

"I am serious, Reese."

She leaned back. "In hindsight, it was stupid. I didn't realize it would affect me that badly. I won't do anything like that again." She narrowed her eyes on him. "But don't think you can tell me what to do, Keen Albrecht. You have no say. You're marrying my sister, for goodness' sake. From now on, I'll do what I have to in order to survive."

He sighed and stared at the ceiling. "What am I going to do with you?"

"Those are my thoughts. What am I going to do with *you?* You drive me nuts when you're near, with all your bossiness, but…I don't like it when you're gone." She scrunched her nose, remembering how distraught she'd been when he left her at the tavern. When she worried she'd never see him again.

His emerald eyes were warm. "The feeling is mutual."

Illa entered the room without knocking, and Keen rose swiftly from the bed. She glanced at him curiously, then at Reese. "You look much better. How do you feel?"

"Like I'll live. I'm sorry I worried you. That was…more painful than I thought it would be. And a bit frightening."

Illa came closer and placed her soft hand over Reese's. "You were in and out of consciousness for three days."

What the…? "Three days?"

"Exactly," Keen said, looking over his shoulder at her, mouth firm.

"Well, crap, no wonder I feel like I've been run over. Were Elena and Derek this sick?"

Just then, Elena entered, followed by Derek, Hakon, and Camille.

"No," Illa answered. "From what I understand, both Derek and Elena recovered after a few hours."

Reese slouched. Hell, she really could have died. She hadn't intended to put her life at risk. She truly thought she'd have the same experience Elena had. "I'm sorry I worried you. I really am okay now."

Reese swung her legs over the edge of the bed and stretched out her toes. A wide gap separated the hem of her pants from her ankles.

She stretched her arms out in front of her—and the sleeves of her shirt were short as well, and tighter all around.

She jumped up and stumbled into the nightstand, her head spinning. Everyone in the room lurched for her, but she held up a hand. "I'm fine. But check it out!" She stood tall. "You guys can't make any more short comments."

Elena raised her eyebrows.

Keen's mouth pulled back on one side.

Hakon looked to Illa. "What is she talking about?"

"I believe she is demonstrating how…*tall* she has grown after drinking the Allon tea."

Reese peered at the faces in the room. "Why do you look unimpressed?"

Elena came over and stood in front of her. She still had a few inches on Reese. "You grew about"—she scanned her—"three inches. Not worth risking your life over."

"I wasn't trying to grow taller," Reese grumbled. "I was trying to increase my powers, but how come none of you are impressed with my awesome new height?"

"Because you're still the shortest one in the room?"

"I've got to be five foot nine now."

"Yes," Keen said blandly from behind Elena. "Short."

Reese shook her head. "Fine. I'll always be short compared to the rest of you. What about the other stuff? My powers. How soon will I know what cool new things I can do?"

Elena glanced at Derek. "Immediately. There wasn't a latency period for Derek or me. We might not have known exactly what we were capable of, but our powers were there as soon as we recovered."

REESE SPENT hours with Elena inside the castle laboratory trying to figure out her enhanced abilities. So far, all she got was a stronger, almost visceral sense of what someone was feeling. And she could easily block it, which *was* a bonus. Emotion overload was real.

"Maybe that's all you've got?" Elena offered unhelpfully.

"All that pain I went through, only for more of the same? How am I supposed to help you in the fight?"

"By staying alive?" Elena lit a candle on the lab table with her finger.

Reese gestured at her. "See, now look at that. I want powers like yours. I want to be able to kick Fae ass."

"You could totally whoop my butt in hand-to-hand combat."

Reese frowned. "That's not saying much. Anyone could kick your butt in a physical battle—if your powers were hindered."

"I want to be offended, but I can't because it's true." Elena grinned. "In any case, don't worry about fighting Newlanders. Derek and Camille are working up a plan." She returned several glass bottles to their shelf. They were using them to see if Reese could move things with her mind. Turned out she didn't get that cool new skill either.

Elena's eyes turned sad. "I am leery of this battle after the last one. But if we could save my mother's people from Portia after what's happened, it would be worth it."

Reese asked her next question knowing she might not like the answer. Or that she'd like it too much and want to see him. "What about Keen and Illa? Are they still here?"

"They're here, along with your father and Ulric. It seems Ulric left without permission and can't return to New Kingdom without harsh punishment."

"How did he get out in the first place? Doesn't that go against his oath to Portia?"

"That's the thing. Ulric never made an oath. Not all of her soldiers were ordered to, only the highest-ranking men and anyone Portia was concerned about. By the time Ulric showed his true allegiance—you know, when he stormed out of the battle with Illa in his arms?—it was too late."

"Never knew Ulric had that kind of ability. He practically disintegrated the door."

"Well," Elena said, "his powers are even stronger now

that he's drunk from the Ancient Allon. He's been working with Derek's men while you were recovering."

"I'm happy Derek agreed to take him in. No saying what Portia would do to him, and he's grown on me."

Elena nodded. "All kinds of changes going on around here. With Ulric, this is the first time in Old Kingdom history they've had a Newlander on the guard. And if my aunt convinces the Sunlanders to help us? History in the making right there."

"Sunlanders? You mean the third kingdom no one seems to care about?"

Elena pursed her lips. "It's not so much that they don't care about Sunlanders...more of an unspoken agreement to leave them alone. Sunlanders don't want royal court drama. They're passive and non-combative."

"So why doesn't everyone live in Sunland? It sounds fantastic."

"Silly Reese." Elena smirked. "Sunland has no power or wealth."

"But they're Fae. They have abilities, right?"

"Sure they do, but Oldlanders have honed their powers and weapons over thousands of years, thanks to crafty alchemists and the Ancient Allon growing inside their castle. Newlanders have strong angel bloodlines and wealth from trade with humans, making New Kingdom and Old Kingdom closely matched in power. I'm sure once they duke out who's on top, the winner will clobber Sunland and take it over."

"Tirnan sucks."

"Truth."

"So what do we do now? I vote we leave this backward place and take our friends with us. No one will know they're Fae if they pretend to be ex-basketball players."

Elena smiled sadly and tossed what looked to be an old-school brass magnifying glass on the counter. Come to think of it, everything in this laboratory looked ancient. They kept things original around here. "Derek was right. I can't in good conscience leave my people in Portia's hands."

"*Your people?* So you acknowledge them now?"

She let out a deep sigh. "I do. You've seen what Portia's capable of. I don't trust her not to continue her killing spree for power. And what if she decides to take over the Earth realm? Rules don't apply in her mind, and every time I imagine asking Camille to take me home, I get this gut-wrenching pain in my stomach."

"Like the one you have now?"

"Like that one." Elena cocked her head. "Don't underestimate your heightened ability. It's got *freak factor* written all over it."

Reese grinned proudly. "Aw, thank you." And then her face fell as she considered their predicament. "If it makes you feel any better, I don't like the idea of leaving Keen behind as Portia's bitch." She bit her lip, tasting blood.

Abandoning Keen—strong and stubborn though he might be—made Reese sick, and it was one of the reasons she'd taken a chance on the tea.

"You're worried about my bodyguard now?"

Reese shot Elena a look that said, *I know what you're doing.*

Elena was digging for information. Reese hadn't revealed her feelings for the Fae warrior and how much things had changed between them. "He's not your bodyguard anymore. He's Illa's fiancé and Portia's servant."

"Maybe, but that's gonna change. We have more warriors from Emain coming to Old Kingdom to help with the takeover. We can't bring everyone—someone needs to guard the university—but Marcus is one of the biggest warriors they have, and he's bringing a few of his buddies."

"Marcus?"

"One of the Emain soldiers who helped guard me on campus. You should have seen him and his guards crammed around our dining table the night before I left for Tirnan."

"When did I miss a meal with a horde of hot soldiers?"

Elena cringed. "It was before Derek and I came here to cure the virus and get you back. A last meal, so to speak...in case we didn't make it home."

"So, good times. And here we are again, saving Tirnan from Portia."

"There's one more thing," Elena said hesitantly. "Keen's here now, but not for long. He'll need to return to New Kingdom. He was able to leave under the pretense of escorting his fiancé to her homeland so she could prepare for the wedding."

Reese's throat went dry. "Right. Of course he'll need to go back."

Elena walked to where Reese gripped the lab table. "What's going on with you two? And don't tell me 'nothing.' I've suspected something since you met Keen in our apartment weeks ago."

"I didn't even know him then," Reese said.

"No. But there was...something. Wasn't there?"

Reese swallowed. When she'd first met Keen he'd just been Elena's tall bodyguard—after she'd dropped the bombshell on Reese about all things Fae. It had been a lot to take in at the time, but meeting Keen had made things worse.

He had always treated Reese differently. He never flirted —quite the opposite. He criticized her clothing, or lack thereof. But Elena was right. There had been a spark, even when they were arguing. *Especially* when they argued. "I didn't think so at the time, but I know him better now. I mean, he's still an arrogant ass. But he's a good guy."

Elena smiled. "So, what's changed?"

"Everything. I know he cares for me. And the way I feel about him... I've never felt that way about anyone before. It's intense, and it's not only a physical attraction. I find myself wanting to see him happy—willing to do whatever it takes to see that he's okay. And we..." Reese gave Elena a telling look.

"Oh. *Ohhhh.* Really?"

Reese nodded and looked away. "But it's done. I don't know what we thought we were doing—not denying ourselves for once, I guess. But we can't be together."

Elena nudged Reese's shoulder, lightening the mood with a wink. "The heart wants what it wants."

Reese choked out a laugh. "Don't start quoting pop songs. The situation is bad enough as it is."

Elena chuckled, but her expression turned more serious. "It will be okay. Everything will work out. Look at Derek and me. He's the king of Old Kingdom and I'm supposed to be the queen of the opposing land—his sworn enemy? I mean, come on, he and I have no business being together. But we're working it out. You never know what will happen."

"But you sort of do, don't you? Has there ever been a lasting Fae-Halven, or even Fae-Human, relationship?"

Elena's mouth twisted and she looked away.

"Exactly."

CHAPTER

TWENTY-SIX

Keen found Reese in the kitchens with the cook, shoving a danish down her throat, her pert rear facing him as she leaned over the large wooden table used as a makeshift dining surface for servants.

"Keep 'em coming, Theresa. You know I like the buttery ones."

"You'll eat me out of castle and hearth, Miss Reese." The cook's ruddy face wore a scowl, even as she piled more food under Reese's nose.

"I'm growing, didn't you hear?"

"*Grew.* The Allon leaves have a one-time effect." Theresa the cook was more handsome than beautiful. Some were more blessed than others, even among Fae. "No longer applies. But you needn't remind me of the young. I have a strapping boy of my own. Twice your size and twice the trouble."

"Oooh, do tell. How do Fae boys get into trouble? In New Kingdom they took me to a brothel—"

Keen had heard enough. Reese didn't need more ideas

on how to get into trouble. She got into enough of it all on her own. "I've spoken to Radnor," he cut in.

Reese spun around in surprise. He might have entered quietly. And ogled when she wasn't looking. But he couldn't help himself. He wanted to soak her up while he still could.

Her gaze skimmed down his body, just as his had drunk in hers moments before.

She crossed her arms, clearly still upset that he'd agreed to marry her sister after he and Reese had...formed a connection. But he'd had no choice. Portia had been waiting for him after the tavern. If he'd stayed with Reese the way he'd wanted to, it would have gotten them both killed, along with her friends. To forfeit his life was one thing, but hers? Unacceptable.

Keen had deflected Portia's inquiries about the Halven's whereabouts by telling her they'd left the land, and it had saved their lives. Not even Portia dared enter Old Kingdom without thorough planning. And now that she could use Keen to infiltrate Old Kingdom through marriage to Illa, Portia would have everything she wanted without going to war.

He cracked his neck and tried not to think about what he'd been forced to do. He wanted to rip apart Old Kingdom castle with his bare hands to ensure Portia never owned any part of it—never forced her will on others. And that wasn't even what was driving him crazy the most. "Radnor tells me that you will remain in Old Kingdom as his daughter and fight alongside him if needed," Keen said, his voice harsh with frustration.

Her mouth went slack, as though he'd taken her off guard. "Why would he say that? He came by while I was sick, but as far as I know, Hakon has one true daughter. And I'm not her."

"Not according to him."

"What's your point?"

"You will not fight. Ever."

This time her jaw dropped completely. "Come again? Because I think you just tried to tell me what I will and will not do. We discussed this. You have no authority over me. You're not my father. Not my...*whatever*. We're nothing to each other. Right, Keen?"

He let out a slow breath that might have ended on a growl. "As soon as it's safe, you will return to the Earth realm."

She tossed another bite of food in her mouth and chewed slowly as she studied his eyes. He wanted to kiss her mouth and lick the flakes of danish off her lips.

Heat filled his body, and he glanced past Reese to the cook, who also had her arms crossed.

"Been a mam for many years, Keen Albrecht. Don't like the way you're looking at Miss Reese. You're engaged to another. Keep them eyeballs in your head."

He stared heavenward. This was not what he needed.

He'd controlled his attraction to Reese for weeks, with one exception, which would be branded in his mind forever. He needed to just get through this last conversation...

Last.

Keen had told Reese he wouldn't leave her, but physically he had to. He didn't trust himself around her, and the sooner he left the castle, the better. He wasn't breaking his oath to not leave her—not really. His heart and mind would always be with her.

He rubbed his eyes. "As I said, Reese, you will not fight. Even if your father wishes it."

Reese glanced over her shoulder. "Theresa, will you excuse us for a moment?"

Theresa scowled.

"Oh, don't worry about this one," Reese said. "He's no threat to me. In fact"—she turned to glare at him—"Keen should watch himself. I'm not very happy with him right now."

Theresa smirked and exited out the servants' door. That was when his little one stalked forward.

His eyes dropped to her mouth. She still had the faintest flake of pastry there.

She was killing him.

"I don't wish to argue with you," he said. "I'm on my way out. This is the last we will see each other." Had his voice come out choked?

He took in her beautiful face, her determined, lively eyes. She'd stunned him silly from the moment they met, and she still had the capacity to bring him to his knees.

He understood it now—her effect on him. She'd taken hold of his heart from the moment she talked back to him, and he would never be the same. But if there was one thing his kind did for those they loved, it was protect them. If that was all he could do for Reese, it would have to be enough.

She seemed taken aback at his words. "The last time, eh? I thought you said you wouldn't leave me?"

He reached across the miserable space that separated them and gently lifted the flake of food from her lip. Her warm breath left her abruptly at his touch. "I want you safe."

She looked away, her face strained. "I'm fine. You don't need to worry about me."

Keen felt his face tense, his chest and arms go taut. "It is impossible for me to not worry about you."

Her gaze flashed back to his. "Because you don't think I can take care of myself?"

Would she never understand? "No, that is not why. I explained it to you when you were sick. Do you remember?"

"*I* haven't forgotten a single thing. *I* remember everything we've done together."

And just like that, heat and lust consumed him. He wanted to pull her into his arms.

He remembered—he simply couldn't act on his feelings.

He reached out and cradled her head in his hands. "Please. Do not fight. I couldn't stand anything happening to you."

Her eyes grew glassy. "I can't promise that. I need to take care of my friends and myself. You're not the only one who's been wronged by Portia."

He dropped his hands. "No."

And that was why he was in this situation, betrothed to Reese's sister. Because he'd made an oath he could not break. And because appeasing Portia had been the best way to protect Reese. "I am sorry for what you've been through. For your friends' losses."

"Anything else you're sorry for?" Her voice turned bitter, like that of a scorned woman.

He stepped closer and lowered his head until his lips hovered above hers. "There is nothing I regret. Not with you."

Reese swallowed.

"Goodbye, little one." Keen turned and strode away before he did something he *would* regret.

TWENTY-SEVEN

Reese trained with Ulric in one of the empty castle rooms they used for swordplay. Weapons hung on the walls, and large gashes marred the floor where targets had been missed and the ground had paid the price. There was no padding in the room, no sweat cloths, or any other luxury afforded by New Kingdom's posh exercise room, but it worked. And throughout the training, Reese let out her pent-up aggression.

Keen had said goodbye. Whatever they had or didn't have, it was over. She needed to accept it and move on.

Somehow her heart and body hadn't gotten the memo.

Her chest ached and her throat was constantly dry and stinging, as though she'd been crying. She would not cry over Keen. Okay, she'd cried a little, but she'd quickly wiped away those tears and sternly told herself that he was just another guy who didn't care enough to stick around.

Only that wasn't true. He'd done so much to protect her. She'd felt how he cared, even if he'd never voiced it. Even if she couldn't read his emotions like she could everyone else's. She knew it was there. And that was the part her head and heart couldn't reconcile. But they would. She'd train until she wiped the memory of him from her mind. Or at least, until she'd pushed it toward the back.

So far, no luck.

Reese lunged at Ulric. He was actually sweating and appeared to defend himself for real, rather than casually blocking her blows.

"You're looking a little peaked," she teased.

Determination filled his eyes and he made a counterattack Reese quickly blocked with a parry and a kick to his stomach.

Ulric grunted and fell back.

One good thing came from drinking the tea of the Ancient Allon. Reese hadn't only grown in height, she'd become exponentially stronger and faster.

Keen had asked her to stay out of any fighting, but Reese had never agreed to it. She was here to help her friends, and that was what she would do.

"Am I disturbing you?"

Reese turned to find Illa at the entrance to the room. "Not at all," she said, and relaxed her stance.

Illa grinned and stepped forward. She wore the Fae black uniform—the stretchy pants and top Reese had grown fond of. Fae battle clothes were formfitting but really comfortable, and they could hold about fifty weapons, which was just cool.

"Do you want to join us?" Reese asked.

Illa's face brightened. "I'd love to."

Ulric groaned. "I believe we learned our lesson the last time."

He was referring to when he'd accidentally cut Illa while showing Reese sword maneuvers.

Illa chose a blade from the wall. "Don't be silly. I'm in

battle gear now. The court dress and shoes would have made anyone slip."

She made a couple of practice moves, then went into *en garde* position against Reese.

Reese was in love with Keen, whether she wanted to be or not. Anyone paying attention knew it. But Illa hadn't once taken it out on her. In fact, she'd remained the devoted sister. Something Reese never thought she would have.

"If you go to battle, don't underestimate the Newlander queen," Illa said.

"I would never underestimate Portia. That bitch is crazy."

Illa feinted to the right, then struck on the left—crashing into Reese's waiting sword. "Yes, exactly. Crazy. And now grieving over the loss of her only daughter. Stay away from her if you can."

Illa knew Reese better than Reese gave her credit for, because Reese had no intention of staying away from Portia. Not when the oppression Portia inflicted stood between freedom for Reese's friends and this land.

"What about you?" Reese lunged forward with her sword, but Illa quickly dodged the move. "Portia could just as easily turn on you."

Her sister's sadness struck Reese's chest like a punch. "Unlikely. The queen needs me... She won't harm me while I'm able to give her what she wants—or, at least, the means to get what she wants."

Reese swallowed. "And after the marriage?" Once Illa and Keen married, Reese would never go near Keen again. She'd never commit adultery the way her parents had. And she'd never betray her sister. "Will you be safe?"

Illa's gaze lifted to Reese's, compassion in her eyes. "Do

not worry about me, sister, when it is I who am worried for you. We will figure out a way to make everything right."

Reese nodded tightly, not certain she knew what Illa meant, but afraid she really did. She needed to work on her poker face.

No wonder Fae were expressionless. They had such acute senses that their most telling weakness—their emotions—had to be kept under lock and key.

Reese and Illa practiced several more battle tactics, and much to Reese's relief, they were evenly matched. With Reese's improved strength and agility, she even found herself holding back, where she hadn't needed to with Ulric.

"That's enough for now," Ulric said, his body tense as he watched them. His feelings for Illa had grown passionately stronger, and Reese could do nothing but commiserate. They were in the same situation, loving someone who wasn't free to love them back.

Illa grinned at Reese, her chest rising and falling lightly on winded breath. She moved across the room to return the sword to the wall, and Ulric joined her. He said something too softly for Reese to hear, but she caught Illa's surprised expression and felt the jumble of excitement and fear that coursed through her sister.

Illa closed her eyes and let out a breath. "I cannot. This is the only course."

Ulric sheathed his sword at his back and turned, storming toward the door. He was furious, his anger, pain, and frustration pelting Reese like hail.

Illa approached hesitantly, glancing nervously at Ulric, who stood near the doorway, his back to them. "I must go. There is a fitting. For the gown..." She glanced away. "I am sorry. For the marriage. It isn't a choice for him. You understand that, don't you? Keen would not marry me if there was another way."

Reese swallowed and plastered on a smile. "He'd marry eventually. He may be an ass at times, but he's a good man. I'm happy he's found a woman he might actually deserve." Her words were playful, but in her heart, she was dying.

Illa glanced one last time at Ulric, then turned to leave.

Reese grabbed her arm. "What about you? Are you happy with the marriage? It seems that your affections might lie elsewhere."

Illa pressed her mouth into a tight smile. "We do what we must, but if I had a choice, I would not marry the man my sister loves."

Reese's head notched back. "Loves? No..."

"You might read emotions as you read a book, but your feelings are transparent as well. As are Keen's. He loves you too."

Reese shook her head, prepared to argue. Fae were only marginally beginning to tolerate Halven. Yes, she'd made love to Keen, but that was because they had crazy physical chemistry; the universe could be cruel sometimes. But Keen could never...

"You know it is true if you search your heart," Illa said. "His feelings for you were clear the moment I saw the two of you in the same room." This time her smile was sincere.

Keen was attracted to her, she'd admit that. He wanted to protect her. He cared about her, or he wouldn't have been upset when she was ill, but love? "Is love the same for Fae as it is for humans?"

"No..." Illa said sadly, and walked toward the door. She passed Ulric and his back tensed. "It runs deeper," she said before exiting the room.

Ulric gripped the door—to close it or rip it off the

hinges, she wasn't sure. "Let's find food," he said. "I no longer have the desire to train."

Reese scurried after him, following down stairs and past twists and turns until they made it to a large room where a fireplace that could roast a deer took up one wall. The place she'd found on her own, and where she'd often grabbed bits of food from Theresa, must have been an antechamber. This room was the *real* kitchen.

There were multiple prep tables along the walls and a large cutting board in the center. Wheels of cheese hung from nets, colorful fruits from baskets, and a somewhat modern stove stood in the corner.

Ulric glanced around searchingly. Only two servants scurried about, and he walked right past them toward a closet in the back. He opened the door and stepped inside, pulling out bowls and bags of foodstuff—scavenging the way Elena's cousin Mateo did when he visited them at their college apartment.

Men. Food scavenging must be inherent.

Which Reese could now appreciate. Ever since she'd regained her strength, she'd become ravenous. The ample meals sent to her room no longer filled her up.

Ulric slapped a loaf of bread onto one of the tables, and what looked to be a slab of ham, but shit, it could be anything. They didn't have pigs in Tirnan, which made Reese question some of the food in front of her.

She walked over and peered into the pantry. "You got anything vegetarian in here?"

Ulric crossed the room and grabbed a wheel of cheese, along with a giant knife, then proceeded to cut thick slices of cheese, bread, and the mysterious Fae meat. He set out two plates and stacked a sandwich onto his own, with what looked like allon leaves instead of lettuce.

"You're eating the leaves?"

He grunted and handed her some.

She stared at them, her lip curling back. "They aren't from the Ancient Allon, are they?"

"No more Ancient Allon for you. These are regular allon leaves. Healthy, but not so magical that they would harm you."

Reese made a sandwich with cheese and leaves and sat at the table across from him. "Why won't you fight for her?" Might as well throw it out there. "Is it against Fae soldiering duty to put one's woman ahead of the kingdom?"

He looked up and scowled.

She took a bite of her sandwich, studying him. He was pissed. Really pissed, which she'd noted from his angry-man glare. The stuff she sensed beneath the surface was more complicated.

Ulric felt desperate but resigned, as though he were trapped—or maybe Illa wasn't cooperating? That would be the more likely scenario. Reese's sister was too self-sacrific-ing. She'd agreed to marry for kingdom, not for love.

"So, Illa," Reese said around another mouthful of food. The sandwich wasn't half bad, and this darn Tirnan cheese was heavenly, though she still didn't want to know which animal it came from. Ignorance was bliss. She chewed and swallowed before continuing. "You're in love with her, right? I wasn't sure at first, because your emotions were more of the angry sort when she was around. Then I figured out it wasn't exactly *anger*...more like frustration. Of the sexual variety. You'd be surprised how similar the two senses can come across."

He shifted his jaw. "I am a Newlander and she is an Oldlander. I am a soldier and she would be a princess if

Derek's father hadn't fought Hakon Radnor and won the throne. Illa is not for me. And she is to marry another." He snarled at his sandwich like it tasted foul.

Reese nodded. "All good points. Except for one thing. She doesn't love Keen, she loves you."

His head shot up and he stared. Then his gaze wandered to the side. Ulric knew just as well as anyone about Reese's ability to sense emotion.

Joy filled the burly soldier's body, then deflated just as quickly. "It is of no matter. She must do her duty."

Reese dropped her food on the plate. "What is wrong with you people? Portia is *one person* and she has everyone tied up in knots. Why do all of you obey her every word?"

His jaw firmed. "You don't understand honor. Once a promise is made—like Illa's to Keen Albrecht—it cannot be undone. And the threat of a second disease has everyone on edge after the first one nearly consumed my kind. Illa told the queen she would marry Keen, and she will."

"*If* there's another disease. The possibility of one is a good enough reason to move swiftly before Portia can make good on her threat. But as far as Illa goes, people change their minds all the time. Illa hasn't made an oath to anyone. Not until her wedding day, when she'll pledge herself to Keen." Reese's chest tightened just saying the words, but she continued. She had to, because Ulric and Illa seemed to have given up. "Illa *can* change her mind. Shoot, I change mine all the time. You might not believe this, but when I first met Keen, I hated him. Well, I thought he was hot, then he spoke, and *then* I hated him."

Ulric rolled his eyes. "Everyone knows that."

Reese sat back, shoulders slumping. "Really?" She thought she'd hidden her feelings pretty well in the beginning. "Well, anyway, the point is, Illa thought she wanted to marry Keen—for whatever reasons she deemed important at the time—and now she's changed her mind. It's as simple as that."

He seemed to consider her words, then shook his head. "It is not that easy. She cannot undo what has been put into motion. They are to be married in two days."

Two days? It couldn't be that soon. She wasn't ready—she *wasn't ready*. "How will we amass an army before then?"

She hadn't realized that stopping the wedding was something she'd considered until the words had left her mouth. There had to be a way to get her sister and Keen out of Portia's clutches. Preferably unmarried.

Ulric set down his sandwich. "You've answered your own question. We *can't* build an army that quickly. The marriage will take place, and you and I must live with it."

But that was the problem. She didn't think she could.

TWENTY-EIGHT

The next morning, while soldiers gathered in preparation to take back New Kingdom, Reese trained with Ulric one last time, then went in search of Elena. She no longer feared that she lacked the skills to survive a fight with a Fae. Sparring with Ulric and Illa since drinking the tea proved she'd be able to hold her own.

Reese had always known who she was, and it wasn't the debutante her mother had painted her. Or the quiet daughter her father hoped would stay out of his way. She wanted more for herself. It was why she pushed hard in school—why she trained in martial arts. She'd dreamed of becoming a blond Lara Croft when she was a kid, but practicality trumped those desires. College and graduate school became her adult ideals.

Until Tirnan.

Now Reese's original dreams didn't seem that far-fetched.

Elena had worked with Fae on the virus, and Reese wanted to take things a step further. If she could fight alongside Fae now—a.k.a. Halven Lara Croft asskicker—why not train with soldiers in Emain and protect her fellow half-bloods? She was a political science and philosophy double major. Becoming an Emain soldier would give her the physicality she craved, and she could apply her political science and philosophy background creating diplomacy with Halven, Fae, and humans. Besides, if things went down the way Ulric predicted, Keen would remain in Tirnan with his bride, and Reese would return to Emain and the Earth realm. She wouldn't have to see him again, or be reminded of what he meant to her. Her memories of him were punishment enough.

After only a few wrong turns, Reese found the door to Elena's bedroom and entered to discuss her new idea. If nothing else, it would keep her mind off weddings and battles.

Elena's room looked just like Reese's, except Derek lay across the bed, sound asleep, while Elena wrote at a desk in the corner.

"Looks like I caught you at a bad time," Reese whispered.

Elena stood and ushered Reese out. "He hasn't slept in twenty-four hours," she said as they walked down the hallway. "He's been working hard to get things arranged. Let's go to Camille's, where we can talk."

They rapped on a door and Camille called out for them to enter. But once inside, Reese discovered Camille wasn't alone either. She stood in the center of the room, speaking to several robed alchemists, including the one who'd given Reese the broth that had helped her heal from the Ancient Allon tea.

The alchemists glanced at Camille and, without a word, made their way to the door.

"They have prepared more null bombs," Camille said after the alchemists left.

"What do you mean, null *bombs*?" Reese asked. "Elena called them *guns* before."

Elena's eyes lit up for the first time since her mother had been killed. "It's my newest invention. And it's wonderful, if I do say so myself."

Elena described how she'd created the bombs, which went right over Reese's head. Because *science* and *chemistry*. *Blech*.

"Newlander powers control nature," Elena said. "That's the one major advantage they have—*we* have, since I'm a Newlander too. We can cause an earthquake, create a fireball, or zap someone with lightning. All deadly and, at the very least, debilitating. Oldlanders can be equally lethal, but most mental abilities require proximity. Null guns give Oldlanders an even playing field by incapacitating the attacker until the soldier can get close. With null bombs, we can wipe out the elemental powers of an entire group in one blast. Genius, right?"

"Yes," Reese said hesitantly. Bombs of any kind sounded bad, but Reese understood where Elena was going with this. If they neutralized Newlander elemental powers, the battle would be hand-to-hand combat—or sword-to-sword. That close, Oldlanders could also inflict their powers on the opposition, weakening them further.

"It's really a necessity if we're to have any hope of winning the battle," Elena said. "I don't trust how far Portia will go to maintain control."

Reese thought back to a previous conversation she'd had with Keen, and most recently with Ulric. "Are you referring to the threat of a second disease?"

"Yes, and it's completely disturbing." Elena shook her head. "How can she even think of doing that again?"

"Because she's Portia? Psychotic she-Fae?"

"The whisperings should not be taken lightly," Camille said. "It's why we are moving swiftly to stage a second attack."

"How can we stop it if she decides to release the disease before we get to her?" Elena sounded desperate, and her emotions confirmed it. "I barely stopped the last virus in time. I can't do it again—I can't. Who knows how many people would die before I created a cure? It could take me days. And what if this one kills Halven too? I'm the last of the transmutation wielders. If I died and couldn't cure it, what would happen?" Elena sank into a wooden chair. "I understand now why Leo spoke about breeding."

"Excuse me?" Reese said.

Elena looked up in exasperation. "Leo, a scientist in Emain. He mentioned producing more Fae with transmutation abilities. After the havoc caused by the first disease, he seems open to breeding Halven with my ability."

Reese stared at her. "You realize how that sounds?"

"Like I'm livestock they want to mate with their pure Fae studs? Yeah, I do, but that's Leo. They try to keep the royal bloodlines strong, and they do it by any means necessary. Right now I have one of the most powerful abilities. They won't risk losing it."

"Are you seriously considering having babies with these people to produce another transmutation wielder?" Reese asked.

"Of course not, but at least I understand why Leo brought it up."

"Well, get off that line of thought," Reese said. "There

are other ways to defend ourselves. Other ways to keep peace between the kingdoms. We just need to find them."

"We have the null bombs…" Camille said. "And now we have Deirdre." She grinned, brimming with excitement. "Deirdre has been organizing Sunlanders willing to fight against Portia. It has taken a great deal of time, given their beliefs about violence, but she's finally managed to convince them to join our cause. They've already used the Ancient Allon leaves I sent, and they arrive this evening. Between the Sunlanders, the Old Kingdom soldiers, additional Emain guards we've recruited, and the null bombs, we have the strength to stage an attack."

Reese looked at Elena. "Who's Deirdre?"

"My aunt. The last time I was here, I watched her take down an Oldlander soldier two times her size in under three seconds. She's sweet, but vicious. We definitely have an advantage with her on our side. Her husband was my mother's brother, who was also a transmutation wielder. He was the first one Marlon and Portia had killed. You could say Deirdre would do just about anything to get Portia out of power, even convince her fellow pacifist Sunlanders to help. Especially after what Portia did to my mother…"

"So she'll be properly pissed," Reese said to distract Elena from the sadness that washed over her. "But what about Keen? How will he and Illa survive if we go blasting in there with null bombs and taking out Portia's military by any means necessary?"

Elena turned to Camille.

"No one wants to see Keen or your sister hurt," Camille said, "but we will battle them if they fight against us."

"And Keen would, the honorable bastard," Reese muttered.

"It is about honor, yes," Camille said. "But we are also

bound by our word. It's difficult to explain to a human or Halven who know of no such magic, but we physically cannot go against our word."

"That makes it worse." Reese feared what would happen when they attacked, knowing Keen would protect Portia with his life.

Elena walked over. "Have faith. Keen is on our side, whether he's sworn fealty to Portia or not."

"What about Illa and her father? What happens to them?"

"You mean your sister and your father?" Elena asked.

"He's only my father in the technical sense. In every other way, he's not been there for me."

"We can argue about that later, but yes, they'll have to decide which side they're on, but at least they have a choice, unlike Keen."

Elena was right. Keen had no choice whose side he was on. He'd given up that right after Reese had nearly died in the dungeon. And he'd done it to protect her.

"With this news about the Sunlanders, we can step up the timing of the attack and make it the night of the wedding. Derek's been working to get everything in order by then, but now that we have Sunlanders, there's no reason to hesitate. It's the perfect time to access the palace. Portia is allowing some of us inside as a unifying measure; we'll simply sneak in a few more."

"Why has Hakon supported Keen and Illa taking Derek's place? Is he that desperate to gain power?"

Elena rubbed her eyes. "It's complicated. Hakon would have controlled Old Kingdom had Derek's father not subdued him by murdering his family members. And if we're speaking technically on that front, Keen has an even better claim to the throne."

"And now that Derek's father, Osulf Niall, is dead..." Reese said.

"Keen can rule if he gains enough support. And takes the kingdom from Derek," Camille finished.

Elena's eyes hardened. "But Keen would still be Portia's puppet, and Derek won't give up the throne to a cruel dictator."

"Why not put Hakon in charge?" Reese's biological father seemed like the best middleman.

Camille crossed the room and picked up an amulet. It was the same shape as the ouroboros on Reese's wrist. "Hakon is no longer interested in politics and ruling the kingdom after Niall murdered most of his family to take control. As long as Niall's heir doesn't rule, Hakon is content to support another in charge."

"But if Keen ruled, that still puts Portia indirectly in control," Reese said.

"Along with Hakon's daughter," Camille agreed. She handed the amulet to Reese. It dangled from a gold chain similar to the one around her wrist. "Hakon wanted you to have this. It is the mate to the one you wear on your arm."

The ouroboros was beautiful, with rubies for snake eyes. It should look creepy, but it was stunningly crafted and somehow elegant.

Hakon had given her a gift that connected her to his family. He wasn't trying to pretend she didn't exist, or pawn her off the way her father back home had done so many times in order to return to his work. The necklace was a sign to all that she was his daughter.

She blinked several times, pushing back what she hoped weren't tears, but she feared they might be. "Tell him thank you."

Camille gave her a light nod.

Reese cleared her throat. "So we storm the palace the night Illa and Keen marry, and imprison Portia?"

"That's the plan," Elena said. "Though only some of us will be allowed in. The rest will go via Camille's portals."

Camille grinned mischievously. "The Ancient Allon worked. I can now portal fifty men with ease, and do it several more times afterward. Not many can boast of such powers where I come from."

"Aren't you from Sunland?" Elena asked, holding up Reese's new pendant and admiring it.

Reese sensed nervousness from the Fae woman. "Camille?"

"Yes, I'm from Sunland," Camille finally said. "But originally I came from somewhere else."

Whatever Camille was about to say was big. Her emotions were all over the place, spiking in panic and pain.

"What do you mean, somewhere else?" Elena asked, slowly handing Reese back her necklace. "There are only three kingdoms."

Camille's beautiful sky-blue eyes pierced them with her stare. "Not true. There is a fourth kingdom—one so unimaginable, many do not believe it exists. It's located inside the Land of Ice, where the Dark Fae live."

TWENTY-NINE

"Dark Fae?" Elena repeated. "You have black hair, while everyone else here is either blond or redheaded, or at the very least, a light brunette, but what do you mean, there's another kingdom?"

Camille sat on the edge of her bed, her back straight. "It is difficult to survive in the Land of Ice. Few leave, and even fewer manage to find our land without perishing first. That is the reason we've remained separate from the rest of Tirnan."

"But you're here..." Reese stared at Camille, not understanding any of this.

"A few of us have left over the years, but there has been no way to communicate once we've gone. The kingdom is isolated, the land encased in minerals that block magic. We can't reach out to our brothers and sisters back home without making the return trek, risking our lives again in the process. Those in the Land of Ice assume death to any who try to leave. It is the most logical conclusion."

Reese had read something about the Land of Ice in the

book Enid had given her, and she thought she remembered Amund saying he was from there. Which made Camille's story all the more plausible—not that Reese had doubted her. "Why did you leave if the chances of survival were slim?"

"For the same reason Elena's mother left her people. I was promised to a man I despised. My parents agreed for me to—*breed* with this man against my wishes. His wife wasn't happy about the arrangement either, but he was powerful and could do as he pleased. He wanted a child, and his wife had not succeeded in providing him one."

"They would have forced him on you?" Elena asked, her voice high. "My mother was a princess and had expectations put upon her. I don't think they do that unless…"

Camille raised an eyebrow.

"Oh," Elena said, looking surprised. "You're…noble? Exactly how many noble Fae are there?"

"Not as many as you would think. There's a reason you and I and the others battle for control of the kingdoms. It's because we carry strong abilities and bloodlines—angel blood powerful enough to rule this land. In any case, I was young and foolish. Thousands of miles separated us from civilization, and there was almost no vegetation between the Land of Ice and here. I took the risk, but I barely survived the journey, even with my power to create portals."

"You said civilization," Elena said slowly. "The Land of Ice is uncivilized?"

"Compared to here? Yes. And the queen wanted me dead after her husband wished me for his concubine and broodmare."

Reese snorted in disgust. "Are there any decent noblemen in Tirnan?"

Camille shrugged noncommittally, then peered at Elena. "Your mother was an exception."

Camille had run away from someplace no one could get to or from, and she might or might not have an evil queen after her. Tirnan was intense.

"Are you safe?" Reese asked. "They aren't coming after you, are they?"

Camille stood and looked out her window. A dirt berm surrounded the castle, protected by a moat. Different castle, same green forest beyond as New Kingdom, with tons of guards milling about. "Safe is subjective. I have been untouched for hundreds of years in Sunland, but that does not mean the queen has forgotten her husband's infatuation. If there was a way for her to reach me and make good on her promise to have me killed, she would."

"But you're the only Dark Fae to survive the journey," Reese pointed out.

Camille turned to her. "I am the only Dark Fae in any of the three Kingdoms, that I know of, though Amund said he was from the Land of Ice when we met with him in the tavern. It is possible there are others. Amund has the build and look of Dark Fae. If the rest of my people succeed in bridging the distance between our lands, they will attack, and not only me. The king was extremely ambitious. He dreamed of ruling all of Tirnan."

"Jesus," Reese muttered. "The royal Fae and their need for control. No one will be left once you guys are through duking it out."

Camille tilted her head. "Quite possibly, though it's in our blood to dominate—a side effect of being Fae."

Elena threw up her hands. "Okay, well, we can't worry about that right now. One major battle at a time."

"Right." Reese nodded. "And this one we're planning

against Portia... What exactly happens if we manage to capture her?"

Elena swallowed and twisted her hands together. "I've spoken to Derek about that. If we capture Portia and gain control of New Kingdom...Derek is willing to give up his claim to the throne."

"What?" Reese blurted. Camille stared in surprise as well. "Derek talked about giving it up before, and now you're supporting him. Why?"

"Hakon has been kind to Derek, but he doesn't approve of him in charge," Elena said. "He doesn't want any blood of Osulf Niall's running this land, and I can't blame him after what Niall did to his family. At the same time, he doesn't want to rule either—but he would support Keen."

"Wise." Camille nodded. "Hakon is a powerful influencer. Derek holds this land, but just barely. With Hakon's support, a man could rule with little conflict."

"Exactly," Elena said. "If Derek agrees to cede the throne to Keen and Illa after their marriage, Hakon will get everyone behind our cause against Portia. Most of the soldiers already are, but it doesn't hurt to have more." At Reese's look, Elena said, "It's not so bad. Hakon believes Derek would make a great liaison between the kingdoms while we work out a truce. The goal is to bring New and Old Kingdom together."

But that wasn't what had Reese's face turning to stone. "So there's no hope of preventing the marriage? Between Keen and Illa? We're attacking the night the wedding is to take place. If we leave early enough..."

Elena was silent as she glanced at Camille, then back to Reese. "I'm sorry," she said. "Camille will start bringing soldiers to New Kingdom before the ceremony begins tomorrow night, but she'll have her hands full with the numbers we need to battle Portia's military. We can't bring people over early, or the Presence Charm will announce their arrival too soon; Portia would know something was up. She expects several of us to come for the wedding, but not an army. And not hours before the wedding. By the time we're ready to act, Keen and Illa will be married."

Reese swallowed and nodded. She'd hoped, but... Yeah, hope was a silly thing. "You've forgotten one problem. Entrapping Portia and putting Keen in charge isn't the solution. He swore an oath to protect her. If she's alive, he has to fulfill his commitment to her."

Elena's mouth twisted. "That's the weak link in the plan. And protection is ambiguous, don't you agree? Would Portia be in danger if we placed her in comfort while locked away? We wondered how she managed to keep everyone in line. The second virus was her trump card. No one would have gone up against her with that hanging over their heads; they were all too terrified after witnessing the destruction the first virus caused. Without a threat of revolution, Portia didn't need to enforce a stronger oath from her soldiers. Protection was more than enough."

She looked between Reese and Camille. "We attack now before Portia has a chance to release the second virus. If the oath Keen made to Portia becomes a problem, preventing him from making decisions that would hurt her physically or mentally, Hakon has agreed to rule over Old Kingdom. Though he'd prefer not to."

"You could kill Portia." Reese shrugged. "Just a thought."

Elena shook her head vehemently. "We're not like her; we're not murderers. Imprisonment and stripping her of her power will be punishment enough. The situation isn't ideal, as your father hasn't a taste for leadership. Osulf Niall destroyed any ounce of ambition Hakon once had on that front, but Hakon wants someone trustworthy in charge. He's agreed to do what he must to keep peace between the lands. Apparently, other noblemen in Old Kingdom would never cooperate with Newlanders. They're all too ambitious."

Reese understood why Elena didn't want to kill anyone. But she feared that leaving Portia alive was a bad idea. Still, Elena and Derek knew the politics of Tirnan better than she did. She trusted them.

"Then it's settled," Reese said. "We'll get Portia out of power one way or another...and Keen and Illa will marry."

THIRTY

Reese looked in the mirror. She wore a black uniform different from the one she'd received in New Kingdom, but it was essentially the same. A tunic-style top that fit all manner of weapons in stealthy pockets and straps, sleek, stretchy black pants, and kick-ass black boots even her mother would approve of. The boots fit her calves perfectly, with good height that gave her spring when she jogged across the room to test them out. In short, they were super comfortable and she felt like she was walking on a cloud.

She'd braided her hair in a loop around her head from crown to nape to keep it off her face. She would fight alongside the rest of Elena and Derek's makeshift army, even if drinking the Ancient Allon leaves hadn't done much to improve her magical abilities.

Elena entered the room and scanned Reese. "You look like a warrior."

Reese grinned. It was the best compliment she'd ever received. Particularly when she was feeling vulnerable after Keen.

Hmm, the first time she'd felt vulnerable after inter-acting with Keen she'd gone to the fraternity party alone—and ended up in a Fae realm. And now, after conceivably the last time she'd ever see him, she was heading into a Fae battle. There was a warning sign somewhere in all of this, but her path was set. She would help her friends. And by the time they arrived in New Kingdom, Keen and Illa would be married.

Just thinking about it made tears bloom behind her eyes. She quickly sucked in a breath. No way would she cry. Not when she was in badass warrior mode.

Elena wore a similar outfit, but her tunic had delicate gold embroidery along the edges of her sleeves—embroidery to indicate Elena's true status as a royal who belonged on the New Kingdom throne. "You look beautiful. Like a queen."

Elena's face fell slightly. "Do you think this is right? To try to take it back? I don't need it—not for my pride, or for anything else."

"That's not what this is about. Portia killed many Fae —with help from my half-brother—all for power. *She. Is. Psycho.* She shouldn't be in charge. From what I heard when my New Kingdom seamstresses thought I wasn't listening, Portia infected the royal family with the virus first. She wanted them out of the way. The only reason your mom survived was because she'd been separated from her family at the time." Reese stepped forward and squeezed her friend's hand. "You're the last one, Elena. You're also one of the most powerful magic wielders in the kingdom, and you have a good heart. If there's anyone capable of protecting these people, it's you. Unless you don't want to..."

Elena's hazel eyes shot up. "I want to protect them. I

just wish it were my mom on the throne. Wish I'd had more time with her..."

"It wasn't much," Reese agreed, "but it was quality. I watched your mother with you. I've never seen—or *felt*—that kind of love and devotion. It was beautiful, and if I could play back what I'd witnessed through my ability so that you could experience it too, I would. For now, you'll have to take my word for it and know that there was no other choice for her when it came to saving your life. She wouldn't have changed a thing. Maybe you were always meant to be the one leading New Kingdom."

A tear slid down Elena's cheek and she quickly wiped it away. "If that's true, I'd rather not have to go to battle to get it back. People will die, Reese."

"People will die no matter what. Portia doesn't negotiate. She won't see reason. The longer she's in power, the more people she harms and forces to do things against their will. Let's get there before she does irreparable damage."

A knock sounded at the door and a petite—by Fae standards—redheaded woman with short hair entered the room, smiling at Elena.

Elena quickly walked over and gave the woman a hug, turning with her arm around her. "Reese, this is my Aunt Deirdre."

Reese stepped forward and shook Deirdre's hand. "Elena told me you were a huge help the last time she was here, and to not make you angry because, despite appearances, you were a fierce warrior."

Deirdre grinned. "I am good with a machete."

A machete. Reese looked to Elena.

"Long story." Elena waved her off.

Deirdre gestured toward the door. "Everyone is in the main hall. We should join them. Illa and her father left for

New Kingdom hours ago, and Camille has begun taking over soldiers in shifts, hiding them until the time is right. The ceremony begins any moment."

Reese's chest rose on a shaky breath. Keen could be marrying Illa right now—and there was nothing Reese could do to stop it.

She bit her lip and turned as the others filed out of the room. She allowed a choking sound to escape her throat when she thought she was alone.

But warm arms wrapped around her, curly, dark hair tickling her cheek.

She glanced over her shoulder. "Sorry."

Elena stepped back. "You don't need to apologize for caring about him. I'd change everything if I could. My mother...you and Keen. As powerful as Fae believe me to be, I can't fix this."

Reese glanced at the ouroboros amulet she wore around her neck. A tear streaked down her cheek and she wiped it away. "No, but we can do what's right. I never fit in my parents' world. I never wanted to be the debutante, intent on climbing the social ladder. I hated the phoniness. But in this world...in some twisted way, I fit. With you and Derek."

"Well, I hate to burst your bubble about Tirnan, but you'll still get the social climbing. Except here it's more of a battle for who's most magical. I mean, crap, they *mate for bloodlines*."

Reese nodded. "True, but I don't believe they're right. Look how powerful you are, and you're not full Fae. They need to change their thinking."

Elena laughed. "You're preaching to the choir. Believe me, I'm working on them. But an ancient people don't change views nimbly. Just look at this place." They both glanced at the wooden furniture and tapestries from another century. "It's stuck in sixteenth-century Scottish Highlander land. This is some *Outlander* shit right here." She grinned, and Reese gave her a wobbly one too. "Seriously, though, they can't keep things the same without the risk of losing it all to someone like Portia. They need our help." She bumped Reese in the arm. "And we need *you*."

Reese had never felt needed. Wanted by frisky fraternity guys? Sure. Used as a shopping buddy by her mother? That too. But truly valued? Never. "I'm here for you. For as long as you need me."

A sad look crossed Elena's face. "It'll be okay—with Keen. I don't know how, but things will work out."

Reese tried to smile, but she was pretty sure it was a fat fail. "We should get going. More important things to worry about and all that. Give me a second, though? I'll be right behind you."

Elena gave her a look that said she wasn't fooled, but quietly left the room.

Reese walked toward the window overlooking the berm, filled with soldiers organizing in groups. Some of the soldiers protected the gates. They'd remain behind and guard the castle while everyone was away. The others waited their turn to portal to New Kingdom.

In Tirnan she was Halven, needed by her friends, and by the stubborn-ass Fae, though they'd never admit it.

Even so, for this moment—while the first guy she'd truly loved committed himself to another—she gave in to a broken heart.

THIRTY-ONE

The room they'd put Keen in had belonged to Beortric, Theda's brother, a New Kingdom prince before he'd married and become a Sunlander in order to pursue science. Everyone agreed science served a purpose, even among immortal Fae, but it was...unpopular. Only the weak chose that path. Battle mastery and magical pursuits were the norm among his kind. It was unheard of for a noble Fae with magic and strength to practice science —until Beortric had given up everything for his passion.

For the first time in his life, Keen understood why a man would do such a thing. Marrying Illa was for the best, but Keen's heart beat heavy and unsettled inside his chest.

He had never been one to dwell on something he couldn't control. The angels had promised millennia ago that they would watch over their children. Belief in the fates was at the root of their culture.

Fae fought to protect what was most precious to them —the land, their magical gifts. But that was the problem. They'd been sired by angels with different abilities—New Kingdom with their elemental abilities and Old Kingdom with their mental powers. Those forefathers had held grudges against each other, and somehow the grudges transferred to their children. This notion Elena had of bringing all of Tirnan together would never work, and now she'd convinced Reese to risk her life based on the idea. It infuriated Keen to no end.

The fates of Fae were entwined and tangled in a way no Halven could undo.

Another knock sounded at the door. There had been several over the last hour, and still Keen ignored it.

This time the guard used a key and entered. Keen lifted his eyebrow at the man's blatant disregard for authority. "My apologies, sir. But they are waiting." The guard shifted nervously. "The queen refuses to wait any longer."

Keen had never shirked his duty. Not once. It was why he'd risen among his fellow soldiers, despite being banished from Old Kingdom years ago. He was a ruthless warrior who always followed orders—unless he was the one giving them.

Somehow, this duty to marry Illa weighed on him like the barrels of gold New Kingdom mined and sold to humans. He couldn't bring himself to walk down the stairs. To do so felt as though he were betraying Reese, his tiny Halven.

His Halven. She was his. He'd made it so when he claimed her in the bedroom of a tavern. And he'd do it again.

Keen was calm under pressure, faithful to his people. Never had he experienced the sheer frustration Reese brought out in him. He wanted to throw her over his shoulder and lock her away half the time, and kiss her insolent mouth the rest. In short, she drove him insane. The thought of not having her in his life, not knowing if she was okay and where she was... It was eating him alive.

While most men cowered before Keen, Reese—small and proud—had stood her ground from the beginning. She was strong, his little one, and her heart was beautiful. Her strength weakened him in a good way—allowed him to be quiet while the rest of the world fought. How would he live without her?

He'd do anything to protect Reese, which meant he'd agreed to marry Illa, because to disobey Portia put all of them at risk. He'd risk his own life, but not Reese's.

He wanted her with him—always. But if he married Illa, he could never be with Reese again. This was what had him pacing Beortric's old room, unable to walk out the door to face his future.

Keen scrubbed a hand down his face and glanced at the ceiling. Then he did something he'd never done in his life. Not since he'd been old enough to realize he was an orphan and his family had been murdered. Not after he'd grown and learned the truth of his noble blood, and how his right to the throne had been torn from him.

He prayed. For *her*.

Keen spun on his heel and stormed out the door in front of the guard who was still waiting. His heart was cold and shredding inside. There would be nothing left of it after what he was about to do.

Tirnan didn't build houses of worship the way the Earth realm did. There was no need. Tirnan *was* a part of the heavens—created for the children of angels. Royalty wed in their castles, and the rest wed in their homes surrounded by loved ones.

Keen walked in an escort of his guards, his legs suddenly leaden with what felt like the weight of the ocean that surrounded Tirnan. But he was good at hiding his feelings, showing strength in the line of duty.

They approached the entrance to the salon where the wedding was to take place. Radnor stood outside the room, his expression emotionless, though Keen suspected more lay beneath. Next to Radnor stood Portia—and about fifty of Keen's men.

He led the men, but they didn't answer to him. Not anymore. Keen was the master of the guard, but these men had sworn fealty to Portia. The power Portia bestowed upon Keen was for show. And they all knew it.

Portia's eyes flared as Keen stopped in front of her. "How dare you make me wait? Do you think this a joke?"

"My apologies. It isn't every day a man commits himself for life to another."

"Don't be foolishly sentimental. This is a political marriage that will bring you power. Or have you forgotten?"

"Power..." He let the word roll over his tongue. Funny— Keen felt powerless. All because he loved a Halven and was desperate to protect her.

"Yes, power, you ungrateful beast. Or do you plan to betray me? For I shall unleash the heavens upon you, should you try."

It was a curious threat, given Portia's recent actions. Murdering his people. Threatening the innocent. She honestly believed she had the ear of the angels?

No one had seen their forefathers in thousands of years, but none doubted the angels' eyes on them.

"I am here. Shall we proceed?" he said without answering her question directly.

Portia's eyes narrowed. But she must have decided his words were good enough, because she spun in her deep purple gown, the likes of which Keen hadn't seen worn by any royal, and swept into the salon. She had made good use of the royal seamstresses, shouting her power and wealth to the world by whatever means necessary.

Keen proceeded to follow her, until Radnor held up a hand.

"A moment." Radnor's voice was firm. He waited for Portia to continue on before he said, "The queen is anxious for this union. But are you?"

"I do what I must to protect my people."

Radnor seemed to take him in. "Which people? Fae? Or is there a beautiful Halven you consider your own?"

The older man had surprised him, but Keen kept his expression blank. "I am protecting the innocent."

"I see. You must mean *all* the innocent."

Keen nodded.

"I do not disapprove. I simply wish to confirm you will not harm one of my daughters in your attempt to protect the other. Illa is my Fae-born child, but I consider Reese no less mine. I believe your—*sentiments*—fall with my Halven child. You've been placed in quite the predicament. But hear me now—should you harm either of my daughters, I will destroy you." Radnor slapped him on the back. "Best wishes."

With that, he walked inside the salon after Portia.

Keen took a moment to compose himself. He didn't fear Radnor. If Keen harmed Illa or Reese, he'd welcome death. But Reese's father was correct. Keen felt nothing but brotherly affection for Illa. His feelings for Reese were another thing entirely. She had him tied up in knots and desperate for her.

Instead of attempting to figure out how he'd get through this, he simply moved his legs forward in long strides and didn't think. He was a warrior. He acted.

To protect the greater good—no matter the cost.

THIRTY-TWO

Camille portaled them to New Kingdom palace, the end of the portal emptying into a small room off to the side of the ceremony. Maybe *small* was misleading. It only appeared small—because of the hundreds of soldiers Camille had brought over previously, who were all lined up and waiting.

Reese's group climbed to their feet and she caught sight of half a dozen guards slumped to the side.

"Dead?" she whispered to Elena, her nerves picking up.

This was real. This was happening.

Elena shook her head. "Unconscious. One of our magic wielders knocked them out first thing. Should last a few more minutes. Enough time for us to squeeze inside the salon where the ceremony took place. There's a reception going on in there now. That's where we'll find Portia."

Reese drew in a breath and nodded briskly. They had a job to do. Nothing more. She wouldn't think about the marriage that had just taken place.

Her stomach dipped and she pressed her arm to it, holding back the pain.

Everyone in the room touched the shoulder of the man or woman beside them, wasting no time. Then Derek Blended the army, making them invisible to the outside eye. More of their soldiers hid behind the palace walls, prepared to fight.

They slipped single file through a side door, careful to remain along the walls. Most of the guests stood in the center of the room on either side of an aisle. The antechamber where the portal had tossed them was large, but this room could hold a small airplane with space to spare. And it looked nothing like a church.

Very little furniture was inside the room, and the floors were bare except for a massive rug underfoot. Instead of a pulpit, a throne stood at the head, where Portia was regally seated. There were no religious symbols that Reese could see, only a twenty-foot statue of an insanely handsome angel and a child at his knee behind Portia.

The figure was made of marble, the strong lines of the angel's face more beautiful than any masterpiece. Broad shoulders, arms bulging with muscles, his hand gently resting on the child's head. He had full lips made for sin, lightly hollowed cheeks, and strong cheekbones that swept up into a broad, refined forehead as he gazed down at those in the room.

If that statue was an accurate representation of the angels, no wonder Fae were so beautiful.

Reese glanced back at Portia, still feeling the weight of the angel's stare, though it was nothing but marble. Even the pretty child at the angel's feet felt real. But as Reese took in Portia's expression and emotions, all thoughts of the statue faded. Because Portia was pissed.

What had happened?

Portia wore a deep purple gown, her eyes inflamed—

which seemed odd, since she'd gotten what she wanted. She held the power in New Kingdom, and if she had her way, she'd soon hold the power in Old Kingdom too, now that Illa and Keen were married.

Reese swallowed. There was nothing she could do about the marriage. It was done. But she could prevent Portia from taking control over anyone else's lives.

The soldiers around her carefully drew arms while maintaining contact with one another. Silently, invisibly—thanks to Derek's ability to Blend them—they prepared for battle. And that was when Reese caught sight of her sister across the room next to Hakon. Illa held her head high, and she was utterly beautiful in a pale gold gown with a beaded train and thin veil.

Reese cared about Illa—was coming to love the sister she'd never known—but in this moment she wanted to bum-rush the woman who'd married Keen.

Then Reese realized Keen was nowhere in sight.

Illa was alone.

And the queen was still pissed.

Reese glanced questioningly at Elena, who shook her head, her brow furrowed in confusion.

Portia slammed her fist on the armrest of the throne. "Enough! Seize him!"

Just then, people stirred and all heads turned toward the entrance of the chamber.

"No need." Keen sauntered inside, looking handsomer than any man should. He wore emerald court dress the precise color of his eyes.

Keen had only ever worn his soldier's uniform—and he already looked good enough to eat in that. In the courtly fitted pants and a tunic with shimmery embroidery at the wrists, the top stretching the breadth of his shoulders—he was tall, powerful, and so, so beautiful. Reese wondered for a split second why she'd ever thought he would want to be with someone so plain, because in this moment, Keen glimmered like the angels from whom he was descended.

And then her spine straightened. No man was better than she was—equal, certainly, but Reese was as good as the next person, and she deserved a guy who loved her wholly.

Keen was looking straight ahead at Illa, but the moment he passed Reese's large group, his perpetual insolent smile dropped a fraction. No one else seemed to notice, but Reese had.

He glanced around and held on the area where Derek stood with Elena and their soldiers, scanning briefly and discreetly until his gaze landed on Reese. That was when a frown pulled down his handsome mouth.

How did he know?

There were hundreds in the room. He could listen in on any number of thoughts, but not Reese's. Yet somehow, she'd swear he sensed her.

Or maybe he'd picked up on the thoughts of some of their soldiers? Keen couldn't read thoughts from those he didn't know, but unfortunately, he knew quite a few of their warriors, and none of them knew how to block Keen's ability the way Derek and Elena had learned to do.

Elena and the others had never told Keen of their plans to invade New Kingdom, though of course he'd suspected. Which was why he'd ordered her to not fight before he'd left Old Kingdom.

Keen was an Oldlander, unlike the rest of the guests inside the chamber. He had a mental ability, and thus, could detect Derek's disguise if he paid attention.

Apparently, he was paying attention. And listening.

Not good.

Keen had to protect Portia. And right now, he knew they were here, aiming to take control from the queen.

"He knows," Reese whispered out of habit. No one could hear their voices while Derek had them Blended.

"Are you sure? There are so many in the room. He can't possibly listen in on everyone's thoughts." Elena appeared doubtful, but there was enough nervousness mixed in that she must be worried. "How do you know?"

"I just do."

Elena leaned toward Derek and told him Reese's suspicions. A change of plans was made rapid-fire, and all the while Reese's gaze was fixed on Keen and Illa at the head of the room.

Keen brought his hands to Illa's face and held her pretty cheeks, staring into her eyes with such intensity that Reese had to look away, her heart breaking again.

It was over—should have never started to begin with. They were never meant to be.

Before Reese knew what she was doing, she dropped Elena's hand, the only thing keeping her Blended, and pulled out her sword.

~

She was here.

Even if Keen had not felt Reese near, he would have known something was up the moment he sensed a large army in Derek's signature Blended state. The disguise was good, particularly in the dim candlelight of the ceremony about to take place, but Keen saw it. The shimmer. The refraction of light that occurred when one was Blended. There had to be hundreds of them—soldiers likely preparing for battle. And once he picked up on a few of their thoughts, he knew for certain.

He'd heard of Derek's increased powers, but this was the first time he'd seen what the young Halven could do. No wonder Derek had gained the respect of so many in Old Kingdom. He was as powerful as his deceased father, Osulf Niall, but with a conscience and morals.

Keen feared they'd eventually attack, though Radnor had only hinted at such a possibility. Radnor's information was the reason Keen had sought out Reese before he'd returned to New Kingdom. He'd not wanted her involved in anything like this. Didn't want her hurt.

Of course she didn't listen.

Keen sighed and glanced at Portia, who'd just waved the officiant of the ceremony forward.

He turned to Illa and cradled her head between his hands, the butterfly-thin fabric of her veil pulling taut over her face.

He couldn't speak. Couldn't warn her. And his ability only went in one direction. He could listen to another's thoughts, but not the other way around. But Illa and Keen had known each other a long time. He knew of her abilities and she knew of his. He tried to speak with his eyes, and he listened in on her thoughts.

What's wrong? he heard her say inside her mind. Her eyes flickered nervously to Portia.

Keen glanced at the back wall—and the hundreds of Blended Oldlander soldiers tucked in every leftover space of the room.

Illa followed his gaze. She was Oldlander, like Keen, and more adept at detecting their magic than Newlanders.

Just as he'd hoped, she paused on the Blended Fae, and her eyebrows rose. *They are here?*

His mouth firmed in subtle assent.

I understand your promise to the queen, but I made no such oath. I wish to help my sister and her friends.

Keen nodded, indicating he would not hold her back.

Illa's face hardened and she took a careful step toward the guard nearest her. Before she could make another move, a war cry sounded.

And Keen recognized that voice.

He turned abruptly to find Reese visible and on her own, her sword drawn. And she was furious.

Out of all the soldiers and hardened warriors, his little Halven had started the fight. She was larger than life. She *was* life.

Illa twisted to the side and grabbed the wrist of the soldier nearest her, who was pulling out his sword.

The man looked dazed, and stabbed the guard next to him—instead of the insurgents made up of Fae and Halven warriors now visible and attacking the New Kingdom guards.

Illa's power was most fascinating. She had the ability to redirect a person's actions with one touch. Instead of attacking an Oldlander invader, the guard had attacked one of his own men.

Keen still couldn't fight alongside Reese and her friends, but he made it his mission to protect Illa while she disoriented the soldiers around her. Portia was protected by dozens of guards and wasn't in danger. At the moment, he needn't be at her side.

And Keen kept his eye on Reese.

Reese had grown stronger, her agility and strength ten times what it had been when he'd trained her in New Kingdom. At least the Ancient Allon had given her that. It wasn't enough to completely keep her safe, but it offered him hope she would live long enough for him to reach her.

As Keen and Illa made their way toward Derek, Elena, and Reese, it appeared a Newlander had switched sides: Ulric was making his way to Illa, cutting a swath through soldiers in his path.

Radnor watched the proceedings for a moment, then he too fought on the side of his daughters. He had made an agreement with Portia to help unite the two kingdoms, but that was when Keen and Illa were to marry.

They were not married, and they never would be.

To marry Illa would be to betray the one he loved. And Keen would never betray Reese, no matter what he'd agreed to with Portia. He didn't know when he'd made the decision, but it felt like it had been there all along. He'd simply needed to acknowledge it.

THIRTY-THREE

Reese lunged for the guard in front of her, stabbed him in the gut, and used the weight of her sword as a counterbalance to give him a neck-breaking roundhouse kick to the head.

And she didn't stop there. She tore through the guards, one after another—stabbing, kicking, and dodging past Portia's defenses as she made her way to the throne where Portia stood looking about smugly.

The woman thought she had things under control? Well, think again.

Portia was the reason for all of this—the reason Elena had been forced to save Fae from the only virus ever to affect their kind. The reason Reese had met Keen in the first place. If not for Portia, Reese wouldn't have fallen in love with him. She wouldn't have had her heart shredded into a million pieces that even her powerful best friend couldn't fix.

Keen had held Illa's face tenderly, the candlelight highlighting their beauty, just as he'd held Reese's when he'd pleaded for her to stay out of any battles. Only this time, he'd cradled the face of his wife.

Reese knew how things would be once she'd arrived. Knew Keen would be lost to her forever, but she hadn't expected to see such tenderness from her stoic Fae toward another. And it tore her apart.

Someone would pay for all she'd lost, and for what so many others had suffered. And that person was Portia.

The man in front of Reese pulled out a dirk from behind his back as she fought off the sword in his other hand. With a flick of his wrist, he slashed her thigh.

Her hand slipped on the pommel of her sword, but only for a split second. She balanced on her good leg and used the power of her injured leg to strike the Fae in the chest, knocking him into other fighters.

Reese's stomach roiled as she caught sight of the blood gushing down her pants.

Her attacker scrambled to regain his footing. But even as she limped away, her leg was healing, much like a full-blooded Fae.

She made it past more soldiers and toward Portia, her leg completely functional again, her determination even stronger. Portia stood at the front, focused on the battle, arms relaxed at her sides. Her emotions confirmed her confidence, and for a moment, Reese worried.

Portia had to have known Derek would attack again, with Old Kingdom at risk after the marriage. But had she prepared for them to return this quickly? They'd thought they would catch her off guard, but now Reese wondered. There hadn't been time for Portia to release the rumored second virus, had there? What if she'd been more prepared than they believed?

Camille flashed to a spot near Hakon, and stabbed a guard about to behead him.

Reese's heart dropped and she gripped her sword. She hadn't formally acknowledged Hakon as her father, but he was. He hadn't raised her, but he cared about her. He'd shown it when Reese nearly died from the Ancient Allon—and before, if she thought about it.

The next place Camille sprang up was across the room, where she knocked the skulls of two guards together. She was so fast that Reese could hardly keep track of her.

Lives could be lost. *Would* be lost. She needed to keep a clear head.

Speaking of heads, a fireball flew past her, singeing the tips of her golden hair and landing square in the chest of a guard on her right...with a pickax a foot from her face.

The Fae with the pickax crumpled to the ground. Not dead, but injured enough that he wouldn't be up for a few precious seconds. Enough time for Reese to keep moving.

Elena flashed her a smile and held up her thumb, before aiming a null bomb at the back of the room where a horde of Newlander soldiers had filed in. Between the water, fire, and other earth magic Newlanders wielded, they'd take the damn palace down if they weren't careful.

A loud *boom* sounded, and then a slippery-looking, bubble-like film seeped over the guards Elena had targeted. They waved their hands—attempting to use magic?—and swiped at the clear film covering them. When their magic didn't work, they pulled out swords and knives and attacked Elena's guards with brute force.

Reese made it a few more feet, then dodged the sword of a seven-foot-plus Fae guard—and elbowed him in the family jewels.

Yep, that was how it was going to be. She'd fight dirty if

she needed to. Being shorter than the rest had its advantages.

The man sank to the floor, groaning, and Reese hopped over him, making steady progress toward the front.

Portia no longer looked so smug, and Reese was closer to Illa now, along with Keen.

She didn't want to look at him, but she couldn't help it. And when she did, he was scowling.

Of course.

His gaze dropped to her leg. It had completely healed, but it was still covered in blood.

He had asked her not to fight, but screw that. He had no say in what she did. She was her own woman. A warrior, just like the rest of them. In her heart, she'd always been one, and now she was in truth. She loved her parents back home, but she was also Hakon's daughter.

One of Derek's soldiers crept up behind Illa's back. Keen broke the Fae's neck before he could do any harm to Reese's sister. Not all of the men they'd arrived with understood the complexity of Hakon and Illa's roles, even though they were fighting on the same side.

Keen continued to block anyone who got near Illa, but he also seemed to keep tabs on Reese as well.

She sighed. He needed to stop that. Things were confusing enough as it was.

Reese stabbed the Newlander next to her, who thought it would be fun to launch an electric bolt her way. The sparks in his hands died and blood bubbled from his lips. Okay, so she might have stabbed him in the lungs. Still, the guy would recover, but not before she swept past him and made it to Hakon.

Her father nodded at her, and continued fighting the Newlanders as he worked his way toward Derek's men at the back of the room. But Reese was on a mission. And so, it seemed, was Elena. They were both making their way toward Portia, along with a contingent of Derek's best men and several Newlander renegades who'd fought alongside Theda before Portia had her killed.

Portia wouldn't get away with it. Not murdering Elena's mother, nor so many Fae. Reese would spend her last breath to make sure of it.

Just then, a group of men and a few women in what looked like peasant garb cleared a swath of attacking soldiers from Reese's path, touching them and dropping Portia's military to their knees with what Reese assumed were mental powers.

These people had to be the Sunlanders Deirdre had convinced to fight. Their working-class dress, the fact that Reese hadn't seen them at the Old Kingdom castle with the rest of the mentalists, and Deirdre fighting beside them were the top indicators. Sunlanders were historically passive, but after Portia had unleashed the disease in Tirnan and murdered half their population, they must have decided battle had its place in their world.

"Sister."

Reese spun and caught sight of Illa. Her sister reached back and touched the arm of a Fae about to grab her. The Fae's eyes went blank and then he spun around and grabbed his comrade instead, who seemed none too pleased with the headlock the man had him in.

"You need to go to Derek and the others," Reese said. "Hakon is making his way there too."

Instead of answering, Illa ducked, touched the ankle of a Fae attacking Keen, and stood as the Fae stabbed himself instead. "You must retreat as well. There are better fighters than the two of us."

"Nope," Reese said, and clubbed a guard in the back of the head with the butt of one of her larger knives.

He spun on her angrily, but Reese kicked the side of his knee, breaking it and knocking him into other fighters.

"Sister, you are good," Illa said. "As good as the average soldier, but these men are experts trained to fight for the crown. They will not back down. Do you understand what I'm saying?"

Reese didn't bother glancing over. She was too busy clashing swords with a seven-foot guard with short white-blond hair who had decided she needed to die, given the ferocity sweeping off him. She feinted to the right, then kicked him in the chest, hearing the crunch of ribs snapping, before a different white-blond Fae moved up behind the guy and broke his neck.

Keen's eyes blazed at Reese over the body that now lay on the ground, slowly writhing as his neck healed. "Take Illa and leave. I've already ordered Ulric to get you out of here."

She swung her sword down and stabbed the guard on the ground in the foot. His broken neck was healing too quickly, and she had a few choice words to give to the arrogant Fae in front of her. "Illa can leave. I'm staying and fighting."

Keen plunged his sword back and stabbed someone through the stomach—rather brutally, twisting it with a nasty crunch. He hadn't even looked to see who it was, but Keen read minds, so...

"I do not have time to sit and argue with you about this. It is not up for discussion."

"Oh good, because I have Fae ass to kick. Excuse me." She turned to make her way to Portia, who was so close...

Just a half a dozen feet more and Reese would be within arm's reach.

But Keen moved in front of her, his large chest blocking her and forcing her to take a step back. "Do not make me throw you over my shoulder."

Okay, now that just pissed her off. He would totally make good on that promise, and she couldn't attack Keen the way she did these other assholes. As big a bossypants as he was, she didn't actually want to *hurt* him.

Which made no sense. He deserved to feel pain. Her chest burned like the fires of hell just from thinking of him married to her sister. "Get out of my way, Keen—" Reese said, and then she felt it.

Not simple hatred, or determination, but a magnified mix of the two that was so powerful it smacked her in the gut like a punch. And it was coming off Portia. Who was staring at Hakon.

Reese ducked around Keen's long legs—another privilege of being shorter than the rest—and raced toward her father.

Keen called after her, but she ignored him, focused on Hakon and whatever the hell Portia had planned. Reese scanned the area. And targeted one of Portia's guards moving steadily to her father. The guard had no weapons—nothing that Reese could detect, anyway. But death—death was what he would inflict. Reese sensed the sour, dire finality of it in his body language and the flashes of feeling he gave off.

The guard was two feet away from Hakon—within striking distance. Reese didn't know what he would do, but she wasn't going to get there in time. She had been headed toward Portia, not her father, who was closer to Derek.

She glanced back. Derek and the others were fighting

for their lives. Even if they could hear her above the din of battle, they wouldn't be able to do anything.

The man reached for Hakon, and his hands were glowing...

Illa can confuse people—make them do the opposite of what they intend...

Reese closed her eyes and focused on the Fae's emotions. She thought of happiness, life...serenity.

Seconds later, she blinked, fearing the worst.

But Hakon was still there, angling his large shoulders into the gut of a younger Fae who couldn't take the bulk of the older man. The two of them toppled to the ground. And Portia's Fae guard—the one with the glowing hands—simply stood nearby, looking confused, shoulders tucked close as though he didn't want to move. Or touch. Or harm.

And he didn't. Reese could read it in his emotions.

Had she done that?

She glanced around the room and targeted a Fae attacking Elena. Elena seemed to have the upper hand with the electric shocks she was sending the guy, but he wouldn't quit going after her, no matter how many times she struck him.

Reese sent emotions of serenity and happiness his way, just as she had the man attacking her father, and the guard stepped back, brow furrowing. He backed against the wall, looking as though he wanted to escape.

Holy shit. If she could change a Fae's emotions, she could change the course of the battle.

Already there were bodies lining the ground, no longer moving. Most were injured, but some had died, and there would be more death to come. But if she could make everyone calm?

Simply making everyone happy wouldn't do it, because

some of these men were bloodthirsty. They got off on the power of taking a life. No—it had to be kindness, contentment, and love that she spread.

Reese closed her eyes, and this time she thought of her love for her friends, her love for Keen, the contentment of finding her place in the world, and projected the emotions into the room. She focusing it on each point at which she sensed anger, a thirst for blood or violence, and greed.

Bit by bit, a change came over the room, with the exception of one target. But his emotions were worry and determination, not hate.

Reese opened her eyes and saw Keen staring at her. He looked around at the men who'd slowly stopped fighting.

With their two abilities blocking one another, Keen couldn't listen in on her thoughts, and she could never read his emotions. It made sense he wouldn't be affected by her new power.

But when Reese looked up at Portia, she too seemed unaffected. And Portia was staring straight at Reese with all the hatred and anger her soldiers now lacked.

Portia stepped forward and grabbed a gun from the holster of the closest Oldlander guard—and shot it straight at Reese.

A roar erupted from Keen.

The blast echoed in Reese's ears, and she grabbed her chest, wiping feverishly at the film covering her. Not blood. Portia had stolen a null gun, eliminating Reese's powers and her ability to calm the room.

Just as quickly as the anger had disappeared, it seemed to fill the space again. Fighting broke out like before, except this time, Reese found herself surrounded by guards. They lifted her, kicking and screaming, and took her toward Portia.

Keen was battling four men at once—his own men attempting to hold him back from reaching her.

Portia glanced at one of her head guards. "Bring in the rest of the soldiers. The ones infected with the modified disease. Show these"—her expression turned to one of disgust—"poor excuses for warriors what it means to have absolute power."

Her gaze landed on Reese, still struggling in the arms of Portia's men. "And you. I tolerated your filthy presence, but I see diplomacy is overrated." She looked over Reese's head, and Reese turned too. Keen had broken away from the guards and stood behind her, staring at the queen.

"Kill her, Keen Albrecht."

CHAPTER

THIRTY-FOUR

Reese wasn't sure how it happened. One moment she was being held by several of Portia's guards, the order for her to be killed ringing in her ears, and the next minute, she witnessed something she believed impossible.

Keen lunged forward and stabbed Portia through the chest.

Portia looked down in confusion, the men around her nearly ripping Keen's arms out of his sockets as they detained him, and then Portia laughed. She bent over, holding the gaping wound pouring blood down her amethyst gown, and laughed manically.

She came up for air seconds later and wiped tears from her eyes. "You broke your oath to protect me, you fool." The rush of blood from her wound had already slowed. "And your attack was sloppy—my heart is intact—though I suppose that's because you're forbidden to harm me. I'm surprised you managed to get this close." She tsked. "Didn't you know your oath would protect me, even if you didn't?

You would never have hit my heart, no matter how precise your attack. And now you will die for it."

Keen groaned and wrenched his arms from the guards. He clamped his hands on either side of his head and sank to the ground.

"Keen!" Reese fought to break free from the guards holding her. "What's happening?"

The nasty white-blond Fae who'd tried to kill her earlier tightened his grip. "Death, you filthy Halven. Death comes to those who break an oath."

"But he did it for me! He can't die."

The guard grabbed her chin and twisted her face toward him. "And what a waste it was."

She jerked away and stared after Keen. He was writhing, his pale skin ashen.

Reese began yanking and pulling with all her strength, her mind suddenly taking in everyone's emotions, unable to control her own, let alone block the others. Anger, pain, frustration, exuberance—they came from all directions and she couldn't block any of it. Not while her emotions swung out of control.

The guard held her tightly and lowered his mouth toward her ear. "He dies, and then you will. Slowly. Painfully—"

Before he'd finished his sentence, Reese swung her head back and cracked her skull into his nose.

Keen wouldn't die. *He wouldn't.* She wouldn't allow it.

The Fae behind her grunted, and she didn't wait for him to react. She slammed the heel of her booted foot into his shin. His grip finally faltered, but when he didn't let go of her completely, she slammed her arm back and hit him where it hurt. Again, not the most sporting move, but effective.

The blond Fae coughed and dropped his arms from around her immediately. The others nearby were too busy watching Keen die a slow and painful death—that no one ever died from because they never broke their oaths—to care that she'd fought her way free.

Reese rushed through the crowd and knelt beside Keen. "How do I make it stop?"

"Can't," he said.

One word? That was all she got from the guy who loved to tell her what to do whether she wanted to hear it or not?

"Why did you do it?" she screamed as tears streamed down her face.

Sweat beaded on his brow, blood dripping from his ears and nose. Reese lay over him, pressing her ear to his still beating heart. She didn't care that he was married to another.

He was *her* love.

He'd given his life for *her*.

In that moment, her emotions overwhelmed her—*hers*, no one else's. Sadness, fear, and love...so much love.

Her flesh tingled, her heartbeat hammering. An energy filled her until all that emotion burst in an invisible wave and flooded the room, the effects of the null gun having worn off.

While the Fae around her stood in a stupor born of Reese's emotions, she went straight for Portia, taking out a knife and aiming it at the older woman's heart.

Reese had never killed before. But she wanted to right now.

Portia's eyes narrowed. She was the only Fae not affected by Reese's ability. She allowed Reese to get closer, her emotions eerily calm. But Reese wasn't worried about that.

She should have been.

Reese thrust her arm forward, aiming for Portia's heart —and hit a wall.

Portia smiled from two feet to the right, no longer standing in front anymore. "A glamour. You really should educate yourself on the powers of your betters." Portia knocked the knife from Reese's hand, and pulled out her own, dragging Reese to her chest and placing the knife at Reese's throat.

"Let him go," Reese said. "Don't let him die because of me. He's the best warrior you have."

Portia laughed. "A fool in love with a fool. I have no use for him. And I have no control over the angel's oath. None of us do. It's why we are so careful not to lie. And now he's sacrificed himself for nothing. Pity."

The knife cut into Reese's throat and her eyes searched for Keen. His head was drawn back, anguish contorting his handsome features. But he saw her in Portia's arms, and that seemed to have him writhing on the ground even more.

Keen was dying. And Reese would too.

This wasn't how it was supposed to end.

And then all sound ceased.

A light flashed, blinding. The air in the room rushed out in what felt like a vacuum, and Reese choked, unable to breathe. When she was able to catch her breath again, the room looked normal, except for the large shadow of a tall Fae leaning over Keen.

The shadow was just that, all dark translucence, with a bright yellow glow that silhouetted its masculine figure.

He leaned down and touched Keen's head with one finger.

Keen coughed and rolled to his side, panting and shaking. He looked up at the figure, then back at Reese, his focus clearer.

Reese didn't know what was going on, but Portia tightened her grip.

"No," Portia gasped. "He broke his oath." Her voice quivered as rivulets of fear rolled off her.

Reese reached for the knife, but Portia was digging it into the base of her throat. Blood dripped onto Reese's hand.

Keen climbed to his feet, his eyes on Reese as he followed the shadow toward Portia.

Let the Halven go, child, the shadow said. Only the voice wasn't out loud. It was inside Reese's head.

It seemed Portia had heard it too. She shook. "He broke his oath."

But the Halven did not.

"She is nothing. She is weak, an abomination. I do our forefathers a service by eliminating her."

You would kill her out of pride, not justice. The Halven you hold is of my blood, and you will release her. Now.

Reese actually heard Portia swallow, but she didn't let Reese go.

And then Portia had no choice, because one minute Reese was locked against Portia's chest, barely able to breathe, with a deep gash in her neck, and the next minute she was alone.

The dark figure held Portia suspended without touching her. *The only one who has disobeyed the rules is you, my child. Your punishment is to leave this land forever.*

And then Portia and the glowing shadow were gone.

And Keen was pulling Reese into his arms.

Everybody in the room, every face, appeared stunned.

"What just happened?" she mumbled into his strong

chest, her arms locking around his waist. She breathed in his scent—the familiar cedar with a touch of metal from the knives and sword he hid in his clothes. He was alive.

Keen swept a large hand over her head, burrowing his face into her hair.

"The angels returned."

CHAPTER

THIRTY-FIVE

Reese leaned back, still wrapped in Keen's arms, and looked up. "I thought the angels weren't ever coming back."

"They weren't. Their arrival after millennia of absence was most strange, to say the least."

She stared off in the distance, remembering. "On the emotions scale, Portia was off-the-chart evil when I compare her to everyone else. Do you think that had anything to do with it?"

"Possibly." He brushed his thumb along her jaw.

"You were willing to give your life for me." She took a shaky breath. "I couldn't sense your emotions—I still can't—but I'm willing to bet they were the complete opposite of Portia's. The angel might have saved you because your heart was pure and hers wasn't."

"The angel didn't simply save me—he saved you and called you his descendant. If your theory is true, he believed you pure, half-blood or not. And he made a point of letting everyone present know you are special to him, which makes our prejudice toward Halven all the more disconcerting."

He shifted her to his side and looked around at the stunned faces of his countrymen. "Elena Rosales, daughter of Theodora Joelle Rainer Rosales, rules this land now. You will bow to your queen."

Elena and Derek's soldiers did so at once, and slowly the Newlander guards did as well.

Just like that, New Kingdom had switched hands. Fae didn't mess around. When one ruler left, another moved in.

And then Keen did the strangest thing of all.

He grabbed her hand. "Where is the officiant? He will marry us."

Keen was dragging her toward the front of the room where Portia had stood upon the dais, and Reese's footsteps froze. "You married *Illa*, remember?"

He looked down at her, his expression soft. "I did not. I...*delayed* the ceremony, realizing I'd rather betray my kind than betray you."

"You're not married?"

He didn't answer the question, merely twisted his mouth and continued talking. "Though living with you will be problematic, as you seem to defy all of my commands—"

"Because your commands suck," she said, tears of happiness filling her eyes.

"But I cannot live without you, and it seems no other will do. We will marry. Besides, you could be carrying my child."

Reese blinked. "Okay, first of all, I'm not pregnant. I'm on the Pill."

"The pill?"

"Birth control. So I can't get pregnant."

A dark cloud formed behind Keen's emerald eyes, turning them nearly black. "Absolutely not. You will stop taking this pill. Once we marry—"

"Hold up there, buddy. Who says we're getting married? I don't remember you asking."

He sighed and dropped to one knee.

He was *serious*? And Fae proposed on one knee like humans?

Keen grabbed her hand and kissed the tips of her fingers with such tenderness—and blatant sexuality—that the backs of her knees tingled. "Reese Fisher of the Radnors, will you marry me?"

Her eyes grew wide. This handsome, powerful Fae—with a nasty attitude when he didn't get his way—was asking her to marry him?

He could marry a princess. If Derek's father hadn't murdered Keen's family and taken over Old Kingdom all those years ago, Keen would be a prince or a king. He was beautiful, passionate, stubborn—and he was hers. He wasn't taking her for granted, or underestimating her. He was proposing marriage.

"Do you love me?"

His gaze didn't waver. "I love you. I will treat you as my queen and protect you and our children."

Children.

He was serious about this kid thing. The guy who at one point didn't want to touch her for fear she'd get pregnant from the brush of his arm and create one more Halven in the world?

"I love you, you stubborn Fae, but I can't marry you right now." This time his face colored in frustration. "I'm *eighteen*. I have school to finish. You've never even met my parents."

"I already know your father, and I asked his permission to marry you."

"My...? You mean, Hakon? When did you have time to ask him?"

He stood and grabbed both of her hands. "When I risked my life for yours and hauled you to my side. I exchanged a look with Hakon. He nodded his agreement, and expressed it mentally."

She glanced over at Hakon, who seemed to be discussing something important with Derek. "How did he know what you wanted?"

Keen raised a brow. "It was obvious."

"That's how men in your land ask permission to marry someone's daughter?"

Keen shrugged. "More or less. Traditionally, we would have performed a mock sword fight, in which he would have backed down and acceded, but there wasn't time for that."

"That's some...*tradition* you have there." She glanced around, trying to take it all in. People were clearing out the wounded and attempting to put the room back to rights, Elena and Derek shouting commands.

Keen's shoulders tensed. "You said you cannot marry me now, but I have your father's permission. When shall we marry?"

Now he was persistent? So much pushback and now he couldn't have her soon enough? Well, he'd have to wait. "In a few years."

He pulled her flush against his body and lifted her into his arms until they were nose to nose. "I do not wish to wait a few years to be...intimate with you."

She arched her brow, a smile tugging at her lips. "You didn't wait the other night."

His mouth drew into a hard line. "Exactly. I can't wait

when you are near. It is impossible. You could conceive and we wouldn't be married."

She looked at him as though he were dense. "That is what the Pill is for, you Neanderthal. Don't you trust me to only be with you?"

"Of course. I would kill anyone who went near you."

Was he serious? Probably. "Exactly, not that you'd need to. I'm a faithful person. But in any case, we'll wait to get married until we're ready, and in the meantime we could practice *coupling,* as you like to refer to the act."

"Practice?"

She gave him a naughty grin. "Yes, *practice.*"

Keen's nostrils flared and he squeezed her tight, but not tight enough to hurt her. "I like this plan. We will begin now." He walked out of the room, passing soldiers who looked somewhat confused and scattered, and past Elena and Derek.

Elena looked up and saw them. She grinned at Reese and gave her a thumbs-up.

Just outside the door, Illa stood with Ulric. His mouth was on hers, his arms banded around her small waist, and their embrace was...passionate.

Keen turned down a separate corridor and continued walking.

"Does that bother you?" Reese asked. "Seeing Illa with someone else?"

He glanced at her, but continued his determined pace. "Of course not. Ulric has wanted Illa. And she is your sister." He looked at her. "And I love you. Only you." His hand slipped down and squeezed her ass.

"Okay," she said a little breathlessly. "That works."

Keen took a set of stairs three at a time and walked several feet down a wide hallway. He opened one of the doors with the arm that wasn't holding her up, and slammed it closed with the heel of his boot.

This room was huge—a suite more than a room. And very luxurious. "Where are we?"

"Beortric's old room." He brought her into a separate bedroom with a four-poster bed and tossed her on it, swiftly following her down.

"Who's Beortric?"

"Theda's brother. Elena's uncle, but he died in the first wave of the disease." Keen's eyes grew shadowed. "He was a good man."

Reese cradled Keen's face with her hand, still unable to believe they were together. "What happened tonight? Because it seemed like I was close to never seeing you again." The memory of Keen writhing on the floor flooded her mind, tears springing to her eyes.

How had he done this to her? She was the commitment-phobe. And now she was in love and thinking about marriage?

She couldn't stand the idea of what she'd almost lost tonight. Keen would have died if... "Why did the angel come back? Has that ever happened before? An angel returning to help?"

"No. Never."

"What does it mean?"

"I don't know. But then, Portia used humans and Halven to attack our people. That's never been done before, and the angel said Portia had broken a rule. We've fought one another for millennia, but never have we involved the humans or your kind."

"Your rules are intense. Would you truly have died because you broke your oath to Portia?"

He kissed her lips gently, and traced a finger over the

small dimple in her chin. "Yes. And I would do it again. I will always protect you with my life."

Keen had never betrayed her. Had always put her first. It allowed her to love, and to trust.

"Damn you." Tears welled up once more, and she couldn't stop them this time. "I don't ever want to come close to losing you again, Keen Albrecht."

He grinned and kissed her chin. "I will do my utmost not to get killed while attempting to protect you." His mouth trailed from her chin down to her neck and her chest, where he'd loosened her top—by tearing it down the middle.

"See that you do," she said dazedly as he kissed her breasts, seemed to get frustrated with the scraps of cloth still covering her chest, and removed it altogether, along with her bra.

The next items to go were her boots, pants, and underwear.

He grinned, pleased with his work. "You will remain like this when we are alone."

She leaned on her elbows as she watched him reach back and pull his fancy wedding shirt over his head and down his arms. "Is that so?"

But as soon as he removed his boots and pants, she really couldn't dish out any more sass. She decided she liked his plan and would insist it worked both ways.

Keen climbed back over her, hovering, his arms braced and supporting most of his weight.

Reese reached down and grabbed the part of him that was standing tall and reaching for her. "Have I mentioned how much I love your body?"

"You called it too big," he said distractedly, as he thumbed her nipples and pressed his length into her hand.

Her eyes rolled into the back of her head. "I said it might not fit, but it does, so there's nothing to discuss." She squeezed the base of him and ran her hand up and circled the top with her thumb.

He let out a slow breath, as though attempting to remain in control. "And the rest?"

"The rest is very pretty too. When no words are coming out of your mouth."

"You love my mouth." And he demonstrated how much she loved his mouth on her breast.

"You're right," she said as his lips trailed a path to her belly. "I do love your mouth."

He looked up mischievously, and then his head dropped lower.

She glanced down, suddenly wondering about something. "How is it that you guys have all these rules about sex for furthering the species, but oral sex, which produces no output, is just fine? You sure some angel isn't going to catch us? You're not going to go up in flames for being naughty like this, are you?"

He grinned and licked her, and she moaned. He lifted his mouth briefly, and she glanced down. "No...but you will."

And he was right.

THE NEXT MORNING Reese was tucked against Keen's large frame. Large and small, yet somehow they fit together perfectly.

She looked over her shoulder to find him gazing in the direction of the bedroom window, his brows drawn. "Everything okay?"

His eyes swept over her face and he smiled. "Yes. For once."

Keen had been a soldier, committed to protecting Fae his entire life. Which was not to say that he hadn't also found time for pleasure, if the magic he'd worked with his tongue last night and his hands this morning were any indication. And she really didn't want to think about how he'd become an expert on the female body. The point was, he'd never had anything of his own. No family. Military friends, sure. But he'd asked her to be his wife last night. He was the only man in her life who'd given without expecting anything in return—the only man who'd put her first.

She was his and he was hers.

She rolled over and pressed her cheek to his chest. "What do we do now? Will the kingdom really accept Elena as their ruler?"

"Yes, however begrudgingly, or I would have been down there last night with them."

"You've been reading their minds? I always forget you can do that. Maybe because you can't read mine." She gave him a saucy grin. Finally, something she had over him.

He ran his hand over her bare hip. "I believe I can read your mind right now."

Her breathing sped up and her lips parted. Damn him. He could when he did things like that. "Fine, but only under sexual duress." He moved to lift his hand, and she covered it with her own, forcing him to keep it right where it was.

"So you've been keeping track of what's going on? And everyone's accepted the change?"

"Absolutely not. They despise Halven."

She pulled back and covered her breasts with the sheet. He glared down at her hand and attempted to pry the sheet free. "How can they still hate us? We've saved their lives. Twice!"

Giving up on the sheet in her death grip, he sighed. "They accept Elena's actions. They do not accept Elena—"

"But—"

"As Halven. However," he continued, cutting off what was about to be an epic rant on Fae prejudice, "they are coming around."

"Really?"

"No. But they have no choice. Elena is a direct descendant of the rightful ruler, and one of the closest links to our angelic forefathers, with or without her human father. It is why her powers are so strong and why a team of Fae followed her before she'd ever come into her powers. No one can argue she belongs in the kingdom. As for being their ruler? That is under debate. You can depend on an attack on her authority. She'll need to be guarded."

Reese swung her legs over the side of the bed, taking the sheet with her. "Why didn't you say so? We need to get down there. We need to help her keep things under control."

Keen looked at her body, covered by the sheer sheet. "I suppose. Though I prefer to continue *practicing*."

She smacked the Frisbee-sized hand that had reached out to grab her. "We can *practice* later. What happened to the Fae warrior who puts nothing ahead of duty?"

His eyes heavy-lidded, he said, "He fell in love with a tiny human."

Her stomach did a backflip and her heart worked some acrobatics of its own. He was lethal when he put his mind to seduction. "Fine. A quickie. And then we get our asses down there."

Reese went to hop back on the bed, but Keen had

already wrapped his hands around her waist and was lifting her on top of him.

He kissed her, and she could feel him growing. "Didn't we take care of that a few minutes ago?" She wasn't serious. She could make love to him all day if he didn't have a kingdom to manage...and if she didn't have school and a life.

"The Fae have unending stamina," he said, kissing her neck and pulling her up so that he could reach her breasts.

She stared at the top of his head, which she could see from this vantage point. "For real? Always?"

He buried his face in her breasts, and she rolled her eyes. *Men.* "If we want," came his muffled reply.

She inched back down and reached for him. Sure enough, his body was primed and ready.

Impressive.

And just to emphasize that point, Keen rolled her beneath him. "The question is whether or not you can keep up."

That was a challenge if ever she heard one. "Oh, I can keep up." She tried to push him to the side so she could straddle him, but the man wouldn't move. Finally, he figured out what she wanted and rolled onto his back.

Reese climbed on top of him, enjoying her power position. He placed his hands on her hips and then slid them up toward her breasts, a lazy smile on his face. "Test me all you like. I will not fail."

"I'm counting on it."

THIRTY-SIX

Over the next two days, Elena, Derek, Keen, Reese, and the rest of the soldiers and friends supporting them put New Kingdom back in order.

Maybe *order* was a bit optimistic.

Ulric had been forced to imprison a dozen guards, who'd staged a small coup against Elena's authority, and Elena had fought off an assassin with a lightning bolt. Keen and Derek had fought off another dozen idiots who'd thought they could get rid of Elena, but for the most part, the kingdom was getting used to her as their ruler. Particularly after she opened the New Kingdom guard and allowed in several townsmen who'd previously been relegated to farming duty.

Elena had also given several high-ranking guards and courtiers positions within her military elite and advisory committee, and she'd named Ulric her master of the guard, replacing Keen.

Reese had known her sister loved Ulric—she could read

Illa's emotions—but she didn't know how quickly Illa would act on those feelings.

Ulric and Illa were married the day after the attack. Wham, bam, thank you, ma'am. For immortals, they sure made lasting decisions quickly.

Illa and Ulric were holding down the fort in New Kingdom now that the immediate threats had been defused. People were somewhat mollified by town brethren in new guard positions and others filling court ranks, so Derek and Elena took that opportunity to return to Old Kingdom, and Reese and Keen joined them.

In the end, Keen had agreed to rule Old Kingdom as long as he had the majority vote among court Fae, but Radnor didn't think that would be a problem.

"You will live here with me," Keen said as they made their way through the Old Kingdom castle to a bedroom they'd share for the night. Camille had been busy—with what, no one knew—so Derek, Elena, Radnor, Deirdre, Reese, and Keen had traveled the old-fashioned way. By foot.

Traveling on foot wasn't as painful as it would have been before Reese's Ancient Allon transformation, but still. They had electricity, yet no cars? Fae strength made it so that running was literally faster than riding a horse and cart, the way the farmers got around, but this was taking the scenic route too literally.

"That won't work," she said, as he carried her pretty gowns and her new training uniforms over his large shoulder, just as he'd done all those miles to the castle. "I can't live here full time. I want to finish school. Which won't be easy. As it is, I'm going to have to wear flats so no one wonders about my awesome new height."

He rolled his eyes, which she promptly ignored, because her height *was* awesome even if no one here thought so.

"Don't even get me started on how I'm going to keep my physical appearance from my dad, though he's not the most observant when it comes to me; maybe it won't matter. My mom hooked up with Hakon, so it shouldn't be a surprise to her." Reese's mouth twisted. "The moment I get my hands on her, she's getting an earful."

"So visit your family. I don't understand the need to live there."

"I told you, *school*. I have to return to campus for exams. Plus, I'll need to be at Dawson part of the time to train in Emain."

Reese had written a letter to her professors, which had been hand-delivered by one of the Emain Fae. She'd explained that there'd been a family emergency, and asked to turn in her work remotely. Normally, that sort of thing would never have been acceptable long-term, but Keen had connections on campus and got her professors and counselors to agree to the terms. He was less enthusiastic about her training in Emain instead of Tirnan.

Reese didn't want to be away from him, but she saw a future in helping Emain bridge the gap between Halven and Fae.

He growled. "We should have married. Then you would have to do as I say."

Reese bent over and laughed. "You're kidding, right? Since when do I do what you say just because you say it?"

He reached back and swatted her ass.

"Ow! That hurt. Your hands are like meat cleavers."

"Pardon," he said abashedly, then added, "Would you like me to kiss it and make it feel better?"

She cut him a side-eye. "No, you naughty man."

He grinned.

She shook her head and made sure to wait outside while Keen unloaded their things in the room. No way was she going near a bed with him close. The guy had skills. She'd find herself on her back before she knew what hit her, with more *practice* in the works.

THEY DROPPED off their clothes in the large suite they'd been assigned, and Keen tried to tempt Reese into testing out the softness of the bed. Being the only levelheaded one these days—their friends were waiting for them—she'd prudently refused.

He couldn't get enough of her. And he never would.

Keen didn't know how he'd held out against Reese as long as he had. Fortunately, he'd come to his senses.

They made their way to the kitchen, where they met up with Derek, Elena, and Deirdre.

Kitchens were sacred among Fae, given the quantity of food his kind ate to keep up with their fast metabolisms. Theresa, the head cook, might come from humble beginnings, but she was just below the king in terms of importance to the castle. No one crossed her, or they found themselves going hungry.

"Just ain't right," she muttered. "You should be in the formal dining area, you should." Theresa harrumphed, but she set out a massive platter of cheese, meat, and bread.

Keen and a few others in the room visibly relaxed.

Theresa wasn't going to put up a fuss and refuse them food, which suited him, because eating sounded marvelous. Almost as wonderful as returning to the bedroom and seducing Reese. He'd rather be alone with his woman, but she was being difficult. As usual.

Keen made a dash for the food—until Derek cut him off and nearly knocked the platter to the floor.

Derek shrugged, stuffing half a loaf of bread in his mouth.

Reese shook her head as Keen nudged Derek out of the way with his elbow, a smile playing along her pretty lips. Travel to Old Kingdom had made everyone hungry. But Reese's beautiful mouth only reminded Keen of his other hunger...

She wouldn't marry him—*yet*. Wouldn't agree to live with him full time either, but he'd have his way. Though her plans about school and becoming an Emain soldier appeared serious.

A Halven Emain warrior? Had she lost her mind?

No, she was simply Reese. And he loved her, feisty though she was.

He was no fool. He'd give her anything she wanted, as long as it made her happy.

Keen sighed, circled Derek, who'd ignored the not-so-gentle elbow jab, and slid the tray to his side of the table, piling a slab of meat on a plate.

Derek frowned, but didn't complain. His plate was full. Before he could pile more food on he had to eat what was there, though it was rapidly disappearing.

Radnor entered the kitchen and stopped beside Reese. "Here you all are."

Keen dished food on a separate plate and brought it to Reese. She offered him a sweet smile, making his heart beat a little faster.

He had ignored the physical signs that indicated his feelings for Reese from the very beginning, determined to not fall in love with the beautiful Halven—or human, as he'd first thought. He'd never had a mother or sisters, but Illa had once told him that when he found the one he loved, he'd do things he never imagined just to be close to her. As far as Keen knew, Illa had never fallen in love, until she met Ulric in New Kingdom. He wasn't sure how she knew such things at an early age, but she was right. And little did Illa know that Keen would fall in love with her very own sister.

"I assume you will be staying with us, daughter?" Radnor said. "And for that matter, I prefer you change your last name. I've been thinking about it, and you are a Radnor. No more of this *Fisher* business."

Reese choked on her bite of food. "Excuse me? Fisher *is* my last name, given to me by the man who, you know, *raised me*. I won't take your name because you think it's a good idea. I barely know you."

Ignoring her last comment, he said, "That pompous buffoon your mother married? He never deserved her. Or you."

Reese's shoulders tensed.

Keen sighed, because he knew what was coming.

"That *man*," she said, "might not have set a good example for father of the year, but he was there—mostly— and he claimed me as *his*."

"I gave you your name, not your father."

Her brow furrowed. "What are you talking about?"

"I had your mother name you after my own mother, so that you would know you were mine. Would have given you my last name too, but your mother claimed some nonsense about appearances. She put up a fight about it. The woman gets tetchy when she wants her way. You had just been born and I didn't want her to become ill with all of the energy she was expending arguing with me. I gave in on the last name, but not the first. You were named after my mother, Rohese Radnor. Your mother changed the spelling to appear more human—again, not my idea," he said sulkily.

Reese swallowed hard. "You named me...after your mother?"

"Of course. You are my daughter. Would have raised you here if your mother hadn't put up another fuss about that too. I wanted her to leave that...well, your *father,* but she wouldn't. She worried about your life as a Halven in Tirnan. In the end, she was right. It wouldn't have been safe for you, or her. I wasn't thinking clearly. Fortunately, your mother was, but it meant I missed out on the early years of your life."

"You mean my entire life," Reese said dryly.

Radnor waved her off. "Those were but a few years. Many more to come. And this time, you are safe in our land. Relatively so," he amended.

She would be safe if Keen had to take down every Fae who believed her inferior. No one was better than his Reese.

Radnor was correct: their land was relatively peaceful now. Those infected with the new disease had been quarantined and quickly cured by Elena, and Marlon's secret lab inside the New Kingdom palace had been destroyed. Both kingdoms were on stable ground, with reasonable communication between the two, now that Keen led Old Kingdom and Elena ruled New Kingdom. That did not guarantee a truce, for there was much to negotiate that had little to do with whether Keen and Elena got along—his people were a prickly group. But for now, they were safe.

Radnor and Reese spoke softly in the corner, and Keen watched as Radnor reached out and touched Reese's shoulder. She blushed shyly, then smiled. Keen was pleased with their reunion. Anything that proved to Reese how special she was made him happy.

He sighed, remembering. He'd done the opposite when he'd first met Reese. He'd wanted her the instant he saw her, but he'd pushed those emotions down, blocked his feelings for her, making negative comments and taking actions that made her feel less than special. He'd never forgive himself for the way he'd treated her, but he'd also never stop proving to her how much she truly meant to him.

After a few minutes, Reese returned to his side, smiling as she looked out at the room. Radnor approached the scored wooden butcher's table around which they'd all hovered at one point or another, and took his turn at the food platter that had already been refilled three times. Reese slipped her hand into Keen's and he smiled down at her, tugging her closer to his side until her soft curves pressed up against him.

He felt at peace. For once. Utter and complete peace. He was where he was meant to be, with the one person he couldn't live without.

And then the air wavered in the middle of the room, and Keen's back stiffened. The hair on the back of his neck stood at attention, and his muscles tensed.

He set his plate to the side, and tugged Reese behind him.

Derek was in full view—the air wavering couldn't be him in his Blended state. Nothing but magic made air molecules refract in such a way.

"What is it?" Reese tried to peek around him, but he kept her behind his larger frame.

Before he could respond or sound out an alarm, something fell out of the air, crashing into metal pans stacked atop a table in the corner of the room.

Swords were rapidly drawn, daggers slipped from sheaths, Elena's hands held up as though she were about to use the elements...but it was only Camille tumbling in from one of her portals.

Camille scrambled to her feet, her eyes wide. The dark-haired Fae with the crystal blue eyes appeared fearful.

"They are here," she said.

Dear Reader,

I've been eager to write *Fates Entwined* ever since Reese and Keen popped up on my screen in *Fates Divided*. I hope you enjoyed their story! If you have a moment, please click the *Fates Entwined* link above and leave a review.

Continue the Halven Rising series with **Fates Fulfilled,** and discover what the Dark Fae have in store for Tirnan...

Cheers,
Jules

FATES FULFILLED

The Dark Prince has arrived.

The Dark Prince will stop at nothing to save his people—even if it means kidnapping the one woman with the power to destroy them all...

Garrin Branimir, Prince of Dark Kingdom, has been trapped in endless winter for centuries, along with his people. His only hope of saving them is to find the woman with the power to destroy the magical barriers imprisoning Dark Fae. With her by his side, he and his kinsmen will finally be free.

But Lex Meinrad isn't full Fae, and she wasn't raised in his land, content to obey her prince's every order. She refuses to do his bidding—no matter how intense the sparks between them.

Garrin must convince this impossibly stubborn woman to cooperate before his enemies bend her to their will. And, unlike him, *they'll choose force over seduction...*

Grab *Fates Fulfilled*!

ALSO BY J. BARNARD

HALVEN RISING SERIES

Fates Altered (Prequel)

Fates Divided (Book 1)

Fates Entwined (Book 2)

Fates Fulfilled (Book 3)

About the Author

J.Barnard is the fantasy pen name for USA Today Bestselling Author Jules Barnard. Library Journal calls her Halven Rising series "...an exciting new fantasy adventure." To find out more, visit jbarnardauthor.com or follow @jbarnardau-thor on Instagram.

Sign up for J. Barnard's newsletter for writing updates. By signing up here, you'll also be the first to know when new books go live:

Please spread the love for the Halven Rising series and *FATES ENTWINED* by leaving a review or rating it, and sharing the series on all things social. Don't forget to tag me!